AUTUMN'S LIGHT

What Reviewers Say About Aurora Rey's Work

Built to Last

"Rey's frothy contemporary romance brings two women together to restore an ancient farmhouse in Ithaca, N.Y. ...[T]he women totally click in bed, as well as when they're poring over paint chips, and readers will enjoy finding out whether love conquers all."
—*Publishers Weekly*

"*Built to Last* by Aurora Rey is a contemporary lesbian romance novel and a very sweet summer read. I love, love, love the way Ms. Rey writes bedroom scenes and I'm not talking about how she describes the furniture."—*The Lesbian Review*

Lambda Literary Award Finalist Crescent City Confidential

"This book will make you want to visit New Orleans if you have never been. I enjoy descriptive writing and Rey does a really wonderful job of creating the setting. You actually feel like you know the place."—*Amanda's Reviews*

"*Crescent City Confidential* pulled me into the wonderful sights, sounds and smells of New Orleans. I was totally captivated by the city and the story of mystery writer Sam and her growing love for the place and for a certain lady. ...It was slow burning but romantic and sexy too. A mystery thrown into the mix really piqued my interest."—*Kitty Kat's Book Review Blog*

Spring's Wake

"*Spring's Wake* has shot to number one in my age-gap romance favorites shelf."—*Les Rêveur*

"The Ptown setting was idyllic and the supporting cast of characters from the previous books made it feel welcoming and homey. The love story was slow and perfectly timed, with a fair amount of heat. I loved it and hope that this isn't the last from this particular series."—*Kitty Kat's Book Review Blog*

"The third standalone in Aurora Rey's Cape End series, Spring's Wake, features a feel-good romance that would make a perfect beach read. The Provincetown B&B setting is richly painted, feeling both indulgent and cozy."—*RT Book Reviews*

Summer's Cove

"As expected in a small-town romance, *Summer's Cove* evokes a sunny, light-hearted atmosphere that matches its beach setting. …Emerson's shy pursuit of Darcy is sure to endear readers to her, though some may be put off during the moments Darcy winds tightly to the point of rigidity. Darcy desires romance yet is unwilling to disrupt her son's life to have it, and you feel for Emerson when she endeavors to show how there's room in her heart for a family."
—*RT Book Reviews*

"From the moment the characters met I was gripped and couldn't wait for the moment that it all made sense to them both and they would finally go for it. Once again, Aurora Rey writes some of the steamiest sex scenes I have read whilst being able to keep the romance going. I really think this could be one of my favorite series and can't wait to see what comes next. Keep 'em coming, Aurora."—*Les Rêveur*

Winter's Harbor

"This is the story of Lia and Alex and the beautifully romantic and sexy tale of a winter in Provincetown, a seaside holiday haven. A collection of interesting characters, well-fleshed out, as well as a gorgeous setting make for a great read."—*Inked Rainbow Reads*

"*Winter's Harbor* is a charming story. It is a sweet, gentle romance with just enough angst to keep you turning the pages. ...I adore Rey's characters and the picture she paints of Provincetown was lovely."—*The Lesbian Review*

Visit us at www.boldstrokesbooks.com

By the Author

Cape End Romances:

Winter's Harbor

Summer's Cove

Spring's Wake

Autumn's Light

Built to Last

Crescent City Confidential

Lead Counsel (Novella in The Boss of Her collection)

Autumn's Light

by
Aurora Rey

2018

AUTUMN'S LIGHT
© 2018 BY AURORA REY. ALL RIGHTS RESERVED.

ISBN 13: 978-1-63555-272-0

THIS TRADE PAPERBACK ORIGINAL IS PUBLISHED BY
BOLD STROKES BOOKS, INC.
P.O. BOX 249
VALLEY FALLS, NY 12185

FIRST EDITION: OCTOBER 2018

THIS IS A WORK OF FICTION. NAMES, CHARACTERS, PLACES, AND INCIDENTS ARE THE PRODUCT OF THE AUTHOR'S IMAGINATION OR ARE USED FICTITIOUSLY. ANY RESEMBLANCE TO ACTUAL PERSONS, LIVING OR DEAD, BUSINESS ESTABLISHMENTS, EVENTS, OR LOCALES IS ENTIRELY COINCIDENTAL.

THIS BOOK, OR PARTS THEREOF, MAY NOT BE REPRODUCED IN ANY FORM WITHOUT PERMISSION.

CREDITS
EDITOR: ASHLEY TILLMAN
PRODUCTION DESIGN: SUSAN RAMUNDO
COVER DESIGN BY JEANINE HENNING

Acknowledgments

I remain so grateful to everyone at Bold Strokes. You are my people and I love you. Particular thanks to Radclyffe and Sandy Lowe, who have such a passion for the art and business of books. Also, to Ruth and Carsen for wrangling all the important details, not to mention the writers. And Ash—you make me laugh and you make me a better writer. Even more important, you make me a better person.

Thank you to TJ and Tracy for being outstanding beta readers and to Jen for helping me reclaim the library and the lunch hour. I write more and better because of you.

Setting four books in Provincetown has been equal parts fun and challenging. I've learned so much about a place I hold so dear. I owe a heap of gratitude to the people I've met along the way, including Captain Dave of Billingsgate Charters. If you ever want to try your hand at lobstering, he's your guy.

Dedication

For Provincetown and her residents, past and present

Chapter One

Mat checked the GPS tracker on the small screen above her head. Just as she crossed over the desired coordinates, she shoved the freshly baited trap from the rail of the boat. The long coil of rope, along with her gray and green buoy, followed quickly behind. She picked up speed and smiled as the wind whipped her short hair. She was having an exceptionally good day.

"I hate to burst your bubble over there, but we're about full."

She turned to her cousin Dominic and frowned. "What do you mean?"

"The barrels. They're full. I mean, you could maybe squeeze a couple more in, but that's it."

"No shit?" She glanced over. Even from the opposite side of the boat, she could make out the shells of lobsters pretty close to the water line. "How many traps have we done?"

Dom checked the pad where he tracked both their progress and their catch. "One-thirty."

They hauled one hundred and fifty of their eight hundred traps each day. In the eleven years she'd captained her own lobster boat, she'd never filled two barrels pulling fewer than a hundred and fifty traps. She'd known they were in a sweet spot today, but she was surprised by how sweet. Pleasantly surprised, but surprised. "Hot damn."

He looked at her from across the small table that held the banding box. "Does this mean we get to knock off early?"

Mat shook her head and smiled. "It means you're going to fill some empty bait totes with water. No way are we going to chance leaving full traps on the ocean floor." Full traps, left for too long, meant the lobsters might start going after each other—never a good thing.

Dom laughed. "I'd complain, but my head is too full of dollar signs."

"That's the spirit." Mat steered them to their next stop. She pulled up alongside the buoy, snagging it with the gaff. She threaded the rope, started the hydraulic lift. A moment later, the trap emerged. She counted nine lobsters inside. She went about inspecting them, throwing back the females and undersized males. Still, five were keepers.

They continued for another hour, filling three of the eight bait totes they'd brought on board. Dom made a notation in his book and smiled. "And that makes one-fifty."

"Aren't you glad we kept at it?"

"I am. I always am."

Mat smiled and started the journey back to shore. She loved a lot of things about working with her cousin. Near the top of that list was the fact that they were nearly identical when it came to work ethic. Dom might grouse from time to time, but they both believed in the mantra "work hard, play hard." Hauling at the rate they did afforded them one day off each week for bad weather or whatever their hearts desired. The pace was intense, but profitable. And it left just enough time for fun. Mat might take the fun part a little more seriously than Dom, especially since his transition, but he managed to have his share.

Once in the harbor, Mat slowed the engine and steered carefully through the traffic of boats coming and going. Dom texted their uncle and Mat pulled up to their unload spot along the main pier. With the help of the small crane mounted to the pier, they moved their barrels to the waiting Pero Specialty Seafood truck and moved two empty barrels to the boat for the next day. Emilio would deliver their catch, along with that of her uncles and cousins, to restaurants and fish markets in town and to a retailer in Boston.

It was a family business, one that existed long before Mat decided to make her living on the water. Technically, it existed long before she was born. Mat might not see eye-to-eye with her family on all things, but she knew her livelihood was greatly improved by the close-knit nature of it. That included the lessons she got from her father, the boat she was able to purchase from a great uncle, and the well-established family distribution network.

"What about the totes?" Dom asked.

"Give him two. I want to deliver the last one personally."

Dom gave her a suspicious look. "You working a side hustle, Mattie?" The thick New England accent, paired with the family nickname, was a perfect imitation of their uncle.

"I trust Emilio to sell our catch and give us a fair price. I think he might be a little less skilled in the relationship management arena."

Dom snorted. "I'll give you that. Who are you planning to grace with your bounty?"

His suggestive tone made Mat laugh. He knew her well. "Audrey. She's the executive chef at Osteria 160."

"Ah. And are you hoping to cultivate a professional relationship or get in her pants?" Dom waved to their uncle, who pulled away to sort and weigh their catch, and Mat navigated the short distance to their slip.

"You say it like those things are mutually exclusive." At Dom's judgmental look, she chuckled. "Kidding. We do a little friendly flirting, that's all."

He lifted his hands. "Okay, okay. I believe you." Dom hopped from the boat and started securing the ropes.

"I think I might be able to convince her we're the perfect compromise between a distributor and buying direct."

Dom grinned. "If anyone can, it's you."

Mat smiled. She'd never give up the time on the water required to handle the distribution side of the business. That didn't mean she couldn't help it along every now and then. Especially if the customer in question happened to be a gorgeous local chef.

❖

Graham made her way down the gangplank and onto MacMillan Pier. She'd taken the early shifts all week, which meant, even after two tours, she was done for the day before five. She'd just made it past the Dolphin Fleet sign when she heard her name.

"Connor."

Graham turned in the direction of the voice. It was Charles, her boss, calling at her from the deck of the Dolphin IX. She looked up at him, shielding her eyes from the sun. "Yes?"

"Do you want an extra shift on Monday?"

Graham pulled up a mental picture of her calendar. Technically, Mondays were her only days completely off. But she didn't mind the work, especially during the busy season. The more hours she spent on whale watches, the fewer she'd have to work doing something else come winter. "Sure."

"I'm putting you with the intern. You cool with that?"

Graham smiled. Just two summers ago, she'd been the intern. It meant a lot that Charles trusted her to be the senior naturalist on board. "Absolutely."

He offered her a casual salute, which she returned, then disappeared back into the boat. She walked along the pier, studying the fishing boats and yachts tied up side by side. She'd noticed that before, but never really thought about it. It struck her as odd that they shared the same space. Was that common or something unique to Provincetown?

Her schedule rarely coincided with the comings and goings of the fishermen. The tides must have been just right, though, because a number of boats appeared to be unloading the day's catch. She slowed her pace to watch as bins of fish and barrels filled with lobster were hoisted via a makeshift crane from boat to pier, probably on their way to restaurants just down the street to be cooked up and served the next day.

Her budget didn't allow for a lot of fresh seafood, but maybe she could justify a trip to the fish market. If she sprang for a couple of lobsters, she might even convince Aunt Nora to do the steaming. Graham sighed at the thought of fresh lobster, dipped in drawn butter.

Her gastronomic daydream was cut short by the appearance of a woman she'd not seen before, standing on the deck of one of the fishing boats. She wore a black tank top and faded gray work pants. Her jet black hair was cut short and the deep bronze of her skin looked like more than just a tan. She handed bins to a guy with similar features, who stacked them along one side of the boat.

Graham realized her mouth was hanging open. She quickly closed it. She bit her lip and stared. Wow.

As if sensing the attention, the woman looked her way. Graham could tell she had dark eyes, even from such a distance. The kind of eyes that felt infinite.

Graham knew she should look away, but she found herself transfixed. The woman paused long enough to offer Graham a slow smile. Not the kind of friendly smile Graham usually exchanged with people she passed on the pier, the kind of smile that made tourists feel welcome or the kind residents and workers shared amongst themselves. No, this smile had more of a come-home-with-me energy. Or at least it felt that way to Graham.

Just as quickly as the moment began, it ended. The woman returned to her work and Graham was left standing in the middle of the sidewalk with a goofy smile on her face. She barely resisted a face palm. With more intention than before, she strode toward Commercial Street and away from making a complete idiot of herself.

She was just at the point where pier met dry land when she ran into Will coming the other way. They wore matching Dolphin Fleet polo shirts, although Will paired hers with cargo shorts and Graham went for more feminine capris. "Hey, Will."

Will flashed a smile. "Hey back. How have I not seen you in almost a week?"

Graham shrugged playfully. "I hear you've been busy."

"Stop." Will blushed, then frowned. "I mean it. I miss you."

"I was teasing. We've just been working opposite shifts."

"Right." Will closed her eyes for a second and shook her head. "Sorry."

Although her friend Will and her Aunt Nora had been together for over a year, Will had only officially moved into the inn with Nora a few weeks ago. Graham was pretty sure they were still in the honeymoon phase of that, a fact that made Will hilariously shy. "I was just thinking of inviting myself over for dinner."

"I'm sure Nora would love to see you, even more than I would. I can check her schedule and I'll get back to you with a couple of dates."

"Excellent. Ask her if she'll cook lobster if I bring it."

Will laughed. "If she doesn't want to, I will."

"Deal."

Will glanced at her watch. "I have to go."

Graham waved a hand. "Sorry, sorry. Didn't mean to make you late. Text me."

Will resumed walking down the pier. "I will."

Graham turned to watch Will board the boat she'd just left. Once she was out of sight, Graham allowed her gaze to drift back to the lobster boat. The boat remained but the woman was gone. Graham tried not to notice the stab of disappointment.

Maybe she'd take a little stroll back down the pier. Even if she didn't see the woman again, she could check out the boat, see if it was local or just passing through. Graham made a point of studying each of the boats she passed. Some were old and some were new. A few had been designed for play, but most had the scuffed paint and piles of rope and mechanical equipment that indicated a working vessel.

As she approached the one with the mystery woman, Graham walked past it quickly, afraid the woman might reappear and catch her staring. At the end of the pier, she spent a moment looking out at the breakwater. She breathed in the salt air and let the sun beat down on her face. Gorgeous woman or not, Graham couldn't imagine a single place on earth she'd rather be.

She made her way back toward the boat slowly, searching for signs of life, but also details that might tell her more about its crew. It looked to be about twenty feet long, with three walls and a covered area instead of a fully enclosed cabin. The deck had been hosed and scrubbed clean and the white paint on the outside looked like it had been applied this season. Across the transom, in dark burgundy paint, she read *Paquette,* Provincetown, MA.

Graham swallowed the flutter of excitement. The boat was local. That might mean her crew was, too.

"Dom, are you there?"

The sound of a voice—a rich, deep, yet utterly female voice—sent Graham scurrying. She didn't slow down until she reached Commercial Street. Nor did she look back.

Rather than turning left toward home, Graham made a right. Maybe she'd pop by Aunt Nora's for a bit now. She'd be in the middle of happy hour, but that was okay. Graham had nowhere to be. She could make herself useful or relax in the garden. Then she and Aunt Nora could catch up and she could sweet talk her way into that lobster dinner.

Chapter Two

Mat stopped at home long enough to take a shower. She didn't want to seem like she was trying, but she also didn't want to walk in smelling like diesel and bait. She put on a pair of dark jeans and a black button-down, her favorite boots, just a touch of paste in her hair.

It was taking a chance, but she drove to the restaurant, and pulled her truck into the spot reserved for deliveries. She was, after all, delivering something. She took the tote from the back of her truck, careful to hold it away from herself, and headed to the back door.

Preparations for dinner service were well underway, but the kitchen lacked the frenetic pace of the dinner rush. Mat snagged the attention of a guy slicing lemons. "Do you know if Audrey is here?"

He nodded. "She's out front going over specials with the waitstaff."

Mat frowned, unsure of how long that would take, or if she should wait. Before she could decide, the door from the dining room swung open and Audrey came through. Her white chef's coat fit like it had been tailored for her curves. As did the black pants. Rather than detracting from the look, the rubber clogs left no doubt she meant business in the kitchen. She looked in Mat's direction and smiled. "Well, hello, stranger."

"Stranger? Is that any way to talk to someone who comes bearing gifts?"

Audrey's eyes sparkled. "A present? What did you bring me?"

Mat set the tote on an unused square of counter and flipped open the lid. "The freshest catch in town."

Audrey peered inside. "Did these come in today?"

Mat smiled. In addition to being gorgeous, Audrey had a keen appreciation for Mat's line of work. "I hauled them myself."

She watched as Audrey did a quick count and, likely, estimate of their weight. "What did I do to deserve such an offering?"

"It's what I know you'll do with them that matters."

Audrey narrowed her eyes, but her tone remained playful. "Are you after dinner or a date?"

It was almost too easy. "I'd never say no to either, but at the moment, I'm here with a business proposition."

"Oh?" Audrey raised a brow and Mat couldn't tell if she was intrigued or disappointed.

"We both know you're one of the hottest new spots in town. On top of that, you're elevating local seafood to a new level." Mat lifted a hand. "Not that I have anything against lobster rolls."

The rich, sultry sound of Audrey's laugh made Mat wonder if maybe she should angle for the date instead of the business. "I should warn you that, unlike most chefs, my ego isn't running the show."

Mat grinned. "I'm only calling it as I see it. And as I see it, we should be partners."

"Tell me more."

Mat leaned against the counter. "You need a more consistent supply of fresh lobster than one person can provide."

"Agreed."

"But going through a wholesaler means you're paying a middle man. On top of that, you don't know exactly where or how your product was caught."

Audrey nodded. "Also true."

"Pero and Sons can offer you the best of both worlds."

A guy in an apron brushed past them with a crate of vegetables. Audrey nodded. "I want to hear more, but I've got a hundred things to do before dinner service starts."

"Don't let me keep you. Maybe we could grab drinks one night after your shift."

Audrey quirked a brow. "I didn't realize lobstermen stayed up that late."

Mat tipped her head slightly. "We just need a good enough reason."

"Should I feel honored to be on that list?"

Mat smirked, then nodded at the tote. "You enjoy those. I'll stop back in a couple of days to pick up the bin and you can tell me about all the delicious things you made."

Audrey looked Mat up and down. "I'll look forward to it."

Mat left the way she'd come, climbing into her truck, and making the short drive home. Tomorrow wasn't a day off, but since she'd gone to the trouble of getting dressed, she considered going out for a drink or two. A quick text exchange later, she'd wrangled Dom into joining her.

Since he'd only requested a few minutes to get ready, Mat stood in the driveway of the building where they each had an apartment. She leaned against her truck and let her mind wander. But instead of Audrey, Mat's thoughts went to the woman from earlier in the day, the one she'd caught staring at her from the pier.

Even from a distance, Mat could tell she was beautiful. The strawberry blond hair and blue eyes gave her a look that seemed to hover somewhere between all-American girl and Irish beauty—striking, but in an innocent, almost unassuming way. Mat wondered if she lived in town or was just passing through.

Dom appeared at the top of the back stairs and waved. When he reached the bottom, he raised a brow. "So, how'd it go?"

Mat nodded. "Good. We didn't really get to talk, but she seemed impressed with what I had to offer."

Dom chuckled. "Again, I'm not sure if we're talking about you or lobsters."

Normally, she'd go back and forth with him, topping one another's double entendres until they crossed the line into the ridiculous. For some reason, tonight she didn't. "I think we might be able to get her as a regular."

Dom narrowed his eyes, but didn't comment on the directness of her answer. "That would be really great."

It would be. There were only a couple of restaurants they supplied exclusively. Those relationships, the confidence they implied, were like a feather in her cap. Even better, the more they sold locally, the higher the profit margin. "Don't say anything to Uncle Emilio yet. I'd like it to be a done deal before he swoops in."

They started the stroll into town, debating between the beer garden and the After Tea Dance. As they walked down Commercial, Mat scanned the faces they passed. The diverse press of people that spilled into town during the day had thinned, leaving a crowd that was predominantly queer. That was why she liked evenings best.

She found herself looking for the woman. It surprised Mat she'd invaded her mind to that extent, given they'd not even spoken to one another. It didn't bother her, though. Whether she ever saw her again or not, appreciating a beautiful woman was one of her favorite pastimes. Sharing a moment of mutual appreciation was its own pleasure.

Graham walked along Commercial Street with her roommate, Jess. Aunt Nora had been exceptionally busy, so Graham made plans for dinner the following week and bid her good night. She'd headed home, feeling mildly restless. She'd readily accepted Jess's invitation for a walk and a slice of pizza. Not only would that provide a nice diversion, it meant she didn't need to think about cooking.

"You seem distracted."

"Huh?" Graham looked at Jess.

"Exactly. I said you looked distracted."

"Oh. Yeah, I guess. A little."

"What's on your mind, sunshine?" Jess studied her with concern.

"Nothing bad. I just saw this crazy hot woman earlier and I was thinking about her."

"Crazy hot, huh? Tell me more."

Graham shrugged. "I'd just left work and was walking along the pier, looking at the boats. And there she was, looking rugged and sexy. I kid you not, I stood there with my mouth hanging open like a complete idiot."

"Did she look back?"

Graham thought back to the brief interaction, to the way her body responded. "Yeah."

"And? Did you talk to her?"

"God, no. We exchanged a look. Fortunately, after I managed to pick my tongue up off the sidewalk."

Jess gave her a look of complete exasperation. "Why didn't you introduce yourself, make a little friendly conversation?"

"She was working. On top of that, I'd just gotten off work. Not my best look." It had nothing to do with being a tongue-tied, blushing mess.

"But what if you never see her again?"

Graham tried to ignore the pang of disappointment the idea created. "It's not like it was love at first sight or anything." She offered a playful shrug. "Lust, maybe."

Jess shook her head. "Haven't you spent the last six months lamenting your lack of a love life? You can't just ignore opportunities that fall into your lap. You must act."

Graham laughed at the vehemence in Jess's tone. But then she let the words sink in. She'd never been the forward one in dating scenarios. Well, aside from her clumsy and ill-fated attempt to hook up with Will, which had crashed and burned. Things had all worked out for the best, obviously, but it certainly hadn't helped her confidence on that front. "I don't think I'm cut out to be the aggressor."

"Nonsense. And it's not about being the aggressor. It's about putting yourself out there, making it easy for the other person to make the first move."

Graham had a vision of herself wandering up and down the pier in a dress and heels, waiting—quite literally—for her ship to come in. It wasn't a pretty picture. "I'm not sure that applies in this situation."

"Sure it does. You just have to figure out a way to make sure you cross paths again. Do you think she lives in town?"

"Maybe. The boat's local."

"That's a good sign. Is she our age? Do you think she goes out?"

"You know, I have no idea." She had a hard time picturing the woman at a bar or in a club, but maybe that was unfair. A Dolphin Fleet uniform and being surrounded by little kids probably seemed incongruous with the kind of girl who liked to go out, too. Graham tried to envision the woman in a dim space, drink in hand, surrounded by people. From there, it wasn't hard to imagine what it might be like to dance with her. The woman's hand on her lower back, guiding their bodies in synchronous movement. "Oh, my God."

"What?" Jess looked at her with alarm.

"She's right there."

Jess looked around. "Where?"

"On the patio of the beer place. Don't look."

Of course Jess looked. "Who? Which one? Oh, wait."

Before she could continue the conversation and embarrass them both, Graham pulled her friend past the restaurant and out of the woman's line of sight. "Are you trying to kill me?"

"Whoa, whoa, whoa. Relax. We're not trading state secrets here." Jess leaned back and glanced in the direction they'd just passed. "Short dark hair, black shirt?"

Graham closed her eyes and nodded. "Mmm-hmm."

"She is hot. Like, really fucking hot."

"I know."

"You have to talk to her." Jess placed exceptional emphasis on the "have."

"Now?"

Jess spread her hands in front of her. "No, next week. Of course now."

Graham dared to lean back so she could catch a glimpse of the woman. She was deep in conversation with the guy next to her, the same guy from the boat. She let her gaze linger for a moment. The jeans and button-down shirt were casually sexy and answered any question Graham might have had about whether she was the type to go out on the town. Although, truth be told, Graham couldn't decide which of the two looks appealed to her more. She reluctantly returned her gaze to Jess. "I don't know."

"Well, I do. We're going to march in there, grab a drink, and just so happen to find ourselves right next to them."

Graham nodded, her stomach suddenly filled with butterflies. "Then what?"

"Then you make eye contact and smile. She'll smile back. And then you'll say, 'Hey, didn't I see you on the pier earlier?' It's not rocket science."

"I know it's not." She might not have a ton of experience making moves, but she wasn't completely socially inept. Something about this woman had an effect on her. The kind of effect that made her worried she'd turn into a blushing, blubbering fool if the woman actually spoke to her. But it seemed like the universe might be telling her something, or even better, giving her a gift. She didn't want to waste it. "Okay. Let's do it."

Jess rubbed her hands together with delight, which made Graham laugh. "Follow me."

Graham did, being careful not to look in the woman's direction and run the risk of losing her nerve. They went inside to the bar and she let Jess order them both a pint of apricot wheat. "Drinks are on me," Graham said.

"No argument here."

Graham slid money across the bar. They picked up their glasses and headed to the patio that faced Commercial. It was a fairly big space, so it took them a moment to wind through the groups of people standing at the high-top tables. When they got to the right spot, it was empty.

"Where'd they go?" Jess looked back the way they'd come.

Graham glanced up and down the street and saw the back of the woman, along with her friend, heading to the West End. She nudged Jess's shoulder and pointed. "There."

"Damn it."

And then they were gone. Disappointment vied with relief. "It's okay."

Jess hung her head. "I can't believe we missed them."

"Yeah." Graham took a long sip of her beer and set it down. "But you know what?"

Jess did the same. "What?"

"If she changed her clothes and was out having a beer, that's a pretty good indication she lives here."

Jess raised her hands in celebration. "Yes. You're right. We just need to create opportunity for you to run into her again."

Graham took another sip of beer. "She was with the guy I saw on the boat. Maybe they're together."

"Highly unlikely. There were all kinds of studly lesbian vibes coming off her."

Graham sighed. She hoped so. "They did look kind of similar. Maybe they're related."

"Absolutely. The lobster boat is probably a family business." Jess nodded and she continued formulating her theory. "I bet she's part of an old Portuguese fishing family who's been here for generations."

"You're probably right." Graham liked the idea of that. It sounded so romantic. It also increased her chances of seeing the woman again. Now that she was looking. The prospect of flirtation, and maybe more, lifted her spirits. "Hey, do you want to splurge on dinner here instead of pizza?"

Jess grinned. "I love the way you think." She lifted her glass. "Here's to the thrill of pursuit."

"I'm not sure I'd go that far, but cheers all the same." Graham clinked her glass to Jess's, then picked up a menu.

Chapter Three

Graham carried the ice chest, trying to ignore the thwapping that came from inside. For the tenth time, she reminded herself that lobsters don't have a central nervous system. Short of being a full vegetarian, cooking and eating lobster was about as humane as it got.

The next thwap caused the cooler to shift in her hand. She swallowed the squeal that bubbled up. Barely.

She let herself in the side gate that led to Aunt Nora's garden and the back door of the inn. She set the cooler at the bottom of the porch steps and headed into the house. She found Tisha in the kitchen, singing and arranging cheese on a large wooden board. She spotted Graham and smiled. "Hey, girl. I haven't seen you in forever."

Graham crossed the room and gave her a hug. "It feels that way, doesn't it? How's it going?"

"Well, other than living in the middle of a honeymoon, I'm great." Tisha rolled her eyes, but laughed.

Graham smiled at the description. If someone had told her a year ago that her aunt would be blissfully happy with a live-in girlfriend—who happened to be Graham's friend—she'd have scoffed. And yet, here they were. Her unrequited crush on Will felt like a distant memory. "That bad, huh?"

Tisha shook her head. "It's adorable. I just feel it's my right to tease Nora about it."

Tisha was the summer manager at Failte, and one of Aunt Nora's closest friends. When Will and Nora had temporarily split, Tisha was Graham's biggest ally in nudging them to get back together. Graham put an arm around Tisha and gave her a squeeze. "It's your right and your responsibility. Aunt Nora needs to remember it's not good to be so damn stubborn."

"Who's stubborn?"

At the sound of Nora's voice, both Graham and Tisha turned. Nora stood in the doorway to the dining room, a look of mild curiosity on her face. Without missing a beat, Tisha said, "You."

Nora nodded and shrugged, making Graham snicker. "We were discussing how blissfully happy you are now that Will has moved in."

Rather than protest, Nora's face softened and she smiled. "It's so much more practical, not to mention economical."

"Economical?" Tisha stuck her tongue in her cheek. "Is that what the kids are calling it these days?"

Graham couldn't suppress another snicker. Nora gave Tisha a bland look. "Really?"

Tisha picked up the board she'd been arranging when Graham arrived. "This is ready to go out."

Nora accepted it and turned to leave. Before she pushed through the swinging door back into the dining room, she said, "I wonder sometimes why I like you."

Unfazed by the insult, Tisha laughed and called after her, "You and me both, woman."

When she'd gone, Graham turned her attention back to Tisha. "Are you joining us for dinner? I brought four lobsters in case."

Tisha offered her a warm smile. "It's sweet you thought of me, but I got plans of my own."

"Hot date?"

Tisha raised a brow. "I might have met one of the new cooks at the Lobster Pot."

"Is he good looking or did he offer to make you dinner?"

Tisha's eyes gleamed. "Girl, what makes you think it's not both?"

"I should have expected nothing less. We'll miss you, but I'm glad it's for such a good reason." Graham looked around the kitchen. "Is there anything I can help with?"

"No, you take a drink and go relax."

Graham eyed the pitcher of sangria that had yet to be put out for happy hour. "You don't have to tell me twice."

She poured herself a glass and headed to the backyard, figuring most of the inn's guests would congregate on the front porch and in the sitting room. She picked one of the benches in the shade and made herself comfortable. The garden was in full bloom. Graham inhaled deeply, appreciating the fragrance as much as the flash of color. She closed her eyes and let out a contented sigh.

It took less than ten seconds for the image of the lobsterwoman to fill her brain. For the last few days, Graham had made a point of wandering the pier before and after her shifts. A couple of times, she even used her lunch hour to try and catch a glimpse of the *Paquette* and its sexy captain. She'd succeeded three times. Two of those times, the woman had looked her way. Both times, she offered the same easy, knowing smile.

Graham opened her eyes and huffed out a breath. Her worst fear was to spend the rest of the season half admiring, half stalking this woman, and never even learning her name. But it seemed unlikely the woman would leave her boat to talk to Graham. If only she could run into her somewhere else. Neutral territory, ideally with Graham wearing something nicer than her Dolphin Fleet polo shirt and a pair of khakis.

"Why do you look so perturbed?" Will stood near the side gate, a look of concern on her face.

"I'm not perturbed." She wasn't. Mildly frustrated, maybe.

"Could have fooled me." Will, dressed in her own Dolphin Fleet uniform, angled her head and met Graham's gaze.

"Do you know that I've lived in Provincetown for over a year, not to mention the whole summer before that, and I haven't hooked up with a single woman that whole time?"

"Do you want a hookup?"

Graham sighed. "I don't know. Maybe? I want to do something. I've had exactly two dates. No girlfriend. No action. None."

Without waiting for an invitation, Will sat next to her on the bench. "I hear you."

"It just feels a bit pathetic, to be in a town teeming with lesbians, completely celibate."

Will nodded. "I felt the same when I first moved here, even knowing I was just out of a relationship and needed to regroup."

"Yeah, I'm grouped. I'd like someone to come and," she waved her hands back and forth, "muss me up."

Will chuckled at the description. "Is this a general feeling you're having or has someone stirred your pot?"

It seemed ridiculous to confess her pseudo-obsession with a woman she'd never actually spoken to. And, really, this woman only stirred up feelings that had been there all along. "General, I'd say."

Will narrowed her eyes. "Really?"

She appreciated that Will knew her well enough not to take everything she said at face value. "I happened upon an exceptionally hot woman the other day. She may have brought things to the surface."

"Who is she? Do I know her?"

"I doubt it. She works on one of the lobster boats that moor at MacMillan Pier."

Will folded her arms and leaned forward. "Oh, a townie. Intriguing. Tell me more."

"There's not much to tell. I saw her. She's hot. That's about it."

"Have you spoken to her? Do you know if she's local? Is it her boat or does she just work on it?"

"We've not spoken, so I know nothing. I'm not even sure how I'd initiate a conversation." Graham thought about Jess's many and varied ideas for doing so.

Will looked at the sky. "How about, 'Hi, I was admiring your boat. Do you come here often?'"

Graham snorted. "Okay, that is truly terrible."

Will shrugged. "Do you have something better?"

Graham let her shoulders slump. "No."

"Well, maybe beggars shouldn't be choosers."

"Maybe we could not use the term beggar to talk about my love life."

Will leaned over, bumping her shoulder against Graham's. "Sorry."

"It's okay. I'm feeling pretty awkward and pathetic already. Beggar isn't much of a leap."

"I was kidding. You're lovely." Will looked at her earnestly.

"And single."

"And beautiful and smart and a total catch."

"And single." She paused between each word for extra emphasis.

"Oh, Graham."

Will frowned and Graham could see that she was truly worried. Graham made a point of smiling. She squeezed Will's leg. "It's okay. I'm being dramatic."

Will sighed heavily. "No, I understand how you feel. It's hard."

Graham shook her head. She did not want to wallow. "It's not that bad. I'm not looking to get married or anything. I'm twenty-five. I've got time for that. Maybe you're right and I should just put myself out there a little more."

Will perked up. "That's the spirit. Talk to your lobsterwoman."

"Maybe."

"You could also—" Will's suggestion was interrupted by Nora calling to them. Will said, "We're out here."

Before Nora had a chance to join them, Graham placed a hand on Will's arm. "Can we keep this between us?"

Will offered a knowing nod. "Of course."

"How's the party?" Graham asked as Nora approached.

"In full swing. Six of them are teacher friends. Who knew teachers were such party animals?"

"I'm not surprised." Will stood and gave Nora a kiss. "I bet teachers are excellent at relaxing."

Graham laughed at the idea. "They'd have to be, right?"

"Can I help with anything?" Will asked, sliding an arm around Nora's waist.

"Not a thing. The food is under control and my guests are so chatty with each other, I didn't even hesitate to sneak away to come search for you two."

"Aunt Nora, are you playing hooky?" Graham opened her eyes wide and used her most scandalized voice.

Nora straightened her shoulders and tossed her hair. "I am exploring a more relaxed management style."

"I see." Graham bit the inside of her cheek and tried to decide if it was okay to laugh. A peek at Will and the serious look on her face told her maybe not. "Well, I think it's great. And everything about a stay at Failte is so perfect, I can't imagine your guests will mind one bit, if they even notice."

Nora folded her arms. "You can say it. I have a tendency to overdo."

Graham shook her head. She knew better. "Nope. I know no such thing."

Nora's expression turned to one of playful exasperation. "You didn't hesitate to make your feelings known when I broke my arm last year, or when you decided to meddle in my love life."

Now it was Graham's turn to be exasperated. "You're really going to complain about that?"

Nora turned her head and planted a kiss on Will's cheek. "Not one bit."

"Okay, then. Did you two decide who's going to cook the lobsters I bought us?"

Will raised a hand. "Nora made dessert, so it's all me."

Graham smiled. "I love teamwork."

It was just after seven when the last of Nora's guests cleared out for dinners or shows or walks along the beach. Tisha was long gone. Will took charge in the kitchen, insisting she had everything under control. She wasn't squeamish, but Graham had no problem at all being far, far away when the lobsters went into the pot. She helped Nora set the table out in the garden, in part because it was a lovely night and in part because it would make cleanup a lot easier.

Will came out with potatoes, corn, and three small bowls of drawn butter. She made a second trip for the main course. Nora opened a sauvignon blanc. Before long, they were seated together, each with a huge lobster tail in front of them. They took turns with the kitchen shears, snipping the shell up one side and down the other.

Graham pitched her shell into the bucket at her feet and smiled at the plump, succulent meat in front of her. "Thanks for cooking."

"I think we're the ones thanking you," Will said, raising her glass.

"Agreed." Nora dipped a forkful into the butter. "This is lovely and indulgent."

Graham thought about the lobsterwoman, wondered if she regularly enjoyed her catch like this. For the first time since the woman had taken up residence in her mind, Graham considered that she might have a wife. Or girlfriend. Or husband. Good God, please don't let her have a husband. That would make her unattainable and mean Graham's instincts were way off. She shook her head, forcing the thoughts away. "I'm glad we get to be lovely and indulgent together."

After dinner, Nora brought out a perfect looking lemon tart. Despite being beyond full, Graham had a slice. She knew how much butter went into it. Even with that knowledge, she convinced herself it was a refreshing, if not light, way to end the meal.

They lingered outside until the sun began to set. The air took on a chill and Graham wished she'd brought a sweater. As if sensing her thoughts, Nora offered her one. She accepted it with thanks and a promise to return it in the next couple of days. After hugs and numerous promises to do it again soon, with or without lobster, Graham wished them good night.

As she walked along Bradford Street, Graham thought about Will and Nora, tidying the kitchen, deciding on a movie to watch before bed. She was happy for them, truly. But the mild desire she'd mentioned to Will earlier had grown into a persistent longing. She needed to break out of the rut she'd inadvertently found herself in, whether it was with the striking woman from the lobster boat or not.

Chapter Four

Are you going out tonight?

Mat glanced at her phone, then back in the mirror. Satisfied with her look, she picked up the phone and typed a reply. *Do you really have to ask?*

It was Portuguese Festival weekend. That included the blessing of the fleet at noon the next day, which meant she wouldn't even need to think about rolling out of bed until nine. A rare treat in the summer, and one she had no intention of wasting.

I'll be at your place in ten.

Mat smiled and headed to the kitchen to grab the rest of her things. She stuffed cash and her ID into the slim billfold she liked for going out, then slid it into the back pocket of her dark jeans. Her phone went into the other, and a single apartment key into the front.

While she waited for Dom, she peeked into the bedroom to make sure everything looked neat and tidy. It did. As did the living room and the kitchen. She was just putting on her shoes when a knock came at the door. Before she could answer, much less open it, Dom breezed in. "You ready?"

Mat stood. "Yep."

"The pad all ready for whoever you bring home?"

Mat looked around. Out of nowhere, the image of the girl from the pier popped into her mind. Weird. She shook it off. "Yep."

Dom shook his head. "I was kidding."

Mat shrugged. "It pays to be prepared."

"I think if I tried that, it would jinx me."

"The fact that you only have eyes for Renata is what's jinxing you."

Dom let out a dramatic sigh. "True story."

Since the gesture was more good-natured than truly forlorn, Mat gave in to the urge to tease him. "You know, she's probably waiting for you to make a move."

"I am making my move. I'm just not a sprinter like you, over practically before I start."

"You wound me." Mat slapped a hand to her chest in mock offense. When Dom gave her a bland look in response, she added, "Maybe go for the 800-meter instead of the marathon."

Dom punched her in the arm. "Why do girls find you charming again?"

Mat opened the door and gestured for Dom to lead the way. "I'd be happy to give you lessons."

Mat locked the door behind them. Dom slung an arm around her shoulders. "I think I'll stick with my own methods, thanks."

Mat shook her head. "Suit yourself."

Their first stop was the community dinner. Mat's parents were there, along with aunts, uncles, cousins, and her eighty-seven-year-old grandmother. Enough tourists were there, eating lobster rolls and kale soup, that Mat felt the odd sensation of having disparate worlds mingling together.

"You'll stay for dancing, yes?" Her mother's face was more expectant than questioning.

"Of course, Ma."

"Beatrice's mother says Constance might be gay, so you should dance with her, talk her up."

Mat had known Constance was gay ever since the sixth grade when they made out in the shadow of the monument at this exact event. The idea that she might just be coming around to owning it—or, perhaps more likely, telling her parents—made Mat vaguely sad. "Okay."

"I think she could use a friend is all. Someone in the community."

Mat appreciated that her mother wasn't in a constant state of trying to fix her up. She'd watched her brothers endure relentless attempts at matchmaking from the moment they turned eighteen until the day they got married. But as much as she didn't want it, it bothered her that the reprieve seemed to be solely a function of her sexual orientation. She wondered if that would change now that a nice, eligible Portuguese girl might be right under her nose. "I'll track her down, I promise."

She and Dom grabbed dinner. Mat enjoyed watching him scan the crowd for Renata. The two of them had been talking and flirting for months, but had yet to go on an official date, much less sleep together. It was frustrating to watch; she couldn't imagine living it. He'd always been rather old-fashioned. She hoped it was that holding him back and not some concern about how Renata felt about him being trans.

Mat indulged in a little crowd watching of her own. Between knowing so many people and the feeling that her mother was watching her, she didn't engage in any flirting. Didn't, at least, until she locked eyes with the woman from the pier. She was in a dress this time, a blue one that made her eyes stand out across the room. She appeared to be with someone, but that didn't stop her from offering Mat a smile. Mat returned it, wondering if she'd get a chance to talk with her this time.

Before she could act on it, Mat got pulled into a conversation with her Aunt Dores about the recent negotiations at Osteria 160. By the time Mat extricated herself, the gorgeous redhead with the bright blue eyes was gone. She chalked it up to fate, but not without hoping their paths might cross later.

Eventually, Dom found out from a cousin that Renata was home with the flu. The poor guy seemed utterly deflated.

"We'll go out after, take your mind off things." She slapped a hand on his shoulder, gave it a squeeze. "Who knows? Maybe some pretty girl will catch your eye." She didn't mention the one who'd already captured hers.

Dom shook his head and regarded her with disdain. "I'm pretty sure a bar is the absolute last place I'd go looking for the love of my life."

Mat made a confused face. "Who said anything about the love of your life?"

His only response was to roll his eyes. Mat enjoyed teasing him. It was part of their back-and-forth, not to mention part of what made him an excellent wingman. In truth, she found his quaint sensibilities sweet, even if she didn't share them.

She kept her promise to her mother, seeking out Constance in the crowd. But her concerns had been for naught. Constance, looking far more butch than Mat remembered or even would have imagined, had the rapt attention of no fewer than three women. Mat had to chuckle. Things sure had changed in the decade since she first came out, or perhaps more accurately, since she'd been yanked out of the closet against her will.

She wondered if her life might be different had she come out later, on her own terms. Probably not much. She could imagine her parents tolerating her sexuality a little better than they had at first, but truly supportive? She couldn't picture it. Which was why she kept her worlds nice and tidy and separate. It made it easier for everyone.

She nudged Dom, who also seemed to be watching Constance bask in the attention she was getting. "You ready to get out of here?"

He glanced at his watch. "It's barely nine."

She angled her head. "I don't see this party improving with age."

He snickered. "Good point. Let me kiss my mom good night."

Mat laughed, but spent the next few minutes doing the same. She might not want her worlds to collide, but she loved them both.

A short while later, she and Dom strolled down Commercial Street. "Maybe I should bring Renata some soup," Dom said.

Mat raised a brow. "If she's as gaga for you as you are for her, the last thing in the world she'll want is you showing up on her doorstep when she feels, and probably looks, terrible."

Dom frowned. "I don't care what she looks like when she's sick."

"No, but she might. Would you want her around if your head was in the toilet?"

He made a face. "When you put it that way."

They got to the club and she paid the cover for both of them. "Trust me."

"Thanks, dude. You know, in this one instance, you might be right."

Mat shot him a bland look. "Just this one?"

He gave her a shoulder bump as they walked down the dimly lit corridor. Bass pumped and colorful lights flashed on the floor in front of them. "Maybe a few others. But clearly I can't tell you that. It goes right to your head."

Mat shrugged. "I'll take that."

They approached the main room that held both the bar and the dance floor. The doors to the deck overlooking the harbor were open wide. It wasn't packed, but the crowd was solid and the dance floor more than half full. "Is this the point in the evening where I wish you good luck?"

Mat offered him a devilish grin. "Who says I need luck?"

"Right." He nodded. "Right."

Chapter Five

At Will's third yawn, Graham shook her head. "You should go home."

Will tapped her fingers against her mouth and smiled. "I don't know what you're talking about. I'm having a great time."

"You are a truly terrible liar."

"It's charming, right?"

"Utterly. I mean it, though. Some of our friends from work are here. I'll hang with them. I'm sure Nora is waiting up for you."

Graham couldn't see it in the dim light, but she was certain Will blushed. "Yeah."

"Don't feel bad. I'm glad one of us is getting some."

Will cringed, making Graham laugh. Will closed one eye, peeking at Graham through the other. "Is it weird that I still feel weird talking about it?"

"Not weird. Gallant. Maybe a little old school. Both of which are evidence you and Nora are perfect for each other."

"Yeah." Will got that goofy, faraway look on her face.

"Go. I'll be fine."

Will hesitated, but only for a second. "I'll leave my phone on. Promise you'll text if you need me."

Graham rolled her eyes, but smiled. "I won't, but thank you."

They exchanged hugs and Will left. Graham took a deep breath and surveyed her surroundings. She had a full view of the bar on the opposite wall and could just make out the couples enjoying the dimly lit deck. A handful of coworkers gathered to her left, along with a few people she didn't recognize. The dance floor was starting to heat up—boys mostly, but also a few older lesbians. She didn't know why she expected the woman from the lobster boat to be there. Graham had seen her at the dinner, surrounded by people. They locked gazes exactly two times. But she'd never been alone and Graham hadn't had the nerve to go up and talk to her.

Graham sighed. The woman was definitely a local, and probably still at the dance. She'd likely not deign to set foot in a club that catered to tourists.

Refusing to let herself mope, Graham headed to the bar. After procuring a vodka cranberry, she joined her friends. They talked and laughed about crazy customers and mishaps at sea. Kevin bought her another drink and she let herself get talked into dancing with Marta. There wasn't a reason in the world for her to be disappointed.

Graham was just telling herself that for the tenth time when she glanced at the door and froze. She was there, with the same guy from the boat. Graham said a silent prayer the resemblance meant they were related and not together. Then she allowed herself a moment to stare and simply appreciate the gorgeousness that was this woman.

She had the same high cheekbones and prominent brow Graham remembered, dark eyes Graham could—and desperately wanted to—get lost in. Her hair looked wind tossed, the slightly longer part on top with just a hint of curl. Graham's fingers itched to touch it. The tank top and work pants had been replaced. The dark jeans and shirt more *GQ* than fisherman, even more so now than when Graham had seen her at the beer garden. She still couldn't decide which was more appealing.

And then she looked Graham's way. Their eyes met. Graham's mouth came open. She was suddenly hot and short of breath. Never in her life had she felt such an intense and immediate reaction to another human being. Graham bit her lip, then smiled. The woman returned the smile, with the tiniest nod of acknowledgment.

The guy she was with said something and the spell was broken. The woman turned away and Graham forced her attention back to her friends. Of course, her distraction hadn't gone unnoticed. Marta looked at her expectantly and Kevin's perfectly plucked eyebrow arched.

"Looks like someone has a little crush." Kevin angled his head and put a hand on his hip.

Graham chuckled, not minding the teasing. "Is it possible to have a crush on someone you've never met?"

"Absolutely." Marta didn't hesitate. "Sometimes, those are the best kind."

Kevin shook his head. "She's right about the first part, but not the second. The best kind of crushes are the ones where you get laid."

He was joking—mostly—but Graham let his words sink in. She didn't see herself as the kind of person who'd go home with a different woman every night. But did that mean she couldn't go home with someone ever?

The closest thing she'd ever had to a hookup had been in college. After too many cheap beers, she'd made out with a girl who'd lived on her hall. They'd been casual friends before and agreed to return to that after. The attraction had been mutual, but fueled by alcohol on both sides. It had been easy, and fun.

Sure, her attraction to this woman was about a billion times stronger. Did it matter? Graham realized just how desperately she wanted this woman's attention, wanted to touch and taste and feel her naked body pressing Graham's into a mattress.

"Earth to Graham." Marta waved a hand in front of her face.

Graham resisted the urge to groan over the abrupt end to her fantasy. "Sorry."

"Don't be sorry." Kevin looked at her with exasperation. "Go talk to her."

Graham had a flash of the last time she attempted to make a move—planting a kiss on Will at Aunt Nora's New Year's Eve party. Not her finest moment. This was different, though. She and Will had been friends. If this woman wasn't interested, Graham wouldn't ever have to see her again. Graham nodded, her mind made up. She shoved her mostly full cup at Kevin. "Take my drink so I can go to the bar and get another."

"Happily." Kevin made a point of drinking from her cup, then his own. "Go get 'em, tiger."

Graham tossed her hair over her shoulder and headed to the bar, reminding herself to walk slowly. She positioned herself at an open space, but didn't hurry to make eye contact with one of the bartenders. Instead, she glanced at the woman.

Graham didn't know how long the woman had been looking at her, but she was now. Their gazes locked. Without breaking eye contact, she said something to her friend and started toward Graham. Graham swallowed. Holy crap. She was doing this.

"Hi."

Graham wouldn't have thought it possible, but the proximity intensified the attraction. "Hi."

"I'm Mat." The extended hand seemed casual, friendly, but the look in her eyes was anything but.

Graham reminded herself to breathe. "I'm Graham."

Mat quirked a brow. "Cute name. Can I buy you a drink, Graham?"

Was it as easy at that? "Sure."

"What's your pleasure?"

"Um." Where were her words? "Vodka cranberry, please."

"You got it." In a matter of seconds, Mat snagged the attention of the bartender, who knew her by name. Graham filed that detail away as Mat placed an order—vodka cranberry and a vodka soda. She slid money across the bar and a minute later handed Graham her drink. "Cheers."

"Cheers." Graham lifted her glass and took a sip of her drink, suddenly aware of how dry her throat had become.

They stepped away from the bar and off to the side of the dance floor. Conversation proved difficult over the pulsing dance music, but having Mat's mouth close to her ear as they talked had its merits. They carried on like that for maybe twenty minutes, talking about summer in P-town, seeing one another on the pier. Graham stole furtive glances at her friends, who at least tried not to be obvious in their staring. Graham sipped her drink, not wanting to be drunk, but thinking loosened inhibitions might be a good thing.

"You want to get out of here?"

At Mat's question, Graham leaned back. She tried searching Mat's eyes for meaning, but couldn't be sure what she saw. Maybe suggestive? But also playful. Relaxed. Having never done this before, Graham wasn't sure what signs she was looking for. There was only one way to find out.

She took a deep breath. A tiny voice in the back of her head screamed no. But the rest of her—her body, her ego, and the part of her brain that was tired of doing what she was supposed to do—said yes. Yes, yes, a thousand times yes. She smiled, offered a shrug she hoped was casual, but not disinterested. "Sure."

Mat took her hand and led her through the crowd. The simple gesture held Graham's attention. It was confident, direct, and sexy as hell.

A moment later, they stood on the street. The cool air and relative quiet felt like a shock to her senses. The proverbial bucket of cold water. She could change her mind, beg off. But if she did, any chance she had with Mat would be out the window. And, more importantly, she didn't want to change her mind. Graham looked up at the stars, waiting for Mat to make the next move.

"Would you like to go for a walk? Get another drink somewhere quieter?"

"I..."

"My place is a little ways from here, but not too far. A nice walk, if you're up for it."

Her place. Yes. On top of everything that implied, the prospect of a moonlit walk with Mat had a certain appeal. "Sounds perfect."

Mat placed a hand in the small of her back. "It's this way."

Graham tried not to fixate on the sensation of Mat's hand, the warmth of it obvious through the thin fabric of her dress. She allowed herself to be guided up a side street. They crossed Bradford and kept going. The houses started to feel less like vacation rentals and more like regular houses. Modest Cape Cods, a few ranches, with driveways and yards and the feeling they were lived in. It was strange the difference a few blocks could make.

Before long, Mat gestured to a driveway. "I'm down here."

The house reminded Graham of her place while she was in grad school. "Cute house."

"It's been in my family for ages. My cousin has one of the upstairs units and the other two are rented to seasonal workers."

"That's cool."

"It has its perks, for sure." Mat led her along the side to a door at the back. Mat unlocked the door, then reached in to flip on a light. "After you."

Inside, the apartment was cozy. The small living area and kitchen were one space. A table with two chairs sat against the wall by the door, creating an eating area of sorts. It wasn't overly decorated, but the art on the walls and photos stuck to the fridge with magnets made it homey. From where she stood, Graham could see into the bedroom and the bathroom. "This is nice."

"It works for me. Can I get you something to drink?"

Graham felt like she was in a movie, one of those cheesy straight romantic comedies. "Sure. Whatever you're having."

Mat pulled a pair of beers from the fridge, popped the lids, and handed Graham one. "Cheers."

Graham clinked her bottle to Mat's, then took a sip. Even though she hadn't really wanted it, the cold, crisp liquid helped to calm her nerves. Mat gestured to the sofa. Graham sat. "You've lived here your whole life?"

Mat nodded. "And my parents and their parents and their parents before them."

"I love that."

Mat shrugged. "It drove my brothers nuts. They couldn't wait to leave."

"But not you?"

"I never wanted to do anything but be on the water."

Graham could relate. Even though her family didn't live or work on the ocean, she wanted the same for as long as she could remember. "There's nothing like it."

They talked like that for a little while. The conversation was easier than Graham expected. Before long, she'd finished her beer and felt completely relaxed. Maybe she'd misread Mat's signals. Maybe they were just going to hang out.

She'd just started to process whether she was relieved or disappointed when Mat shifted slightly on the couch. She looked at Graham's mouth, then into her eyes. Such a small thing, but it communicated so much. Graham licked her lip, suddenly full of anticipation. And wanting. She couldn't remember wanting someone as badly as she wanted Mat right now. Mat must have read it in her eyes, because the next thing Graham knew, Mat's lips were on hers.

Graham expected an assault on her senses, a kiss that was aggressive and clear in its purpose. But Mat's mouth was soft, more invitation than demand. That didn't keep Graham's body from shifting into overdrive. Blood roared in her ears and she felt her panties grow damp. She grasped the front of Mat's shirt, heard herself moan.

Mat broke the kiss and pulled back. Graham panicked, convinced she'd let herself get carried away, ruined the moment. But Mat's eyes weren't cool or dismissive. No, they were even darker than before and filled with lust. The idea that Graham had put it there gave her immense satisfaction. Mat smiled slowly. And then she took over. The next kiss was not an invitation. Graham had clearly accepted and Mat was taking it to the next level. Her tongue traced Graham's bottom lip, teased her mouth open. Graham moaned again and Mat took advantage, slipping inside.

Mat shifted again and Graham followed her lead, easing back until her head rested on one of the pillows set against the arm of the sofa. She wondered vaguely if they'd been set there for just that purpose. Mat positioned herself over Graham, sliding a thigh between her legs. Before she could stop herself, Graham pressed against it. She felt Mat smile against her mouth.

Mat's hand was at her side. It moved up Graham's ribcage, then down. Changing positions had caused Graham's dress to ride up, leaving her thigh exposed. When Mat touched her, sliding a hand right over her ass, Graham almost lost it. She started pulling at the buttons of Mat's shirt, desperate to touch, to feel skin against skin. Mat obliged, wiggling her arms free and tossing the shirt to the floor.

God, she was gorgeous. Graham took a second to appreciate the definition of Mat's arms and shoulders, accentuated by the cut of her black sports bra. Knowing it was the result of work, and not hours in the gym, turned her on even more. "You are so fucking sexy."

Mat grinned. There was a cockiness that should have turned Graham off, but it didn't. "I was just thinking the same thing about you." She tugged at the bow holding the top of Graham's dress in place. She eased the bodice down, ran a fingertip across the pink lace of Graham's bra. "See, this is crazy sexy."

Graham flushed, equal parts embarrassment and desire. Instead of speaking, she put a hand on the back of Mat's neck, pulling her down for another kiss. Mat didn't protest. She spent what felt like ages lavishing attention on Graham's mouth, her neck, the top of her breasts. Graham's nipples strained, aching to be touched. Before she could find the words to say as much, Mat slid a hand behind her. In a matter of seconds, Graham's bra was gone. Mat's mouth teased and tortured. She sucked and swirled her tongue until Graham thought she might explode.

Graham continued to move against Mat's leg, wanting to be touched but also wanting to draw out this moment of reckless abandon. When Mat eased away, she literally whimpered. But then Mat moved down her body, pushing her dress up and sliding her panties down. Graham tried to find her voice, to articulate what she wanted, but nothing came out. When Mat's fingers brushed over her, Graham realized she didn't need to. Mat stroked her, gently but with purpose. Graham's body moved with her, as though they'd been together a hundred times.

When Mat eased a finger inside her, Graham thought she might die from pleasure. But then Mat added a second and Graham realized that, if she were to die of pleasure, that would be what did it. She rocked and writhed, using what little brain space she had to marvel that she'd gone so long without sex.

The orgasm crept up on her. And then it crashed over her, stealing her breath and any attempt she might have made to be graceful or pretty. Every muscle went rigid and Mat held her there for longer than seemed humanly possible. Graham finally collapsed, her skin sweaty and her bones feeling like jelly. "Oh, my God."

"Yeah."

Graham opened her eyes and found Mat smiling down at her, looking even more sure of herself than before. Graham bit her lip, unsure of what to say. She settled for, "That was incredible."

"Oh, it was credible. I promise." Mat's smile was smug, but seductive as hell. She stood and extended a hand. "Come on, let me actually take you to bed."

Graham took her hand and followed. She had no idea what the rest of the night would hold and didn't really care. She felt wanted and brazen and up for just about anything. She watched Mat shed the rest of her clothing and followed suit, wiggling out of the dress now bunched around her waist. Mat turned and crooked a finger, summoning her to the bed. Graham went to her, smiling at Mat, but also at herself.

This was what it was like to go home with someone. Why in the world had she waited so long?

Chapter Six

Mat opened one eye and looked down. Graham lay wrapped around her, sound asleep. Mat smiled. It had been a good night.

She hadn't gone out with the specific goal of bringing a woman home, but it was always a welcome culmination to an evening. She hadn't expected the cute girl who'd made eyes at her on the pier would be that woman. But that was one of her favorite things about her life—just how often she got to be pleasantly surprised.

She glanced at the clock on the bedside table. Close to nine. It was later than she usually slept, even when up late. Graham had certainly given her a good workout.

But sleeping late meant she didn't have the luxury of a leisurely morning. She'd finagled her way out of going to Mass, but needed to be in line for the blessing of the fleet. If she bailed on that, she'd never hear the end of it. Ever.

She ran her fingers through Graham's hair, kissed the top of her head. Graham didn't stir, even a little. Mat shifted in the bed. Graham's limbs were dead weight around her. What was it about being young that allowed people to sleep like the dead? Mat chuckled. She missed those days.

She eased herself away and climbed out of bed. Graham rolled into the empty space. Mat chuckled again and headed to the kitchen. She put on coffee, then took a shower. When she emerged a few minutes later, towel secured around her waist, she found Graham sitting up in bed. She had her knees up and her arms draped around them in that way girly girls tended to do. Mat smiled. "Good morning."

The smile Graham offered in return seemed hesitant, or maybe just shy. "Good morning."

"I put coffee on. Can I get you a cup?"

"That would be great." She nodded and her smile grew more confident.

"I'll be right back." Mat went back to the kitchen and poured two cups. "How do you take it?"

"Um, more cream and sugar than you'd think should go into a cup of coffee."

Mat laughed at the description. She doctored one of the cups, brought them into the bedroom. "It's not real cream, I'm afraid. I drink mine black so I only keep the powdered stuff around."

"It's all good." Graham accepted the cup, took a sip. She made a face, although Mat could see she was trying not to.

"Not sweet enough?"

"It's fine. I mean, it's great. Thank you."

Mat raised a brow. "You don't have to lie. Everyone is entitled to do whatever they want with their coffee."

Graham smirked in response. "You don't have to lie, either. Pretty much everyone I know judges me for how I like my coffee."

Mat spread her hands and moved them in circles around her. "This is a judgment free zone." She took the coffee, went to the kitchen, and stirred in another heaping spoonful of sugar.

Graham took it back, sipped, smiled. "Thank you."

"I aim to please." Mat was pretty sure that Graham blushed at the assertion, but she didn't look away. Instead, she bit her lip. It was the kind of gesture that made Mat want to crawl back into bed. Too bad she had places to be.

"I imagine you rarely disappoint," Graham said.

A loaded statement for sure, but Mat didn't figure Graham was looking to discuss the vagaries of living up to expectations. "I had a great time last night."

Again, the shy smile. "Me, too."

"I'm sorry to bail so early on a Sunday morning, but I have to be at the blessing of the fleet soon."

"Of course." Graham set the coffee aside and got out of bed. She looked around and frowned.

"I think the rest of your clothes are in my living room."

Graham giggled. It shouldn't have been adorable, but it was. "Right."

Mat followed her into the living room and watched as she pulled on her clothes. "Maybe I'll run into you again sometime?"

Graham slid into her shoes, then looked at Mat as though she was searching her face for meaning. Eventually, she nodded. "I'd like that."

"I'm sure I'll see you around the pier, yeah?"

Graham lifted a shoulder. "I'm there far more often than the club."

For some reason, Mat found the statement endearing. Maybe because it was true of her as well. "We should exchange numbers, too."

"That would be great."

Mat grabbed her phone, adjusting her towel as it started to slip. "Okay, give me yours." Graham did and Mat sent her a text. "Now you've got mine."

"Cool. So, um, I'll get out of your hair." Graham started for the door, then stopped. "Purse."

Mat grabbed it from the table and handed it to her. She took advantage of the proximity to slide a hand into Graham's hair. "Take care."

She told herself the kiss would be casual, brief. But Graham's lips were so damn soft, and then she opened her mouth and it was like an invitation. Mat slid her tongue inside, enjoying the way Graham tasted like coffee, but with a hint of sweetness. Graham purred and leaned in. Her body brushed against Mat's bare nipples and tempted Mat to ask for much more than a kiss.

Unnerved by the intensity of her reaction, she forced herself to pull away. Graham blinked a few times, clearly affected as well. Mat took a steadying breath, told herself it must be some kind of pheromone reaction.

"Have fun getting blessed." Graham grinned and put her hand on the doorknob. "Would you care to step back before I open the door?"

Mat looked down, realized she was nude from the waist up. She shrugged. "Nah."

That earned her a laugh. Graham opened the door and turned back one final time. "See you around."

Mat lifted her chin in acknowledgment. "See you."

With Graham gone, Mat finished getting dressed for the day. She grabbed her phone and realized she'd missed a text from Dom. *Is the coast clear?*

Mat smirked, even though he wasn't there to see it. *Just. Ready?*

She watched the three dots and waited. *I'll be down in five.*

❖

Graham left Mat's apartment and headed home. Jess was already at work, so she had no one to tell all about her exploits. Well, aside from Athena, Jess's cat, but she was super judgy. Since Will had been with her before Mat arrived, she decided to try her instead. *You'll never guess what I did last night.*

Graham got in the shower instead of waiting for a response. When she emerged, Will had answered. *You met a hot woman and went home with her.* The winky face that followed made it clear Will was teasing her.

Maybe I did.

The scream emoji followed, along with a demand to know what, how, and who.

Even though she and Will were on the same schedule for the week, there wasn't much time for chatting, especially if the content of said chat wasn't G-rated. So, an hour later, before they were both due to clock in, Graham found herself seated across from Will at a small table in The Flour Pot.

She sipped her iced chai, feeling content and maybe a little smug. The afterglow, it seemed, had a direct correlation to the quality of the sex.

"I assumed you were kidding." Will eyed her over the rim of her latte. "But now I'm not so sure. Why do you look like the cat who ate the canary?"

Graham shrugged, let the question hang for a moment. "I had sex with the hot lobsterwoman last night."

Will choked on her coffee. She coughed into one hand while waving the other back and forth in front of her face. When she finally stopped, her face held a mixture of concern and alarm. "You did what?"

"I went home with her. And it was amazing."

"I don't understand. I thought you hadn't even met her."

Graham tipped her head. "I hadn't. Until last night. She showed up not long after you left."

"Are you serious?"

She couldn't tell if Will was surprised, or disapproving. "Please don't get all judgmental."

Will shook her head emphatically. "No judgment. I swear."

"Good. I've never done anything even remotely like that before and I really don't want to feel bad about it."

"You are young and beautiful and single. You should do whatever you want that makes you happy." Despite the positivity of the statement, Will frowned.

Graham folded her arms. "But?"

"I guess," Will paused, clearly choosing her words carefully. "I've just never gotten the impression that's what you wanted."

Graham shrugged. "Not for my whole life, obviously. But I think it might be fun for a little while. I've always been such a goody-two-shoes."

"That's not true."

Graham gave her a withering look. "Yes, it is, and you know it."

"Okay, maybe. But there's nothing wrong with it."

"Will, do you know how many women I've slept with?"

The look of concern turned into one of pure discomfort. Graham didn't know if it was the fact that she'd once harbored a crush on Will or a more general case of too much information. "I don't need to know."

"Two. Two women. My girlfriend in college and this older doctoral student my first year of grad school. That's it."

"You say that like it's something terrible, something to be ashamed of."

Graham blew out a breath. "It's not that. It's just that I'm in my twenties and I want to live a little. Shouldn't I do that now, while I still can?"

Will leaned over and put a hand on Graham's arm. "Like I said before, I think you should do exactly what makes you happy. I don't want you to get hurt is all."

Graham tried not to be exasperated. Will meant well. It was actually kind of nice to have a protective older sister in her life. She decided not to harp on the implication that she was fragile or needy or any other annoying trait she despised. She wanted to revel in last night, not talk about its implications for her long-term prospects. So, instead, she offered a playful smile. "Aren't you going to ask me for the details?"

Will winced. "You want me to, don't you?"

"Well, I'm not going to tell Aunt Nora about it, so you're pretty much what I've got." She offered a smile. "Please?"

Will sighed dramatically. "Fine."

"After you left the bar last night, I was hanging out, lamenting the fact that she wasn't there. And then she was."

"I wish I'd stuck around to get a look at this woman."

"Will, she is so hot. There are no words to match how sexy she is." Graham closed her eyes for a second to indulge in a mental picture.

"Did you get her name?"

"Of course I got her name. Jeez." She gave Will a withering look. "It's Mat. I assume that's short for something, but I didn't ask."

"Ah. Last name?"

Crap. "That I did not get."

"Oh, well. Sorry I asked. I mean, jeez." Will's tone was playful, along with the way she lifted her hands and moved them around.

Graham bit her lip. "I suppose I asked for that."

Will nodded, but smiled. "You did."

"As I was saying, she came in with a guy I later learned was her cousin. It's the same one I've seen on her boat. Or maybe it's his. I'm not sure. Anyway, I walked up to the bar, made eye contact. She introduced herself, bought me a drink."

"Just like in the movies."

"If you mean sexy lesbian movies, then yes. We talked for a little while. She asked if I wanted to go somewhere we could talk. We ended up at her place."

"Are you shitting me? And that worked?" Will shook her head. "I can't believe that actually worked."

Graham shrugged. "Well, I'd sort of already decided to sleep with her, so I'm not sure if it's fair to say whether or not it worked."

"Right, right. So, you went to her place. Where does she live?"

"Sort of West End, but up a bit. Near Stop and Shop. Her family owns a multi-unit house and she's in one of the apartments."

"Nice."

"It was nice. Comfortable. Less cramped than some of the places right in the middle of town. We had a drink. We made out. She took me to bed."

"Wow." Will leaned back and shook her head again, still seeming to be in a state of disbelief.

"I know. I had a couple of moments where I couldn't believe what I was doing. But then I was like, why am I not doing this all the time? I could totally be a slut." Will blanched. Graham laughed. "In a good way. Liberated woman, doing her thing. To hell with societal constraints on female sexuality."

"Yeah."

She could tell Will was trying to be enthusiastic, which she appreciated. "And since you're being so supportive, I won't even inflict the specifics on you."

"I don't mean to be scandalized."

It was Graham's turn to touch Will's arm. "I know. I kind of like that you're romantic and old-fashioned. That's what I'll want when I settle down."

"Settle down." Will chuckled and rolled her eyes. "Just promise me you'll be careful."

"Like about getting tested and stuff?" Graham winced. "Yeah. We should have talked about that. If I see her again, we'll definitely have that conversation."

"I was thinking about your heart. But now that you say it, that, too." Will shook her head. "God, I don't miss dating."

If a tiny part of Graham agreed—longed for romance and true love—she wasn't about to admit it. She did long for those things. Just not now. "Eh, it has its perks."

"I believe you. Speaking of, are you going to see her again?"

Graham thought about the way Mat looked at her, touched her. "I sure as hell hope so."

Will nodded slowly. She looked pensive, like she wanted to go along with what Graham was saying, but was having a hard time. "Shall we head out?"

"I suppose."

They returned their dishes to the counter and headed down Commercial Street to the pier. Will's expression remained serious. "You're not growing bored with Provincetown, are you?"

Graham shook her head. "Of course not. I love my life, my job, my friends. I'm reveling in a little friendly diversion."

"Okay. I just don't want you up and leaving in search of excitement."

Graham laughed. "That's just it. There's plenty of excitement here. I've been remiss in taking advantage of it."

Will let out a small chuckle. "I guess that's one way of looking at it."

Graham gave her arm a squeeze. "Trust me. I know what I'm doing."

Chapter Seven

Mat had every intention of calling Graham, but she decided to give it a few days. Eager beaver was not her style. And she had no desire to change that.

In spite of adhering to her casual approach in action, her thoughts had been the exact opposite. The fact of the matter was, over the course of those few days, she'd been unable to get Graham out of her head. It wasn't just the physical, either. She'd had plenty of thoughts related to the feel of Graham under her, the look on her face as she came, the noises she'd made. But her mind had also wandered to the way she smiled or her playful spirit. They hadn't had that much conversation, and Mat found herself wanting to get to know Graham better.

Instead of focusing on that, she directed her attention to Dom, who'd shown up at the dock with a grin on his face and a bouncy energy that hadn't let up as they loaded bait and made their way to open water. By the time they arrived at the first trap, he'd started to whistle.

"Dude, why are you being all goofy today?" Mat moved lobsters to the banding box. "Wait, did you and Renata finally hook up?"

A slight shrug, but the smile didn't leave Dom's face. "Not by your standards."

Normally, she'd rib him about the universal definition of hooking up. But he seemed genuinely happy and finding out the specifics of why seemed more important. "But by yours? Do tell."

Dom transferred the catch, then looked at her. "I wouldn't use the phrase hooking up at all."

"Yes, yes. You're noble and a romantic and all that crap. Are you going to tell me what happened or not?" She rebaited the trap and shoved it overboard.

"I stopped by her office to see if she was feeling better."

"Please don't tell me that's all there is to the story. That you stood in front of her desk and made puppy eyes."

Dom made notations in their book. The fact that he wasn't immediately defensive told her there was more to the story. After a beat, he said, "I asked her out. And she said yes."

Mat slapped him on the shoulder. "I'm so proud."

"Don't be an ass. I know you think dates are for dorks."

She lifted her hands defensively. "Hey, that's not true." That earned her a look. "Okay, maybe a little true, but I'll have you know I'm planning a date myself."

"Are you serious?"

Mat had told Dom about her night with Graham, but not the fact that her phone number had been burning a hole in her pocket ever since. Not that she never called women, or went out with them a second time, but usually it was for drinks and a mutual understanding of what would happen after drinks. "Yeah. So maybe I should be asking you for pointers."

"The girl from the other night? The redhead?"

Mat nodded. "Her name is Graham. I actually saw her a couple of weeks ago on the pier. I caught her staring at me."

"Of course you did. Let me guess. She's been angling to go home with you ever since."

"I wouldn't go that far." Not that they'd talked about it. "That was the first time we spoke."

Dom shook his head. "I know it shouldn't surprise me at this point, but I still can't believe you'll go to bed with someone after one conversation."

"You can't be shocked that I'm planning a date and shocked that I have one-night stands."

"All right. I'll be shocked about the date since that's more of a rarity for you. Tell me about it."

Mat shrugged, feeling self-conscious all of a sudden. "There's not much to tell. I was thinking dinner, maybe at Audrey's restaurant."

"Nice. That'll require reservations, though, especially if you're thinking Friday or Saturday night. Are you going to pick her up?"

"It's like a ten minute walk from anywhere in town."

Dom rolled his eyes. "Not in your truck, dumbass. I mean walk to her place, then walk to the restaurant together."

"Oh." She'd not given it that much thought.

"That's pretty standard date fare."

Mat sighed. He was right, but she didn't have to like it. "You're going to tell me I should bring her flowers, aren't you?"

"I wouldn't dream of telling you to do that. Even though I've already ordered a bouquet for Renata."

"But you're wooing. I'm not." And had no plans to.

Dom shrugged. Mat couldn't tell if he was judging her or feeling sorry for her. "Maybe you should be."

Mat scowled. She didn't need to woo. The women she connected with weren't interested in that any more than she was. But even as she told herself that, Mat imagined Graham, smiling at a big bunch of tulips. She shook her head and pulled up another trap. "No, thank you."

"Have it your way. You're the one who said she was looking for pointers."

She had, but she hadn't been serious. And now he'd gone and put ideas in her head. "Enough about me. Tell me about your epic plans to woo Renata."

Dom's goofy grin returned. "Well, I ordered flowers. And I went with a reservation at Ciro and Sal's. I feel like it's old school romantic."

Mat couldn't disagree. If she were inclined to be romantic, she'd go with the candlelit wine cellar vibe, too. "And let me guess. Walk on the beach under a full moon when you're done. With a single, sweet kiss good night."

"You are such an ass."

"Yep." She knew he didn't mean it, or didn't really, at least, but his words stuck in her head. Would Graham expect flowers? No, that wasn't the right question. If Graham was the kind of woman who expected flowers, Mat would lose interest pretty quickly. What she wanted to know was if Graham might like flowers. Even more, would buying her flowers be nice or send all the wrong messages?

"Dude, relax. I was just yanking your chain."

She steered to the next trap. "I'm not mad."

Dom gave her a suspicious look. "Could have fooled me. You should see your face."

Now she was annoyed. Not with Dom, but with herself. She'd let him get under her skin, question her MO. She shrugged. "No, man, you just got me thinking about flowers. This is how I look when I think about flowers."

That got her a laugh. "I didn't realize they were such a trigger."

Mat hooked the next buoy and started hauling the trap to the surface. "More like an allergic reaction."

By four in the afternoon, they'd hit their daily quota of traps and called it a day. Definitely a decent catch. They unloaded, docked the boat, and finished cleaning and prepping for the next day. Dom was more focused than usual and they finished in about half the usual time.

"Wait, is this date tonight? Is that why you're in such a hurry?"

"Yeah, dude. I got things to do and places to be."

Mat smiled, feeling a deep wave of affection for the guy who was so much more of a brother to her than any of her actual brothers. "You should have said so. I could have finished on my own."

He smiled. "I'm good. I'm not going to leave you hanging."

They climbed the ramp to the main pier and headed toward Mat's truck. At the divided house they both called home, Mat punched him lightly on the shoulder. "Good luck tonight. I mean it."

"Thanks. You going to call Graham?"

Mat considered. "You know, I think I might."

Dom raised a brow. "No flowers, though."

"You never know, man. You never know."

They parted ways and Mat went into her apartment. First things first. She peeled off her clothes, tossed them in the hamper, and went straight for the shower. A few minutes later, she stood in her kitchen in dark green boxer briefs and an undershirt. She popped a beer and leaned against the sink, phone in hand. She pulled up Graham's number and studied it, quickly dismissing the idea of an actual phone call.

Mat typed a couple of versions, realizing uncomfortably that Graham might not even be interested in a second date. Or would it be a first? She shook her head. She did not like the bubble of uncertainty and couldn't remember the last time her confidence had wavered this much. She settled on a message and hit send before she could overthink it any more.

Hey. It's Mat from the other night. Remember me? She added a winky face to make it clear she was being flirty and not insecure. She waited a beat. Delivered, but not read. Mat set down her phone and walked away.

A minute later she picked it up. No change. She scrolled through her recent messages. Maybe she should distract herself with some company. But as she did so, her brain remained stubbornly fixated on Graham. Since it felt skeevy to hit on one woman while thinking about another, she put the phone back down. She'd almost crossed the room when it pinged with a new text alert.

Hey, Mat from the other night. I most certainly remember you.
She'd added a pair of little flames at the end. Mat grinned. Light, flirty. In short, perfect. *Wondering if you might be interested in getting together again. Perhaps with dinner this time.*

There was no pause this time in the response. *Would love to. Free any evening this week but Friday.*

Thursday would be sooner, but that wasn't necessarily a good thing. She didn't want to seem too eager. *Saturday? Osteria 160? I know the chef and could get us a reservation.*

Sounds perfect. Let me know what time and I'll be there.

Mat promised to be in touch soon. It was a relief that Graham put out the idea of meeting there. It meant she didn't have to think about picking her up. Or getting flowers. Feeling much more relaxed about the whole thing, she opened her fridge and contemplated what to have for dinner.

❖

Graham came home from work vaguely disappointed. She'd looked for Mat's boat, but it wasn't in its slip. She'd then stalled for a good twenty minutes. Still no Mat, and she'd managed to make herself feel silly. Kind of like an eager teenager. Not the vibe she was going for.

Fortunately, she had Jess to prevent her from moping. They threw a frozen pizza in the oven and Jess offered to distract her with the latest of her own escapades. This consisted of meeting a guy at the vet's office where she worked and trying to figure out if his flirtations were casual or in earnest. Jess had decided she wanted them to be earnest, so she was figuring out how to make it easy for him to ask her out. That quickly turned into her deciding she should just ask him out and get it over with already.

Graham appreciated the distraction, as well as Jess's no-fear approach to dating. She liked to think it was rubbing off on her, if slowly. She was about to say as much when her phone pinged. It was Mat. She showed Jess the screen. Jess made an oohing sound. Graham took a minute to decide on her reply before unlocking her phone.

"Just do it. Don't overthink it," Jess said.

Graham bit her lip, typed a response. They went back and forth for a moment. She looked up and found Jess sitting with her legs crossed, twiddling her thumbs. Athena sat on the back of the sofa, her disinterest looking far more genuine.

"Sorry."

"Don't apologize." Jess waved a hand in dismissal. "Just tell me what she said."

"We're going out Saturday." Graham couldn't suppress a smile. She had a date.

"Out for drinks? Out for dinner? Out as nothing more than a pretext for going back to her place?"

"Jess." Graham tried to make her voice stern. It didn't work.

Jess raised her hands and shrugged. "What? It's a perfectly valid question."

It was. And as much as Graham hoped for a repeat of her previous Saturday night, it would have felt weird if the invitation came off as nothing more than a booty call. "Dinner. Well, dinner and probably going back to her place."

"What did she say? Tell me exactly."

Graham looked at the screen. "She said, 'Wondering if you might be interested in getting together again. Perhaps with dinner this time.'"

"Oh, that's good. I like that very much."

"And then she offered to get a reservation at Osteria 160."

"Mmm." Jess nodded her approval. "Classy, but not over the top."

Graham hadn't been there. "She said she knows the chef."

"Nice. I like this woman. What's her name again?"

"Mat."

"Such a cute, preppy butch name."

Graham made a face. "I'm pretty sure she isn't preppy."

Jess shrugged, unfazed. "That's okay. It's still a nice name. What are you going to wear?"

"I don't know. I literally made plans two minutes ago."

"You mean to tell me you haven't spent the last three days thinking about going out with her again and, by extension, where you would go and what you would wear."

She had given it some thought, but didn't intend to give Jess the satisfaction of saying so. Instead, she quirked a brow. "In most of my thoughts, we aren't wearing anything at all."

"Damn, girl." Jess did a little dance from her spot on the sofa. "Looks like someone found your vixen switch."

In truth, she talked sassier than she felt. Still, there was something to be said for fake it till you make it. If Mat was convinced enough to ask for a repeat, she was doing something right. It was her turn to shrug. "Lights on and open for business."

Jess whooped her approval just as the timer on the oven began to beep. Since she was on a roll, Graham didn't want to admit her relief, but she was glad for the distraction. She liked the idea of having a bold, uninhibited side, but the reality of it—not to mention acting on it—still felt a little unnatural.

Graham went to the kitchen and slid the spinach pizza from the oven. She cut it into slices and divided it between two plates. She returned to the living room and handed one to Jess. "Bon appétit."

Jess picked up one of the pieces, blowing on it before taking a bite. "You know, we should probably cook for real at some point."

"Yeah, but this is so good. And cheaper than buying a ton of ingredients." And between pizza, the tikka masala and saag paneer that came in pouches, and the frozen veggie burritos she'd discovered, it didn't get boring.

Jess nodded. "Agreed. It just seemed like what I was supposed to say."

Graham took a bite of her own pizza. It really was good. "If I'm going to embrace being sexually liberated, I'm sure as hell not going to feel ashamed about not slaving away in the kitchen all day."

"Well said, my friend." Jess lifted one of her slices in a toast. "Well said."

Conversation lulled as they ate. Jess clicked on the television and flipped the channel to *Jeopardy*. Graham started thinking about what she'd wear on her date. Her phone dinged again, but when she looked down, it was a text from Will that appeared on her screen, not Mat. *What are you up to? Please don't say an orgy.*

Graham snorted a laugh at the insinuation. *I'm not that girl... yet.*

She filled Will in on her plans with Mat. Will didn't try to hide her relief that it was an actual date. Graham promised to learn Mat's last name, find out whether lobstering was her primary profession, and to be careful. She also promised to join Will and Nora for dinner the following week.

After a cheesy movie with Jess, Graham decided to go to bed early. She picked up her Kindle, but left it on her chest as she stared at the ceiling. She was going on a date with Mat. A real one. And yet, the weird nervousness she usually felt about sex—would they, wouldn't they—had already been resolved. It still felt strange, but she was getting more and more behind the whole idea of having sex not be this monolithic thing. It took so much of the pressure off.

She set the Kindle aside and turned off the lamp. In the darkness, she did a mental inventory of her closet. Despite her joke earlier, she did want to look nice and the right outfit would be key—more dinner date than dance club. Maybe the lime green dress? She wondered what Mat might wear. Then, without really meaning to, Graham started thinking about Mat without clothes. She imagined her hands on Mat's golden skin, her dark nipples hard under Graham's hand.

The image brought with it a quick flash of arousal. Graham pressed her thighs together in an effort to stave off the feeling, the wanting that came with it. Saturday suddenly felt a long way off.

Chapter Eight

Graham arrived at the restaurant a few minutes early, but Mat was already there. She stood on the sidewalk, scrolling through something on her phone and looking sexy as hell. The outfit wasn't all that different from the night at the club, only she'd swapped the dark jeans for black pants and wore a gray button-down instead of black. Her hair managed to look put together and messy at the same time. Graham patted her own hair instinctively. Satisfied it wasn't too windblown, she said, "Hi."

"Hey." Mat looked her way and offered an easy smile. She slid her phone into her back pocket and walked toward Graham. When Mat reached her, she put a hand on Graham's arm, leaned in, and kissed her cheek.

Graham blushed, not because she didn't like it, but because she didn't expect it. Of course, she'd never gone on a first date after having sex with someone. "Good to see you again."

"Same. Hungry?"

"Sure."

They walked the short distance to the restaurant door. Mat put her hand on Graham's lower back. It was a casual gesture, but also intimate. Graham liked it. A lot. Mat opened the door and gestured for Graham to lead the way. In a matter of minutes, they were seated at a table near the window. Outside, the tiny patio was crowded with flower pots overflowing with petunias and impatiens. She agreed with Jess's description—classy, but not over the top.

"How do you know the chef?" Graham asked.

Mat grinned. "I recently convinced her to let my family's business be her exclusive lobster supplier."

"Nice." Graham meant the arrangement, but she also liked that Mat was part of a family business. "Is it you and your parents? Siblings?"

"It's everyone." Mat angled her head and smiled. "Not really, but it feels that way sometimes."

Graham laughed. "I can imagine."

"I operate a boat with my cousin, Dom. My dad just retired. He sold his boat to one of my cousins. Two of my uncles are still at it and a third runs the distribution side of things."

"Wow."

"Yeah. We go way back."

Graham thought about having a line of work so deeply entrenched in the family. It probably came with a fair share of headaches, but it had a certain appeal. "I love that."

Their waiter approached the table to run through the specials and take drink orders. Mat went with an IPA while Graham ordered a glass of sauvignon blanc. They perused the menu, with Mat settling fairly quickly on the steak frites. "I eat lots of seafood," she said with a shrug.

Graham laughed. "Of course. I'm leaning toward the salad with grilled peaches and burrata, but I also want fries. Should I order my own or may I steal some of yours?"

Mat's smile was playful and a little suggestive. "I'll share."

"Perfect."

The waiter returned and they placed their orders. When he left, there was a brief lull in the conversation. She studied Mat and decided to indulge her curiosity. "Why do I get the feeling you don't do this very often?"

"Do what very often? Eat?" Mat sipped her beer, set it down slowly. It wasn't a surprise that Graham would be assessing her, trying to figure her out. That didn't stop it from making her uncomfortable. What did surprise her was realizing how much she wanted Graham to like her.

Graham gave her a knowing smile. "Take a woman out to dinner, on an actual date."

Mat folded her arms and leaned forward, resting her elbows on the table. "Are you accusing me of being cheap?"

"Oh, no." Graham shook her head slowly, still with that smile. "I didn't mean to imply that at all."

"So?" Mat knew where Graham was going, but wanted to hear her say it. Her tone would say a lot about how Graham viewed the two of them, as well as what she expected. "What are you implying?"

Graham crossed her arms, mirroring Mat's pose. "You seem a bit out of your element. It was just an observation."

Mat frowned. She hated being transparent. Worse, she hated the idea that Graham could read her so easily. It meant that Graham had some kind of crazy deep perceptiveness going on or that they had a connection that went well beyond the bedroom. "I think I preferred the insinuation I'm cheap."

Graham laughed, a low, sensual sound that made her seem older than Mat guessed her to be. "Come on, you're making me feel bad."

Mat pointed a finger at her. "Hey, you're the one who started it."

Graham leaned back. Her eyes remained playful. "Well, you never answered my question."

Normally, Mat hated being teased, at least by someone outside her immediate family. So often, it veiled something mean-spirited or held some ulterior motive. But Graham seemed different, genuinely playful. It made Mat want to play along. "Technically, you asked why you had a feeling. I know better than to tell a woman the why or how of her feelings."

Graham considered. "Touché. Let me rephrase. Is this unusual for you?"

"I wouldn't say unusual." Mat angled her head. "Just not my standard MO."

"I see." Graham tapped a finger to her lips. "For what it's worth, I think the trappings of dating can be overrated."

Trappings of dating? Mat swallowed the laugh that bubbled up, certain that Graham didn't mean it in a humorous way. Instead, she focused on the sentiment of the words, which she could totally get behind. "Agreed."

Graham lifted her wine glass, tapped it lightly to Mat's beer. "To breaking with convention."

Mat picked up the glass to make it a proper toast. "I'll drink to that."

Their food came. Graham ate her salad, stealing fries from Mat's plate as promised. She asked about Graham's education—where she went to school and how she chose her field. She figured it was a safer topic than family or work, one that would keep them in nice, casual territory. Graham's answers were thoughtful, with just a hint of self-deprecation. Rather than making Mat feel like they had little in common, she found herself nodding in agreement. Their experiences couldn't have been more different, but Graham had much more of a practical streak than Mat had given her credit for. Not to mention a love for being on the water.

Despite Mat's intentions, Graham asked about her family. Mat went with her stock answer—they were close, but being gay complicated things. As expected, Graham acknowledged how hard that could be, then didn't protest when Mat steered the conversation to lighter topics. She felt a little bad shutting Graham down so quickly, but it was probably better—and definitely easier—that way.

When the check came, Graham put up more than a token argument about splitting it. Mat insisted but promised Graham could pay the next time. It surprised Mat to already know she wanted there to be a next time. They left the restaurant and wandered down Bradford Street. Despite being nearly nine, the last strains of sunset remained in the sky, streaking it with pink, orange, and purple. The thinnest sliver of moon hung overhead.

"Nice night," Graham said.

Mat gave in to the urge to take her hand. "The summer more than makes up for how much the winters suck."

Graham smiled and raised a shoulder. "I love summer, but I don't even mind the winter so much. Everyone huddles in and hunkers down. I invite myself to my aunt's inn when she doesn't have any guests and curl up by the fire all day with a good book."

"I guess there's some of that. I'm thinking about trying to do a day's work when it's ten degrees out."

"Don't you stop for the winter?"

"Definitely the worst of it. By January, I'm glad to come in out of the cold for sure. But even then, I get restless pretty quick."

"You? Restless? I can't imagine." Graham's eyes sparkled with humor.

"There's also the non-existent social scene."

"Ah." Graham nodded. "Now the truth comes out. The off season cramps your style."

"Well." Mat cringed slightly. How'd she manage to walk into that one?

"No, no. I feel you. I've got friends and my aunt, but I can get bored, too." Graham looked away, seemed to get wistful for a minute. "Although, honestly, I'm a homebody at heart."

Mat smiled. "You say that like it's a bad thing."

"Not bad, just," Graham paused, looked at Mat. "This is where I confess that this isn't how I usually go about things."

"This like right now?" Mat pointed back and forth between the two of them.

Graham laughed. "More like last time. Going home with someone from a bar."

"Oh." Mat tried to ignore the sinking feeling in her chest. "Do you regret the other night?"

Graham quickly shook her head. "No, not at all. It was great."

"But?" Mat waited. There had to be a but.

"I should have asked the other night, but I didn't think about it. And I really don't want to be clumsy about this, but I'm pretty sure I am, so please forgive me. I know we're low risk and all, but like, do you get tested?"

Oh. Mat swallowed the sigh of relief, not wanting to seem indifferent. "No, I'm the one who should apologize for not bringing it up. I do, probably not quite as often as I should, but at least a couple of times a year. Clean bill of health."

Graham did let out a sigh. "Okay, good. Thanks. Sorry I was awkward."

"Not awkward at all. What about you?"

"What about me?"

Mat chuckled. This had to be the most endearing conversation about STDs she ever had. "Do you get tested?"

"Right." Graham rolled her eyes. "Me. Yes. It was a year ago, but I haven't been with anybody since."

"Excellent. We're good. Thank you for bringing it up. Really." They continued to stroll. Although they'd not discussed it, there seemed to be a mutual agreement about where they were headed. It struck Mat that she shouldn't presume. "Did you want to stop for a drink? Dessert?"

Graham smiled. "I'm good I think."

"Okay. Were you thinking—"

"I'd love to go back to your place."

Mat gave her hand a squeeze. "Good."

They turned onto Mat's street. Mat stole a glance at Graham, who seemed happy and relaxed. Not that Mat wasn't those things, but Graham's words replayed in her mind and made her think. Graham hadn't been with anyone in a year. It wasn't any of her business, but something about it made her uneasy. Like it didn't compute.

She shoved the questions aside. It wasn't any of her business. Graham didn't owe her an explanation, nor had she expressed any expectations about what their night together meant, or should mean. From the looks of it, she didn't seem to have a care in the world. And that, Mat reminded herself, was exactly what she was looking for.

She unlocked the door to her apartment, focusing on the way anticipation seemed to hang in the air. She closed the door behind them, but Graham didn't move any further into the room. Her hand brushed Mat's arm, settled on her side. Through the thin fabric of her shirt, Mat felt its warmth. She could so easily imagine that hand on her bare skin—touching, grabbing, scratching. Although Graham's initial vibe had been subdued, hesitant almost, she'd opened under Mat's touch. By the end, she'd come out of her shell. She'd been bold, brazen. Mat hoped that was the Graham she'd get tonight.

"Can I get you something to drink?" Mat asked, more out of habit than anything else.

Graham smiled at her, more coy than shy, and raised a shoulder in a casual shrug. "I'm good, actually."

"Okay, then." Mat took that as all the invitation she needed. She closed the space between them and plunged her hands into Graham's hair. She brought her mouth to Graham's, no longer worried about being gentle or light.

Graham's mouth, and her body, responded with enthusiasm. Her tongue came out to tease Mat's and her hands crept under the hem of Mat's shirt. She raked her nails over the skin of Mat's lower back.

"Mmm."

Mmm was right. Mat almost always found something to enjoy in kissing a woman, in taking her to bed. But something about Graham was different. It went beyond pleasure, threatening to take over her brain as much as her body. She set aside any alarm over the intensity of her reaction, focusing instead on getting Graham out of her dress. She ran her hand up and down the back, feeling for a zipper. Not finding one, she grasped the fabric at Graham's hips, thinking she'd need to pull it over her head.

"It's on the side." Graham's words were muffled against Mat's mouth, but Mat got her meaning.

"Got it." Mat found the zipper and eased it down. It created enough give to slide the straps from Graham's shoulders and push the dress to the floor. Graham stepped out of it and Mat took advantage of the space between them to appreciate the view. Her bra was hot pink satin with lime green embroidery and matched the hip-hugger panties. "Much better."

"Fair's fair," Graham said. She made quick work of Mat's shirt and sports bra, then started on her pants.

Mat watched her hands. Something about slim, manicured fingers unbuckling her belt turned Mat on like nothing else. When Graham was done, but before she could push the pants down, Mat grabbed her around the waist. "Let's move this to the bedroom, shall we?"

Once there, Mat kicked off her shoes and let Graham dispense with her pants. They tumbled to the bed in their underwear, then rolled. The next thing Mat knew, Graham was on top of her, straddling her hips. She could feel Graham's heat as she writhed on top of her. Combined with the vantage point—Graham's strawberry blond hair spilling over her shoulders, her breasts peeking out from the top of her bra—the position might have been Mat's favorite.

She sat up just enough to reach around Graham's back and flick open her bra. She cupped Graham's breasts, grazed her thumbs over rosy nipples that hardened on contact. Even better.

Graham continued to move on top of her, driving Mat just the right amount of crazy. She moved her hips, pressing them up and setting a slowly delicious pace. Graham closed her eyes, made little noises that made Mat want nothing more than to plunge into her. But she waited, wanting to draw the moment out, make Graham frantic for release.

When her own need began to throb more insistently between her legs, Mat slid her hands up the front of Graham's thighs. She stilled her hips and used the resulting space to slide her fingers into Graham's panties. God. She was so fucking wet.

Graham's eyes flew open, her gaze fixed on Mat's. Mat offered her a knowing smile. She watched Graham bite her lip, take an uneven breath. And then, without any further coaxing on her part, Graham started to ride her.

It was beautiful to watch. As much as Mat enjoyed having her own orgasm, she preferred this. Watching another woman come undone at her touch.

Graham shifted slightly, coming up onto her knees just a bit. Mat took advantage, sliding her fingers down Graham's slick folds and plunging two into her. Graham cried out and fell forward. She placed a hand on either side of Mat's shoulders, braced herself in a way that caused her nipples to brush Mat's each time she rocked back and forth. Her hair curtained both their faces.

Mat felt Graham tighten around her fingers. Her lips formed a perfect "O," but no sound came out. Mat held her fingers in place. A wave of liquid heat enveloped her hand. Graham's entire body went rigid, then shuddered.

After a long moment, Graham eased herself away. She sat back on her heels and rested her forehead on Mat's stomach. If Mat had any concerns about the intensity of her reaction to Graham, she could at least take comfort in knowing it seemed to be mutual. She patted the mattress next to her. "Come here."

Graham lifted her head and grinned. "No way."

Without another word, Graham inched down the bed. She hooked her fingers in the waistband of Mat's boxer briefs and tugged. Mat lifted her hips to make the job easier. When they were gone, Graham settled herself between Mat's legs. Mat lifted her head, thinking perhaps this view might actually top the one from earlier.

"Talk to me. Tell me what you like," Graham said.

Mat opened her mouth to speak, but before any words would form, Graham's tongue pressed against her clit. She made circles around it, sucked it gently. The throbbing she'd experienced earlier had nothing on this. Mat closed her eyes, content to let Graham do whatever she wanted. "That. Yep. All of it. It's all good."

She thought she felt Graham smile against her. Mat smiled in return, even though Graham couldn't see. Graham continued to work magic with her tongue. She stroked and sucked and did all sorts of incredible things, but never one thing long enough to make Mat come. It was amazing until it wasn't, until the need for release took on an edge that bordered on pain. "Right there. Exactly that. Don't stop."

Graham obliged. Her tongue made long swipes, passing squarely over Mat's clit with each upward pass. It didn't take long for the pressure to build. Mat grasped at the sheet beneath her. She bore down, letting the wave of pleasure radiate outward. She groaned and gave herself to it. Her muscles trembled and her skin flushed hot as the orgasm permeated her entire body.

The ripples finally subsided, leaving her weak and disoriented. She felt sated, but also spent. Mat shook her head back and forth, trying to clear the fog from her brain.

"No? You're shaking your head no. Is something wrong?" Graham's voice held worry.

Mat shook her head with more intention. "No. I'm good. That was good." She picked up her head and saw Graham's face, still between her thighs. "More than good. Beyond good."

Graham smiled, but she didn't seem entirely convinced. "Just checking."

Mat crooked a finger, beckoning Graham to join her. Graham obliged. Mat stretched out her arm and Graham nestled into it, curling against her. "That was incredible. Like, knock-my-socks-off amazing. I swear."

Graham laughed softly. "You don't have to say that. I just wanted to make sure you were okay."

Mat planted a kiss on the top of Graham's head. "I am so much more than okay."

"Good."

"I'm hoping maybe you'll let me show you. Will you stay?"

Graham lifted her head and looked at her like that was the most absurd question in the world. "Of course I'll stay."

Mat smiled. "Great. Just give me a minute to get circulation back to my extremities and we'll be good to go."

It was Graham's turn to shake her head. She reached up and kissed Mat on the mouth. "No rush. We have all night."

They most certainly did.

Chapter Nine

"Ah, fuck."

The expletive yanked Graham from sleep. "Huh? What?"

"Sorry." Mat set down her phone and looked at Graham. "I didn't mean to wake you."

Graham blinked. It was still dark outside. She had no idea what time they'd finally fallen asleep, but it felt like hardly any time had passed. "Is something wrong? What time is it?"

Mat sighed. "Just after four. My cousin is sick."

Graham couldn't remember the last time she got a text at four in the morning. "Is it serious? Is he in the hospital?"

Mat smiled at her. "No, no. He's just not coming out with me today."

"Oh." Of course he'd be calling in sick at this hour.

"He's claiming a stomach bug, but I'm guessing it's a case of morning after."

Graham lifted her head so she could study Mat in the dim light. "Morning after?"

"He finally hooked up with this girl he's been flirting with for weeks. I'd bet money he's looking for round two this morning."

Graham tried to process Mat's explanation, decipher her feelings on the subject. She didn't seem angry. Resigned, maybe. "Does he bail on you often?"

At the question, Mat smiled. "No. He's quite responsible. But he's been boning on this girl pretty hard. And he hasn't dated all that much since his top surgery."

"Ah."

"Yeah. I don't begrudge him this. It just fucks with my schedule. I was hoping to do a double haul today to avoid the storm we're getting tomorrow."

Graham swallowed. The idea of spending the whole day with Mat took root in her mind. She might not have experience, but she was able-bodied and not afraid of a little hard work. "I could go out with you."

Mat rolled onto her side. Even with the low light, Graham could read skepticism on her face. "Have you ever even been on a lobster boat?"

Graham scowled. "No, but I've been on a number of fishing vessels, including a crab boat down in Maryland." She didn't add that those times had been as a research assistant, not a fisherman.

Mat sat up. Graham hoped that meant she was considering the offer. "What did you do exactly on those boats?"

Caught. Damn. "Measured specimens and looked for geographic trends." She could see Mat's expression change. "I also helped to bait traps." The second part was technically true, even if she'd only done a couple to say she had.

"I wouldn't work you too hard. But it is safer to have a second body on board." Mat nodded. "Even if we only haul fifty, the day wouldn't be a total loss."

Graham tried not to bristle at being referred to as a second body. Especially since she really didn't have any idea what the work would entail or if she'd prove herself useful. "When do we leave?"

Mat raised a brow and offered a smile that felt to Graham like a challenge. "Right now."

Without waiting for further direction, Graham bounded out of bed. She was awake now, and ready to go.

Half an hour later, she was aboard the *Paquette*, pulling on a pair of rubber overalls. Closer quarters than what she was used to on a boat, but in a good way, given the company. And the open back kept it from feeling claustrophobic.

Although her initial desire had been to spend a day with Mat, to see her in her element, the prospect of learning the art of lobstering now sat pretty high on her list. She just hoped she didn't make a fool of herself in the process. Mat, who'd gone to collect several bins of bait, reappeared on the dock. "Can I hand these down to you?"

"Sure." Graham wiggled, trying to acclimate to the heavy pants. "They're pretty heavy."

Graham gave her a bland look. "I'm not fragile, you know."

Mat smiled. Graham thought there might be a hint of smugness in it. "Right."

She handed Graham the bin. Heavy, but nothing crazy. Thanks to the gym and helping out at the inn when Aunt Nora broke her arm, her upper body strength wasn't half bad. "Got it."

Three more bins and Mat was joining her back on board. She started the motors and began what looked to Graham like a series of checks. She wanted to ask a hundred questions, but didn't want to make Mat regret taking her along. "I don't want to drive you crazy, but I'd love to know anything and everything you're willing to explain."

Mat nodded. "Okay. Let's get out on open water and then we'll have a little lesson."

"Sounds good."

They moved at a fairly rapid clip, the wind whipping Graham's ponytail around. The air was misty and cool, making her extra glad she'd borrowed a jacket in addition to a sweatshirt. Mat explained where she set traps, how she kept track of them. She also talked about her family's decision to keep with the traditional single trap per line. "The big commercial trawlers like to brag about having fewer lines in the water, but if a whale swims into one of mine, I'm a hundred percent sure it will be able to break free."

Graham thought about her training with the Dolphin Fleet. She'd been taught to highlight the delicate balance between conservation and economic forces, often cited the local lobstering industry as an example of those forces working together. Listening to Mat allowed her to truly believe it.

Before long, Mat approached a buoy with the color markings she'd described as hers. She cut the engine and reached over the side of the boat with the gunwale. She grabbed the buoy with her other hand and slid it into the pulley that stuck out from the top of the boat. "I thread the rope into the hydraulic lift and let it do most of the work." She threw a switch and the rope started to feed through the contraption into a drawer at Mat's feet. She wrapped her right hand around the rope as it came out of the water, sending muck and seaweed flying.

"Are you guiding the rope or cleaning it off?"

Mat smiled and Graham tried to ignore the heat that moved through her and settled right between her legs. "Both."

After about a minute, a trap emerged and Mat cut the lift. With two gloved hands, she hauled the trap onto the wide rail of the boat. Graham counted four lobsters in one chamber of the trap. "We got some."

Mat laughed. "Don't count your lobsters before they're inspected."

Graham watched as Mat unlatched the top of the trap. She pulled one out and gave it the once over. "Nice male here." She set it in one square of the gridded box behind her, then repeated with the second. "See the V?" Mat pointed to a notch in the tail.

Graham nodded. "Yep."

"That means she's a reproducing female. Back she goes." Mat threw the lobster overboard.

Graham was about to ask for explanation when Mat pulled the third lobster out. "Now this one doesn't have a V, but she's got eggs." Mat gestured to the cluster of black on the underside of the lobster. Then she took a small metal tool and cut a notch into one of the flipper shells at the end of her tail. And back into the water she went.

"Okay, I get why you don't keep reproducing females, but I don't know the system."

"Anytime a female is caught with eggs, she gets a notch cut in her tail. That makes her illegal to possess. It takes about seven years for the V to grow out, which is about how long she'll reproduce. So anytime you catch one with a V, she has to go back. And if I catch a female with eggs that isn't marked, I notch her and throw her back."

Graham nodded. So complicated. She understood why they did it that way, but still. Complicated. "You end up throwing back half of what you catch."

Mat shrugged. "It feels that way. Probably more like a third."

"And what about this last one?" Graham eyed the lobster. It was a big one and, based on the claws, looked to be female.

Mat grabbed it by the tail, but she locked onto the wire mesh of the trap and didn't budge. Rather than yanking, Mat picked up one of the small crabs that had come up with the trap. She held it in front of the lobster and, sure enough, the lobster let go to grasp at it. Mat looked at the tail, then flipped it over to check the underside. "No eggs, no V. She's coming with me."

Graham couldn't help but snicker at the saying. "That's funny."

"You'd be surprised what we come up with out here to entertain ourselves."

"I can only imagine."

"Now we bait." Mat took a salt-cured skate from the bin at her feet and speared it, belly up, on the stake in the middle of the trap. She latched the trap closed, but instead of dropping in back in the water, put the boat in gear. "I use GPS to put them back in the same spot every time."

"That's genius."

"I don't know about genius, but it's efficient. I'm all about efficient." They went a short distance, and Mat shoved the trap overboard.

"So, one down, one hundred and forty-nine to go."

Mat tipped her head. "Give or take. How do you feel about banding?"

Graham eyed the two lobsters in the box and decided this was not the time for complete honesty. "You tell me how to do it without losing a finger and I'm your girl."

Mat picked up the larger of the lobsters, squeezing each claw shut. "Get them closed, then switch to grab both in your left hand." She moved the lobster then picked up a tool that looked like a pair of pliers. "Grab the band and pry it open. Slide on, twist, release."

Graham watched as she banded one, then the other claw. Then Mat dropped it into the large barrel to the side of the table. "You make it look easy."

"I'll hold this one so you can get a feel for it."

Graham took the plier thing and slid a band onto it. She got it over the claw, but fumbled the twist part. She got it on the second try, then managed the second claw more smoothly. "I'm not sure how you do this and hold it at the same time."

"Practice."

Graham grinned. "I hope I get lots of practice today."

"You and me both." Mat made a note in a pad on the ledge next to the wheel and they were off. They got to the next buoy and Mat repeated the process of hauling the trap aboard. This one only had two lobsters, but both were keepers. "Want to try and band them yourself?"

Graham nodded, hoping she looked more certain than she felt. She tried to mimic Mat's movements and managed to get the lobster secure and in her left hand. She almost had the first band on when the lobster flicked its tail with more force than she anticipated. Both the lobster and the bander hit the deck. To her complete embarrassment, she let out a squeal. "Sorry."

Mat laughed, but it seemed more empathetic than judgmental. At least, Graham hoped it was. "It's okay. I still have those moments." She bent down and grabbed what Graham had dropped. "Do you want to try again?"

"One, you don't have to say that. Two, absolutely."

She handled herself better on the second try and managed to get both lobsters in the barrel. Mat showed her the tracking system she used. "If you can band and do that, I can handle the rest."

Graham frowned. "That doesn't seem very helpful."

"It's super helpful. I promise."

Graham wasn't convinced. "Okay."

"I have a small area where I'm experimenting with two traps on a line. I'll let you help haul those if you really want to."

Graham tried not to look too eager. "I'm here to help, whatever that is."

Mat steered them around, hauling the first thirty traps she had planned for the day. She stole glances at Graham, both to make sure she was doing okay, but also to appreciate seeing her in this new capacity. She was a quick study and not squeamish—more than

Mat gave her credit for when they first started out. They weren't moving as fast as when Dom was with her, but they were making good progress. "I'm going to take us to another area if you want to sit for a minute."

Graham smiled. "I'm good."

"I'm going to take your word for it. You have to tell me otherwise." When she pulled up to the next buoy, she hauled in a pair of traps. She slid the first down the rail and set the second one in front of herself. "Like I said, I use almost all single-line traps. I'm experimenting with a few doubles, mostly to see if I lose fewer of them over the course of the season."

"That makes sense." Graham moved to stand in front of one of the traps.

"You really don't have to do this part if you don't want to."

Graham squared her shoulders. "I can do it. I want to."

Mat watched as Graham adeptly opened the trap and pulled out its lone resident, a good-sized male. Graham set it in the banding box and, without hesitating, grabbed a skate and speared it onto the spike. She discarded two small crabs and a bit of seaweed, then latched the trap shut. "It looks like you got this."

Graham smiled with confidence and more than a little flirtation. "Does that mean you're glad you brought me along?"

Mat took a second to look Graham up and down. She looked as comfortable in the fishing gear as she did in the bright green dress she'd worn the night before. Mat found the looks equally appealing, a fact that caught her off guard. "Very. You're a natural."

"I can't say I've always wanted to be a lobsterwoman, but I appreciate that."

Mat curled her lip. "Lobsterman. There aren't a ton of women in the profession, but it's a pretty universal agreement not to separate ourselves by gender."

Graham nodded slowly. "Thanks for clearing that up. I definitely don't want to break the lobsterman code."

Mat chuckled. "Don't worry. We cut the newbies some slack."

"Oh, that's good." Graham gave her freshly baited trap a pat. "Well let's keep moving, then. These traps aren't going to haul themselves."

"Yes, ma'am." They did another forty traps and Graham didn't miss a beat. In between spots, she banded and made notations in the book. She moved from one side of the boat to the other with ease. Mat decided to tell Dom he had some competition. "How about we take a break for lunch?"

"You brought lunch?" Graham's eyes lit up.

"Nothing fancy. I make a pile of sandwiches at the beginning of the week and keep them in the fridge."

"I'm not picky at all and completely starving."

Mat felt a twinge of guilt for not stopping sooner. "You should have said so."

"Oh, no. I'm no dummy. I know you work until the boss says it's time for a break."

Mat pulled sandwiches and two bottles of water from the cooler. "Graham."

"Kidding. I didn't realize I was hungry until you mentioned it. Promise."

Mat didn't believe her. She unwrapped her sandwich and took a bite. The truth was, they'd developed a nice rhythm and she'd lost track of time. Despite her plans to tease Dom, she didn't know how she felt about that. "So, um, we can head in if you want to."

Graham finished chewing a bite and looked at her like she'd grown a second head. "Haven't we barely finished half a day's work?"

Mat regretted telling her how many traps she hauled in an average day. "Yeah, but you've worked crazy hard already and I don't want to take advantage."

"Wait. You're not paying me?"

They hadn't discussed payment. And, honestly, Mat hadn't thought about it. But Graham had done more than some of the day laborers she'd taken out in the past. "No, that's not what I mean at all. Of course I'll pay you."

Graham erupted into laughter then. "You should see your face. You looked completely horrified."

"I—"

Graham shook her head, but continued to laugh. "Is it the idea of paying me or not paying me that you find so distasteful?"

"Neither. I feel bad that we didn't talk about it ahead of time." A fact that made Graham seem much more like a girlfriend than Mat wanted to admit.

"I didn't offer for the money. I wanted to help. And I love to learn new things."

It should have been a relief that "spending time with you" wasn't part of that list. Instead, it made Mat feel like a heel. "Well, I appreciate that. But I'm not about to let you work for free. Going rate is twenty percent of the proceeds."

Graham shook her head. "I couldn't possibly. I've not earned that and we both know it."

"You've done more than you think."

"How about you make me dinner instead?"

Mat smiled. "You want me to cook your share?"

"I wouldn't say no, but it doesn't have to be lobster." Graham looked at her seductively. "I'm mostly angling for another date."

Graham seemed to bounce effortlessly between affable sternman and flirtatious minx. It left Mat feeling unbalanced and she couldn't decide whether she liked it. "I would have asked you out again either way. You didn't have to go to all this trouble."

"Not why I offered, I promise. And I really have had a good time."

Mat nodded. "How about I pay you and make you dinner? It would make me feel better."

"Fine. You really don't have to, but fine."

"I wouldn't have pegged you for being so stubborn." Mat took their trash and stuffed it into a bag.

Graham offered her a playful shrug. "I come by it naturally. I'm Irish."

"Right." Mat reached over to tug gently at her hair. Now that the sun had come out, it shone like fire. Although she'd intended to be playful, Mat's brain took a turn and she imagined having Graham's hair in her hands while they were in bed. She swallowed, shook the image away. "Right."

They worked for another couple of hours, checking close to a hundred and twenty traps. Graham never said a word about being tired, but she started to fade. Stubborn wasn't a trait she typically found appealing in a woman, but Graham's tenacity had a definite appeal. As did her curiosity, and her unwavering enthusiasm for learning anything and everything.

When Mat suggested they call it a day, Graham didn't argue. Mat took that to mean she'd officially worked her too hard. She felt bad about that, but otherwise had no complaints. Not only had they had a productive day, she'd had fun. As Mat steered them back toward land, Graham sat on one of the narrow benches. She turned her face to the sun and closed her eyes. Even in the grubby fishing clothes, she was beautiful. Watching her left Mat aroused and unsettled.

Once they reached the marina, Mat called her uncle and they unloaded the day's catch. She tried to convince Graham not to worry about cleanup, but she insisted on helping. "All in a day's work," she said.

After everything was cleaned and stowed, she and Graham walked toward the lot where Mat's truck was parked. The relaxed comfort that had defined most of the day was gone. Mat had never been in this situation with a woman before and couldn't decide what her next move should be. She wasn't tired of Graham's company, but going home together felt entirely too domestic. "Would you like me to drop you at your place?"

Graham rolled her head from side to side. "That would be great."

It was exactly what she wanted to hear, so it made no sense for her to be disappointed. Mat reminded herself of that fact twice on the short drive to Graham's place. When they got there, Graham turned and gestured at the borrowed clothes. "Okay if I return these to you later? I promise I'll wash them."

"Of course." Mat wanted to kiss her, but they were both dirty and smelled of fish. "I really can't thank you enough for today."

Graham waved a hand. "Nonsense. I badgered you to let me come."

"I wouldn't have been able to do it without you."

"I find that part difficult to believe."

"It's true, I swear. Dom and I have an agreement not to go out alone."

Graham seemed to take that much as true. "That's good."

"I'll, um, I'll text you tomorrow?"

Graham's smile was tired, but warm. "Sure."

"I'll have your cut of the profits then."

"All right. But I'm still going to insist you make me dinner." She offered a flirtatious wink, and then she was gone.

Mat waited for Graham to go inside before she pulled away. From the drive home to the shower once she got there, Graham didn't leave her thoughts. It had been such an unusual day, she still didn't know what to make of it. And as she sat on her sofa in boxers and a tank top, sipping a beer and wondering what to have for dinner, images of Graham—naked in her bed, basking in the sunshine, wearing Dom's rubber pants and banding claws like a pro—filled her mind. The desire was still there, perhaps even stronger than before. There was something else, though, something she couldn't put her finger on. Not an unpleasant feeling by any means, but it left her unbalanced. And if there was one thing that made Mat uneasy, it was having her world tilted beneath her.

Chapter Ten

Graham slid into the bath and sighed. Every muscle she had ached, including a few she didn't know she had. As the heat from the water seeped into her bones, she felt her body relax. She was pretty sure she'd never been so exhausted in her entire life. How in the world did Mat do that kind of work every single day?

Graham closed her eyes and allowed memories of the day to play through her mind. There was the look on Mat's face when Graham pulled on Dom's rubber overalls, the respect in her eyes when Graham didn't flinch at baiting the trap. There was the sun and the ocean and learning a whole new way of earning a living from the sea. But more than anything, she loved the moments when she could simply watch Mat work. She seemed so comfortable, so utterly in her element. Sure, she had plenty of confidence in the bedroom, but there was something about seeing Mat on the water that made her seem complete, whole. Graham hadn't known it when she offered to spend the day hauling traps, but she was grateful for having the chance to see Mat that way.

Graham opened her eyes and sighed. Grateful was one word to describe it. Others popped into her head. Words she'd told herself didn't apply to what she had, what she wanted with Mat. They'd connected. Connection didn't have to equate to feelings, or imply anything deeper. Still, Graham couldn't help but wonder how many people Mat let into that part of her life. They hadn't really talked about it, but she got the impression Mat didn't do so often, or lightly.

She'd actually been surprised when Mat agreed to take her along for the day. It didn't seem like the kind of thing that gelled with the idea of a casual hookup. But Graham had offered before she was awake enough to second guess herself and Mat hadn't probed her motivations. That could mean she was more into Graham than Graham realized. Or she simply didn't want to lose a day of work.

Did it matter?

Graham shook her head. It didn't. She liked spending time with Mat. She'd learned that included doing things other than having sex. If it happened again, great. If not, well, hopefully at least the time in bed would continue. Not to be sex-crazed, but that was sort of the point of this whole thing anyway.

Graham pulled herself from the tub before the water cooled completely. She pulled on a pair of cotton pajama pants and a tank top and padded out to the living room just as Jess walked in the door. She set down her things and looked at Graham with a sort of excited curiosity. "Please tell me you're just getting home after an entire day of sexual escapades."

Graham laughed. "Not quite."

"Whole morning at least? After a whole night?"

"You've got the night part right, but that's all the sex there was."

Jess frowned. "Bummer. Was it good, though?"

In the excitement of the day, she'd almost forgotten how good. Well, not forgotten. Momentarily sidetracked. "Oh, it was beyond good. And even though it wasn't a sexcapade, we did spend the day together."

Jess sat in the arm chair, crossed her legs, and leaned forward. She laced her fingers together and propped her chin on them. "Do tell."

"I went out on her boat with her."

"Her lobster boat?" Jess made a face. "Why does that sound completely unromantic to me?"

"It wasn't romantic." Graham sat on the adjacent sofa. "We worked. Her cousin called in sick and she let me go with her instead."

"Wait, wait, wait. You mean you went…lobstering? Is that even a verb?"

"Yes and yes. It was so much fun. I learned a ton."

Jess nodded slowly. "Did you bring any home?"

"No, but I did get her to agree to make me dinner in exchange for my labor."

"As much as I would have liked you to bring home some lobsters, I have to concede that is a better offer."

"Thank you. I think she's going to pay me, too. I told her not to worry about it, but she seemed pretty adamant."

"This is getting more interesting by the minute." Jess stood, continuing to nod. "I want to hear everything, but I really want a shower."

"You shower. I'll make dinner." Graham stood up as well. "And by make, I mean put samosas in the oven and heat up a pouch of saag paneer."

"Works for me," Jess called on her way to the bathroom.

Graham put together dinner and fed Athena, then gave the blow by blow to Jess while they ate cross-legged on the sofa. Jess, who seemed incredulous at first, was practically cheering by the end. Graham said, "I can't tell if you're more excited about the sex or the fact that I went to work with her."

"Uh, both. That's the beauty of it. You're out of hookup territory, my friend."

Graham shrugged, not wanting to get swept up in analyzing what it all meant. "Maybe, but it's not like I'm her girlfriend. Or even want to be."

Jess raised a brow. "Seriously? You don't want to be her girlfriend?"

"It's not that I'm opposed to it. I just—" How could she explain the vibe she got from Mat? The one that made it abundantly clear she wasn't looking to settle down. "I'm not in it for that."

Jess nodded slowly. "Right, right. You're all about playing the field."

"I'm all about having fun. Remember when you told me I needed to do that? Relax a little?"

"I do. And I meant it. I'm sorry I implied you should be doing anything else."

"Thank you."

Jess got up and took their plates to the kitchen. "Want to start that new Netflix series tonight?"

"Don't let me stop you, but I'm beat. Lobstering is hard work."

Jess returned from the kitchen. "I'm sure it is. Of course, it sounds like you didn't sleep much last night either."

"True story." Graham stood and headed toward her bedroom. "Night, Jess."

"Night."

She'd just climbed into bed when her phone pinged. She smiled, imagining a text from Mat. It was from Will, but that was the next best thing. *I'm starting to get worried. Please let me know you're okay.*

Shit. Graham realized that she'd missed three texts from Will during the day. She was used to having no cell reception while away from shore at work, but she'd not thought about it during her day with Mat. *I'm fine. Just seeing your texts. Sorry!*

Are you just getting home? I don't know if I should be impressed or...

Graham chuckled, imagining Will's curiosity warring with her staid sensibilities. *Home a bit ago, but with Mat all day. Not in bed.* She added a winky face.

Will's reply remained true to form. *Dare I ask?*

Rather than trying to text the details of her day, Graham tapped the call button. "Hey," Will said.

"I'm too tired to text. Are you free to chat?"

"I am. It's Nora's bridge night. There is so much cackling coming from the library, you wouldn't believe it."

"I believe it just fine. I've known Aunt Nora longer than you have, if you recall."

"Right. So, too tired to text, huh?"

"And you'll never guess why." Graham launched into the story of her night—slightly more G-rated than what she'd told Jess—and the day on the lobster boat that followed. Just telling the story made her sort of giddy. Despite her exhaustion, she was suddenly wide awake.

"Are you officially dating now? You seem to have sailed right past casual hookup."

"No, no. It's nothing like that." It wasn't. Was it? Why did both Jess and Will seem to think it was?

"Really?"

"No." That's not what she wanted.

"Because she said so or you did?"

Graham sighed. "We didn't discuss it. That's the point. It's not a thing."

"Right." Will's voice was laced with disappointment.

"Will, it's okay. I don't want it to be a thing."

"I know. Sorry. I won't be a downer. I'm happy for you. You deserve to have fun."

"Thank you." Will's heart was in the right place, but the whole exchange left Graham feeling a little flat.

"I love that she's going to make you dinner. That's hot."

That helped. "Yeah. It kind of is."

"And I imagine that will lead to more sexy time."

"Sexy time? I can't decide if you're a little old lady or a twelve-year-old boy."

Will chuckled. "According to my sister, I'm equal parts both."

"That Emerson is smart. How is she, by the way?"

"Good. I think she and Darcy have decided to elope and use the money on a baby."

"Making or adopting?"

"Fertility treatments. They've decided to try to have a baby. Since Darcy is still really close with Liam's dad, they're hoping to use him as a donor. Liam is ecstatic over the idea of a brother or sister."

"Ah. It seems sad to have to choose one or the other. Wedding or baby, I mean."

"Yeah, I agree."

Graham considered what she'd do in that situation. When she finally found Ms. Right, she very much wanted a wedding, but if it came down to having that or starting a family, she'd pick family any day of the week. "Run away to Vegas kind of elope or show up at the courthouse?"

"Hopefully, neither. Nora and I are trying to convince them to do something super small and informal at the inn this fall."

"Ooh, I can help." Graham didn't know Emerson and Darcy well, but she'd met them a few times and liked them a lot. Plus, she loved helping Aunt Nora with parties. "Add my free labor to the offer."

"That's really sweet, Graham. Whether or not they take us up on it, thank you for that."

"I'd really love to. Weddings make me super happy." Graham closed her eyes for a moment. "And since my own probably won't happen for a billion years or so, I'll have to live vicariously through others."

"I'm sorry, friend."

"Don't be sorry. It's not like that. If I told my parents or, Lord, Aunt Nora, I was getting married at twenty-five, they'd have a meltdown. Just because I love romcoms and romance novels and happily ever afters doesn't mean I want to walk down the aisle tomorrow."

"Right, right. You're still such a young thing. You've got ages."

Graham laughed again. "Thank you."

"I'll remember to remind you of that, too."

"Thanks." Although she'd felt wide awake a few minutes before, exhaustion from the day crept back up on her. "I think I need to go to sleep now."

"Yeah, you worked hard today."

"I really did. I'll see you at work tomorrow?"

"Nine and one, right?"

Graham was happy they'd been put back on the same shifts for the next couple of weeks. "Nine and one. I hope those bridge ladies don't keep you up too late."

"You and me both."

Graham ended the call and plugged her phone in. She switched off her lamp and rolled onto her back. She imagined a wedding at the inn. The garden would be a perfect spot and could probably hold close to fifty people. Or maybe thirty if there were tables set up for eating. Emerson and Darcy wouldn't have to worry about decorations or anything. The ceremony could happen right under the arbor where Aunt Nora's favorite bench usually sat.

Graham drifted off to sleep and had dreams of a wedding. Only, she wasn't a guest or helping out. She wore a perfect white dress and walked up a narrow aisle, with the faces of her friends and family all turned toward her. Will stood at the front, holding a book and smiling at her. It took her forever to get there, even though the distance was short. The figure waiting for her wore a dark suit, but Graham couldn't see her face. She had dark hair, though, and felt intimately familiar. When she finally made it to the makeshift altar, the figure turned. It was Mat. Only the eyes looking back at her sparkled with joy and a love Graham had never before seen.

Chapter Eleven

The next morning, Dom was ready and waiting when Mat emerged from her apartment. "Look who decided to come to work today."

Dom shook his head. "Dude, it was awful. I was puking for hours."

Mat raised a hand. "You don't have to play it up. I figured you and Renata finally hooked up and, considering how long it took you to get there, I wasn't about to come bust it up."

Dom looked truly offended. "One, I wouldn't do that, even for Renata. Two, I didn't even make it through dinner. I had to bail on her."

"Oh." Not that she'd really been mad at him, but hearing that made her feel bad for even teasing him. "That sucks, man. I'm sorry."

"It did suck."

Mat climbed into her truck and Dom got in beside her. "If it's any consolation, I got in almost a whole day's work without you."

"What?"

She started the engine and headed toward town. "Relax, relax. I wasn't by myself. I took Graham with me."

"Wait, wait, wait. Slow the fuck down. You did what?"

Mat knew she was going to have to tell him. For some reason she thought she'd manage to make it not a huge deal. Clearly, she'd been wrong. "Unlike your sad sick self, I spent the night with a beautiful woman. When you texted me, she offered to go. She was so damn enthusiastic about it, I decided what the hell."

Dom stared at her like she'd grown a second head. "I don't even know what to say to you right now."

"She works on the Dolphin Fleet, so she's got sea legs and she's not a priss about stuff."

"I'm sorry. I'm still not quite sure I understand. You took a girl, a girl that you're sleeping with no less, out on the boat?" Dom's face registered a combination of disbelief and indignation.

Mat didn't answer right away. She pulled into their usual parking spot and they walked the short distance to the marina. Their uncle had already stacked the day's bait next to the *Paquette*. Mat grabbed the first tote and went aboard. "It's not like that."

Dom followed. "Oh, okay." He set his tote down, then folded his arms and leaned against the rail. "Tell me what it is. I'm dying to know."

Mat didn't want to admit she'd agreed before really thinking it through. Or that she enjoyed Graham's company so much that the idea of spending the whole day with her had more than a passing appeal. "God, you're such an ass sometimes."

"I'm an ass? You're the one who thought I bailed on you so I could get laid." He sniffed. "Which is totally something you would do, by the way."

Mat could tell from his tone that he wasn't actually still mad. "One, it is not something I would do. And two, I totally apologized for that."

Although it was a fake argument, he showed no signs of backing down. "And to add insult to injury, you hook up with a girl who's not only great in the sack, but can haul traps without batting an eye."

"She was a quick study." Mat smiled at the memory. "And she looked way better in those pants than you do."

"You have the goofiest fucking look on your face right now."

"Shut up." Mat moved the last of the bait aboard and did a quick systems check. "Are we ready?" She didn't wait for an answer before starting the engine.

Dom disembarked to untie the ropes, then jumped back aboard. He came up beside her and picked up the notebook. "You did a hundred-twenty traps?"

Mat shrugged again. "Like I said, she was a quick study."

Dom shook his head. "Did you pay her?"

"She told me not to, but I'm going to anyway. She, uh, asked me to make her dinner as payment."

Dom looked even more scandalized than when Mat told him she took Graham out in the first place. "Oh, my God. Are you falling for this girl?"

"Are you out of your mind? We hooked up twice."

"But you're cooking her dinner. Dude, that's girlfriend territory right there."

Mat scowled. She knew it was, but wasn't about to admit it. "She worked hard. I couldn't say no. I'm not a jerk."

Dom raised a brow. "I don't know. I think this one's getting under your skin."

"You're only hating on me because your hot date ended with you hooking up with your toilet." It was much easier to tease him than admit Graham hadn't pressured her into dinner. Mat wanted to do it, and to spend more time with her.

Dom hung his head. "Such a tragedy. But she's not holding it against me. We're going to try again tomorrow."

"That's good. I'm glad it didn't send her running for the hills."

"It did not. I'd like to point out, however, that I am not making her dinner."

Mat leaned over and punched him in the shoulder. "It's a nice gesture. I'm not courting her."

"Is that what you're telling yourself? Okay. Are you going to have sex with her after?"

"I don't know."

Dom offered her a bland look.

"Well, I'm not going to not sleep with her. I mean, if she's interested. I'm not an idiot." Dinner at her place not followed by sex would be even weirder.

"Are you going to buy wine?"

Mat scowled and didn't answer.

"Candles?"

"I will not buy candles."

Dom rolled his eyes. "Let me rephrase. Are you going to light candles?"

"Shut up."

"I wish I had a dictionary on board so I could look up the definition of courting right now. 'Cause that's exactly what you're doing."

"Maybe I just want to get laid again."

"You never have any trouble getting laid. You want this girl to like you."

Mat swallowed the retort on the tip of her tongue. Because the comeback wouldn't be true. As much as she didn't typically put stock in whether or not women liked her, she did care what Graham thought. But that still didn't mean Mat was courting her. Showing off, maybe, but that was different. "So what if I do?"

Dom shrugged. "So, nothing. I just wanted you to admit it."

"You really are an ass." They pulled up to the first buoy and Mat started hauling up the trap.

"And you give as good as you get."

"That's true. Let's even the scales a bit, shall we? Tell me how much you embarrassed yourself in front of Renata."

Dom banded the first of their catch and moved them to the large barrel of water. "You know, the getting sick part sucked, but Renata was really sweet."

"Sweet how?" Mat couldn't fathom wanting a girl she was into within a thousand feet of her if she was sick.

"When I told her I had to go, we were in the middle of dinner. She insisted on walking me home and, when we got there, she stuck around."

"And watched you barf?"

"No. She got a cool towel for my face, poured me ginger ale."

"Did she tuck you into bed, too?"

"As a matter of fact, she did. Or close to it. And then she hung out on the couch all night."

Since it had been Dom and Renata's second official date, Mat was pretty sure they'd yet to sleep together. In Mat's mind, that kind of tending was for a wife, not a would-be girlfriend. "Seems to me you're losing some of the magic before it even starts."

"That's because you have a one-track mind. I wouldn't be seeing Renata in the first place if I didn't think she had the potential to be the one."

For all that Mat had rebelled against the traditional values they'd both been raised with, Dom seemed to embrace them. Especially since his transition, he had a clear plan of finding the right woman, settling down, and starting a family. Mat didn't begrudge him that. In some ways, she could even see the appeal. Truthfully, it wasn't that she had no desire to have a family of her own. What she couldn't figure was how to have that when her existing family—her parents and brothers—would never gel with the one she created. And she had no plans of sacrificing one for the other. "You think Renata is the one?"

She hadn't asked the question seriously. They really had only been on a couple of dates. But Dom got this super earnest look on his face. "I do."

Mat didn't even know how to respond. "Wow. Okay."

Dom didn't seem offended. Rather, he laughed. "I'm an old soul, softie romantic. Does that really surprise you?"

Mat shrugged. "Not that you feel that way, just that it's so quick."

Dom shook his head. "There's just something in the gut, dude. You should try listening to yours sometime."

Mat focused her attention on pulling up the next trap. Trusting her gut had only gotten her into trouble. No, she'd stick with her nice, rational approach to life and love—by keeping each thing in its own little box. There was no reason cooking a meal for Graham before she spent the night couldn't fit neatly in the one she'd set aside for women.

❖

When her second tour of the day pulled back into the harbor, Graham went in search of Will. "Are you done for the day? I was thinking of popping over to see Aunt Nora."

Will shook her head. "I'm on cleanup today."

"I can wait for you."

"Why don't you go on over and I'll catch up? I'm sure Nora would love some time with you one-on-one."

Graham narrowed her eyes. "Why do I get the feeling I'm being set up?"

Will shrugged sheepishly. "Not set up. I did tell her a little about your recent adventures. I'm sure she's curious."

Graham wasn't bothered by that. Apart from her brief crush on Will, she'd always confided in Aunt Nora. From her teen years on, Nora had been more like a wise older sister than an aunt. Graham had held off on telling her about Mat, but now that it was more than a one-night stand, she wanted to. "Oh, that's fine. I'd tell her anyway."

Will waved her hands in front of her. "I didn't tell her any of the, um, details, if you know what I mean. Those are yours to tell."

Graham smiled. "Then I'll get a head start and meet you there."

Graham made her way down the ramp and onto the pier. She crossed the street to see if Mat's boat was there. It was, but there was no sign of Mat or Dom. She hoped that meant Dom was feeling better and the two of them had already finished the day's work. Graham liked knowing what that meant, what it looked like. Even though it was seriously hard work, she hoped she got the chance to do it again sometime, and not just because it meant spending an entire day with Mat.

She walked up the pier into town. They'd entered peak tourist season and Commercial Street was a sea of people. Graham wound her way through, enjoying the bustle and the happy energy of so many people on vacation. She'd just turned onto Nora's street when her phone buzzed with a text from Mat.

Took the liberty of claiming some of today's catch. Dinner tomorrow?

Graham smiled down at the screen. *I suppose I could clear my calendar.*

Don't rearrange anything. I didn't literally bring them home.

Graham imagined a pair of lobsters inching their way across Mat's kitchen floor and giggled. She stopped walking so she could type a more thorough reply. *I was kidding. I'm free and I'd love to. What can I bring?*

Wine? White. Whatever you like.

For some reason, the prospect of dinner at Mat's felt even more exciting than going out. Which was weird, considering she'd already stayed over twice. It seemed intimate, like something a couple would do. She shook her head. That might be true, but she remained more excited by the prospect of what would come after dinner. Even if she had to remind herself that was the case.

Graham got to the inn just as happy hour was winding down. Nora poured them each a glass of sangria and suggested they sit on the porch. They settled in and Nora looked at her expectantly. "Tell me everything."

Graham did. Not the explicit details of the sex, but more than she'd told Will. Nora nodded, raised a brow here and there, and made noises of approval. Graham concluded with the dinner invitation, punctuating the end with a smile and a shrug.

"It sounds like you're having a good time, for sure, but how do you feel?"

Oh, Lord. Graham wondered if the question was pure Nora or if she'd been influenced by Will. "I feel like I'm having a good time."

Despite being like a sister, Nora had a way of looking at her that reminded Graham more of her mother. Nora gave her that look now—stern and knowing. She pointed a finger at Graham. "Don't play coy with me."

"I'm not." Graham sighed. "I feel like women are always supposed to be interested in where things might lead, what everything means. I've been single since I moved here and I want to have some fun."

"I know you've been feeling restless, but are you sure this is how you want to go about it?" Nora's expression had a certain heaviness to it.

"I don't know. Great times and no pressure? I'm thinking maybe I could get used to this way of going about things." Graham smiled playfully.

Nora's expression didn't soften. "It just doesn't seem like you. I'm worried you're settling."

"That's just it. I'm not settling. I'm having an amazing time. Is it enough to satisfy me forever? Of course not. But, for now, it's great. I don't have any weird hopes or expectations that are going to leave me disappointed in the end."

"Okay, then." Nora nodded, as though some important situation had just been decided. "As long as you're in control."

"I am."

"You know, I sometimes wish I'd had a bit more abandon when I was your age. The stakes aren't as high. I might have been less inclined to make stupid mistakes in my thirties."

Graham set down her drink and pointed at Nora. "Exactly. Why is it only boys get to sow their wild oats?"

"Well, it might have something to do with the specifics of the analogy."

Graham snorted out a laugh, which in turn made her giggle. "True. So, we need to coin a new analogy."

Nora quirked a brow. "Something about sampling the oysters, perhaps."

The sparkle of mischief in her aunt's eyes warmed Graham's heart. For all that Graham had considered her a confidante, it wasn't that long ago Nora herself had been a hundred times more reserved, at least when it came to matters of the heart. Falling in love hadn't merely softened her edges, it had given her a playfulness. Or, Graham realized, it had awakened a playfulness that had been dormant for too long. "I like it."

"Did I hear someone say something about oysters?" Will stepped onto the porch. "Does anyone need a refill before I sit?"

Graham and Nora both shook their heads. Nora patted the swing beside her. "We're good. Come join our conversation on female sexual liberation."

Will cringed. "Should I be nervous?"

Will sat and Nora patted her leg. "No, no. We're discussing Graham's liberation, not mine."

"We're talking about Mat, aren't we?" Will looked less anxious, but still concerned.

"We are." Graham reached over and squeezed her other knee. "And trying to come up with the lesbian equivalent of sowing one's oats."

Will sighed and shook her head. She looked at Nora. "And you suggested oysters."

Nora shrugged. "It seemed fitting. There's a reason oysters are a euphemism. So many varieties, shapes, colors. Each one salty and sweet, but with a taste completely its own."

Will made a show of covering her ears and saying, "La, la, la."

When she stopped, Graham looked up at the porch ceiling. "I'm not saying I've given up on mating for life. I've just decided I don't need to think about doing it anytime soon."

Will nodded, as though conceding the point. "That's fair. I just want you to be happy. And I worry about you."

"I know." Graham smiled. "I promise I won't get in over my head."

It was a promise she intended to keep. Even if she found herself daydreaming about Mat at odd times of the day. Or right before she fell asleep. Or the second she woke up. Just because her subconscious had a mind of its own, the rest of her remained rational and realistic. She'd have fun for however long it lasted, then chalk it up to a reckless summer she'd be able to look back on with fond memories for the rest of her life. She most certainly didn't think about it as a story she'd tell her kids about how she and their mother had gotten together.

"Uh, where did you go just now?"

"Huh? What?"

Nora chuckled. "We've been talking to you for the last five minutes."

Crap. "Sorry. I guess my mind wandered."

"I'm sure it did, dear. I'm sure it did."

Graham couldn't help but laugh at Nora's knowing smile. The fact that her aunt was encouraging her—while Will remained the cautious, hopeless romantic—was almost too much. "What were we talking about, again?"

Will stretched out an arm and draped it over Nora's shoulders. "Oysters. Actual oysters. Now that we've talked about them, I have a hankering. Would you care to join us tomorrow for a little ad hoc raw bar?"

"Tomorrow? I think—wait. No, I have plans tomorrow."

Nora turned to Will with a coy smile. "She's busy sampling the other oysters."

Will groaned and Graham laughed. That's exactly what she was doing. And she was resolved to enjoy every minute of it.

Chapter Twelve

Mat stared at the candles. Dom's words echoed in her mind. At this point, not using them would be admitting he was right. A little romance didn't hurt now and again. If she was going to the trouble of making dinner, she might as well set the mood.

She set the table, made the salad. The lobsters were stuffed with linguica and breadcrumbs, waiting to go on the grill. She'd picked up fresh rolls from the bakery and planned to warm them on the grill with the lobster. Not the fanciest thing in the world, but as far as she was concerned, one of the biggest mistakes people made with lobsters was doing too much to them.

Mat changed her clothes and was just about to go preheat the grill when Graham knocked on her door. She looked, as always, pretty and fresh and vibrant. Mat had half a mind to forget about dinner altogether and drag her to the bedroom. That would be poor form though, even if she could convince Graham it was a good idea. She settled for a kiss, which Graham returned with enthusiasm. "Sorry," Mat said when she let her go. "I just had to do that."

Graham smiled and Mat noticed a hint of color rise in her cheeks. "No apology necessary."

Mat took the wine Graham offered and set it on the counter. "Make yourself comfortable. I'll be right back."

She turned on the grill and returned to find Graham watching her from the doorway. "What are we having?"

Mat gave her the menu and enjoyed the way Graham's eyes lit up. "Can I pour you a glass of wine while I finish cooking?"

"Yes, please."

Mat continued making dinner and Graham asked lots of questions. She started to get the sense that Graham didn't do a lot of cooking, but didn't say so. It wasn't any of her business either way. Half an hour later, they sat at Mat's small kitchen table—complete with candles—and ate.

In part because she was curious and in part to keep the conversation going, Mat asked Graham about her work and how she found her way to Provincetown. "Tell me honestly, did you come for the whales, or the women?"

Graham offered a playful smirk. "Yes."

Mat chuckled. "Good answer."

"It's true, though. I knew I didn't want to spend my whole career doing research, so I ruled out a Ph.D. I liked the idea of a commercial operation with an educational mission and a commitment to conservation."

Mat narrowed her eyes and nodded slowly. "Interesting. I would have figured you considered the commercial part a necessary evil."

Graham shrugged. "As long as people want to see animals up close, there's going to be an industry for it. I'd rather that space be filled with reputable companies who provide good information and are responsible with the ecosystem."

"That makes sense."

"It's the same with commercial fishing, right?"

"I don't follow."

Graham took a sip of her wine and seemed to choose her words carefully. "I think a lot of people in my line of work are dubious about those in yours. Not as people, but in how you approach conservation efforts—as a necessary evil."

Mat shrugged. "I'll give you that."

"But you're not like that at all. You get that conservation is an essential part of keeping commercial fishing viable."

"I do. Honestly, I think most small-scale operators do, too. It's the giant trawlers, owned by corporate types and manned by guys who have no connection to the work, that are the problem."

Graham lifted her glass. "See, one more thing we can agree on."

Mat smiled and raised her own glass. The conversation lulled and she moved a second lobster half onto each of their plates. Graham didn't protest and, to Mat's surprise, nearly polished it off.

"This is so delicious." Graham set down her fork and pushed away her plate. "But if I eat one more bite, I might literally explode."

Mat offered her a wry smile. "We can't have that. It sounds messy."

Graham giggled. "Let me wash dishes?"

Mat shook her head. "Nope. It would undermine my nice gesture points if I let you do any work."

"I already told you that you don't need any nice gesture points. I had so much fun."

Mat quirked a brow. "Turns out, I did, too."

"On top of that, you insisted on paying me." Graham pointed to the envelope. "So, we're more than even, which means you should let me help."

Mat considered her options. She didn't want to assume Graham intended to stay over. She hadn't shown up with a bag. Of course, she'd not done so the other times she'd stayed over. "I guess it depends on your plans."

It was Graham's turn to raise a brow. "My plans?"

"Yeah. If you're heading home, my answer is that I'll take care of them after you go."

Graham's smile was suggestive. "And my other option would be?"

Mat wondered if the questions were part of her flirtation or if she wanted, needed maybe, Mat to say the words, issue the invitation officially. It still surprised her that Graham had these flashes of shyness. Even more surprising was how much she liked them. "You could stay. I mean, obviously, we'd want to do them before going to bed."

Graham nodded slowly. "Right. So, really, there's only one question."

"Being?"

Graham shrugged in a way that seemed at once innocent and seductive. "Do you want to wash or dry?"

"I'll wash."

Graham stood, pushed up the sleeves of the light cardigan sweater she wore. "Works for me."

When the dishes were done, Mat poured more wine and they sat on her small sofa. "Do you want to watch a movie?"

Graham shrugged. "We could. I'm also happy to talk."

Mat resisted making a face. "What do you want to talk about?"

Graham laughed and put a hand on Mat's knee. "Don't look so worried. I'm not proposing an interrogation."

Mat chuckled. She needed to work on her poker face. "I'm not worried. I," she paused for a moment. "I guess I'm not much of a talker by nature."

"What if I promise to go easy on you? And we keep the movie option on the table."

She couldn't be sure, but it felt like Graham might be teasing her. Such a change from just a few minutes before, when she seemed almost hesitant. Mat wondered for a second if it was a tactic to keep her on her toes. But everything she'd learned about Graham so far only reinforced Mat's initial impression that she was guileless. "All right."

"You have brothers, right? I feel like I remember you referencing brothers."

"I do. Two, one older and one younger."

"And they don't live here anymore, right?"

As much as they were a central part of her life, Mat was unaccustomed to talking about her family. Even stranger was the fact that Graham remembered the little she'd shared. "Yeah. One is a teacher in Rhode Island, the other is an airplane mechanic in Boston."

"Are they married? Do you have nieces and nephews?"

Mat smiled at the thought of them. "Yes and yes. Luciano has a boy and a girl, Vicente has three boys."

"Wow. How old?"

"The oldest is nine and the youngest just turned one." There'd been a big party for the one-year-old at her parents' house in May.

"I think with five grandkids to spoil, the pressure is officially off for me to provide any."

Graham gave her a funny look. "Was there before?"

"If I'd been straight, definitely. Not being straight complicated things, so it's a relief to have it off the table either way." Mat sensed a follow-up question on the tip of Graham's tongue, so she shifted the focus. "What about you?"

Graham smiled. "No siblings and only a couple of cousins on my dad's side. I always wanted a big family."

"They're messy at times, but I wouldn't trade mine for anything."

"But you don't want one of your own?" The words were out of Graham's mouth before she realized it. She tried to keep her expression light and hoped Mat didn't think she was prying or, worse, plotting.

Mat shrugged casually. "I feel like I have the best of both worlds. Lots of kids and birthdays and big family gatherings, but then I get to come home to my quiet little nest."

"I hear you." Graham couldn't fault the logic. Maybe if she had cousins and nieces and nephews, she'd feel the same. Even as she posed the idea in her mind, Graham knew it wasn't true. She wanted a family of her own. And even though she was open to the idea of adoption, she really wanted the experience of pregnancy—sharing the hope and excitement and worry with the woman she loved.

"But you think I'm crazy, or sad."

Graham shook her head. She hated that Mat had been able to read her thoughts so easily. "Not at all."

"Oh. Well, either way, it's what works for me. And considering I work the hours I do, it's for the best."

"Sure. That makes sense." What didn't make sense was just how deflated Mat's words left her. It's not like she had her heart set on building her family with Mat. Maybe it was Mat's delivery. Despite the upbeat tone, something in Mat's demeanor seemed resigned, like she'd accepted that fate more than she'd chosen it. Resolved not to dwell on it, Graham reached for the bottle to top off their glasses and realized it was empty. "I think we just finished a second bottle of wine."

"I have another if you'd like more."

Graham shook her head. "No, I was just surprised. That's more than my usual limit on a work night."

"Do you feel okay?"

Graham took stock of herself. "Yeah. Probably because it was spread out over a few hours. What time is it, anyway?"

Mat looked down at her watch. "Just after eleven."

Graham cringed. "Are you going out at six in the morning?"

"Not until seven. We have to shift to account for low tide."

"I guess that's a little better. Still, it's late."

Mat gave her a flirtatious smile. "Is that your way of telling me you'd like me to take you to bed?"

The mere mention of being taken to bed turned her on. "Maybe. I promise I won't keep you up half the night."

"Don't be making promises you may not be able to keep."

Graham lifted her chin at the playful challenge. "If I'm a guilty party, I'm not alone."

Mat stood and extended her hand. "I never said you were. And I'm the first to admit, there are things in life far more interesting than sleep."

Graham looked up at Mat, let her gaze linger. "On that, we are in perfect agreement."

Chapter Thirteen

Graham had no idea what time she and Mat finally fell asleep, but she knew she was not ready to get up. Mat slid from the bed. Graham whimpered a little and burrowed down under the sheet and light blanket Mat had pulled over them during the night.

"You can stay if you want," Mat said.

"No, no." Graham tossed the covers aside and sat up. "I have to be at work at eight-thirty, so I need to get up, too."

"Do you want coffee before you go?"

She thought of the last cup she'd had at Mat's—so strong that even a pile of sugar and creamer had barely lightened it. "I'm good. I've got to go home to shower and get ready for work anyway."

Graham pulled on her clothes and looked up to find Mat watching her. Mat smirked. "Maybe you should start bringing a bag."

She glanced down at her outfit. She quirked a brow. "Am I obviously on a walk of shame?"

Mat shook her head. "Not at all. I just want you to feel cool bringing a change of clothes and a toothbrush if you want. It seems like we're past the point of wondering if you're going to spend the night."

Graham swallowed the flutter of excitement. Whether it was the promise of yet another date with Mat, or the idea of moving to some new level with her, she couldn't be sure. "I'll do that. Thanks."

"Good." Mat nodded, adding emphasis to the statement.

"I'll see you again soon I hope." Graham felt more confident saying that, but she still blushed.

"Absolutely." Mat opened the door, but grabbed Graham's hand before she could walk by. She pulled her into a kiss that, while casual, still managed to make Graham's knees wobbly. "Have a great day."

"You, too."

Graham walked home with her head in the clouds. From the food to the conversation to the sex, everything about last night had been perfect. Including the fact that, when it came down to it, there wasn't any pressure. It was such a relief not to have an agenda, or to wonder what every little thing meant. It gave her room to sit back and enjoy it. And was she ever enjoying it.

She walked up the stairs just as Jess came down. "Hey, stranger. Good night?"

Graham didn't even try to suppress the grin. "Great night."

"Nice. You can tell me all about it later. I'll be home at eight."

Graham made a sympathetic face. "Long day. Good luck."

Jess waved a hand in dismissal. "It's all good. I turned off the coffee, but it's probably still hot."

"You're a goddess." Graham kissed her on the cheek. "I'll see you later."

Jess went on her way and Graham let herself in. She considered lounging on the sofa with a cup of coffee, but decided to go ahead and get ready for work. She could take it with her and be early, and hopefully catch Will before the customers piled on board.

A short while later, Graham walked up the ramp to the Dolphin IX, sipping her delicious extra light, extra sweet coffee. Once on board, she spied Will behind the counter of the small cantina on the lower deck. She slid the metal and glass door aside and poked her head in. "Morning, Will."

Will looked up and grinned. "Morning to you, too. You're here early."

Graham shrugged. "I got up with Mat, so I'm running ahead of schedule."

"Ah. I should have guessed it wasn't your own doing."

"Hey." Graham put her free hand on her hip. "I'm punctual."

"You are." Will angled her head playfully. "You're also never out of bed a second sooner than you have to be."

She didn't mind Will's teasing about her not being a morning person, but she felt the need to give as good as she got. "I just don't see why anyone would be."

"Since you stayed over, I'm taking it you had a good night?"

"Such a good night. She made me what might be the best meal I've had in my entire life. And then we talked and drank wine until eleven and then she took me to bed." Graham sighed. "So many orgasms, Will. So many."

Will chuckled. "Well, I'm glad you came by your sleepiness honestly. Want some coffee?"

Graham lifted her travel mug. "I'm good."

"You know, you'd get more caffeine if you didn't fill that halfway with cream."

Graham raised her hand. "It wakes me up just fine, thank you. How was your night?"

"Good." Will got a far-away look in her eyes and a goofy grin on her face. Graham still found it hard to believe that she'd harbored a crush on Will for the better part of six months, not because she no longer found Will attractive, but because she couldn't believe how she'd missed the fact that Will was so completely in love with Nora.

"Let me guess, you didn't get much sleep, either."

Will shrugged, blushed. "Some."

Before Graham could tease her any further, Charles passed along the outside of the boat. She hooked a thumb in his direction. "That's my cue."

"When am I going to meet this studly lobsterwoman?"

"Lobsterman," Graham said. When Will raised a brow, she added, "It's some sort of code, apparently, that female fishermen and lobstermen hate being set apart from their male counterparts."

Will nodded affably. "Makes sense. So, when do I get to meet her?"

"Soon, I hope. But I don't want to jinx anything."

Will smiled her understanding smile. "I feel you."

Graham waved a good-bye and headed up to the top deck of the boat. She found Charles reviewing the logs of the previous day's sightings. "Two new calves yesterday, huh?"

Graham hadn't been the first to see them, but she had laid eyes on both yearlings during her shifts. "Yeah. One with Salt and the other with Tapioca and Roswell."

"What about Grackle?"

"No sign of him yet. I'm hoping that means he broke away to start looking for a mate of his own."

"You and me both."

The boat filled and they headed out. Graham went through her lecture, pausing now and again to point out the birds that swooped and swam around them. Much like the day before, the whales were active. She and Charles tag-teamed the loud speaker and recorded the sightings. Graham didn't think she'd ever grow tired of watching the animals move through the water or hearing the delighted squeals of children and adults alike when they swam particularly close. It made her feel like her life had a real purpose, but one that managed to be fun at the same time.

The second sail of the day was more crowded and included a ton of little kids. Charles had her do the lecture again and, by the time she was done, Graham was the most popular person on board. They swarmed around her, wanting to touch the whale tooth she'd showed or have their picture taken with her. She couldn't decide if it made her feel like a kindergarten teacher or a princess at Disney World. Not that she minded. This was her version, she imagined, of Mat's nieces and nephews.

When the sightings began in earnest, her following quickly abandoned her for a spot along the boat's rail. She picked up her binoculars and helped Charles identify the whales they saw—a lot of repeats from the morning, but a few new ones as well.

When they docked for the second time that day, Graham gathered her things and headed down in search of Will. She found her stacking receipts and counting money from the day's sales. "Hot plans tonight?"

"Martha and Heidi are coming over for dinner and cards."

Graham smiled. Martha and Heidi were two of Aunt Nora's closest friends. She was pretty sure they helped Nora come to her senses when she'd called things off with Will the spring before. "That sounds like fun."

"Do you want to come? I'm sure there will be plenty of food."

Graham dismissed her with a wave. "No, no. You enjoy your couples' night."

"What are you up to?"

"I've got a hot date of my own."

"You're seeing Mat again?" It was hard to tell if Will was surprised or amused.

"I wish. Me and half my wardrobe will be spending some quality time together at the Laundromat."

Will laughed. "You know you're always welcome to use the washer and dryer at our place."

"I appreciate the offer. Even more, I love to hear you call it 'our place.'" Graham put a hand on Will's arm. "Really love it. But if I go to the Laundromat, I can get it all done at once."

"All right. If you change your mind, the invitation stands."

"Thanks. Have a good night." Graham offered a parting wave and headed out. She walked home via Bradford rather than Commercial, in part to avoid the crowds and in part to avoid the temptation to stop somewhere for a glass of wine and to watch the world go by. When she got to her apartment, she found it empty. Athena gave her a disinterested look before going back to sleep.

Sigh. No distractions.

She gathered up her dirty clothes—a basket and a large sack—and loaded them into her car. The Laundromat was near empty so she divvied her things up among three washers and set them to run. She looked around and wished she'd thought to bring a book. She pulled out her phone instead, perusing Instagram and Twitter with mild interest.

Graham resisted the urge to text Mat for about twenty minutes, not wanting to come off as clingy or like she didn't have a life of her own. But as she sat in an uncomfortable chair watching her sheets and shirts progress through the spin cycle, boredom set in. Besides, she reasoned, Mat had issued the last invitation. She clicked to the messages screen and gave in. *Thanks again for dinner. It was amazing and I had a great time. A thousand times more fun than I'm having right now.*

She didn't expect an immediate response, but one came just a few seconds later. *And what are you up to this evening?*

Instead of typing a response, Graham took a photo of the washing machine and sent it.

Mat replied with the emoji of the face whose eyes and mouth were nothing more than straight lines. *That's a pretty low bar.*

Graham contemplated an apology, but decided to tease back. *I did say a thousand times.* She added a winky face, then replaced it with the one that included a kiss.

Oh, well, then. The flashing dots told Graham more was coming. *Interested in joining my cousin and his girlfriend for dinner next week?*

Even though Mat hadn't used it in reference to her, Graham's heart did a flip at the word girlfriend. They might not be there yet, but if Mat was inviting her on a double date, she had to think of Graham as more than just sex. Graham closed her eyes and let her head tip back against the wall. Not her girlfriend, yet. Such a small word, but so many big implications.

She might not be ready to admit it to Mat—or anyone else, for that matter—but it was probably time to be honest with herself. She liked Mat, a lot. More than a lot. Graham wanted to be her girlfriend, complete with all the rights and responsibilities that came with it. Mat might not be using those words, but Graham wanted to believe she felt the same. Sure, she might not be interested in settling down and starting a family, but Graham was years away from wanting that herself.

She hadn't been lying when she told Jess and Will and Nora that she was perfectly content with something casual. She just hadn't expected things with Mat to go so well. Graham couldn't imagine happening upon someone she wanted to spend time with more than she did with Mat. She certainly couldn't fathom having better chemistry with someone else. *I'd love to. Let me know when and where.*

I'll confirm with him and be in touch. In the meantime, enjoy your laundry.

Graham smiled at her phone for a moment, then realized her washers had stopped. She transferred the damp piles to dryers, fed them a pile of quarters. She waited some more, then folded and loaded everything back into her car. She still managed to get home before Jess, so she took the liberty of putting a pesto pizza in the oven and making a salad. She spied a bottle of chardonnay in the fridge and decided to open it. Why the hell not?

Chapter Fourteen

Mat leaned against the doorframe and watched Dom straighten his tie. Ties were a bit fussy for her, at least for a date, but he made her rethink her outfit of charcoal pants and a slim black button-down. "I'm not underdressed, am I?"

"You look great." Dom turned to face her. "I just like wearing ties. Still making up for lost time, I suppose."

Mat smiled at the assertion. "They suit you."

"Just as that," he moved a finger up and down to indicate her clothing, "suits you. What do you call that look, anyway? Sophisticated stud? Sharp-dressed butch?"

"Uh, I don't call it anything."

"Oh, I know. Get-laid chic."

Mat shook her head. "You're ridiculous. And if you don't stop preening, we're going to be late."

"I'm ready. Let's go."

They were halfway down the driveway when Mat's phone rang. She pulled it from her pocket, thinking it might be Graham. The screen read, "Mom." She glanced at Dom. "I should take this."

"It's all good. I told Renata I'd walk by her place and pick her up anyway. We'll meet you there."

Mat rolled her eyes. "All right, Romeo. See you in a little bit." She swiped a finger across the screen. "Hi, Ma."

"How are you, Mattie? How's the catch?" It was how she started every conversation.

"It's good. The currents seem to be working in our favor."

"That's good, that's good. Your father will be pleased. And Emilio says you helped convince some chef to make us their exclusive supplier."

Mat smiled. "I did. Not that I don't trust him to—"

She interrupted with a quick tut-tut. "They don't come more hard-working than Emilio, but suave he is not. You've got a softer touch. The customers like that, especially the women."

Mat appreciated the compliment, even if it was rooted in her mother's wish she'd take over the business side of the family operation instead of heading out to sea every morning. "I'm happy to play salesman every now and then, especially if it improves the bottom line."

"Emilio may not say so, but he's glad for the help." Mat thought this might be the lead-in to a lecture, but she was spared when her mother said, "But that's not why I'm calling."

Mat chuckled. "What's on your mind?"

"I'm making sure you're coming to Dores and Martin's party next weekend."

"Ah." Her aunt and uncle, Dom's parents, were celebrating their fortieth wedding anniversary. They'd shunned anything formal or fancy, so the party had turned into a massive Sunday dinner at their house. "Of course. I wouldn't miss it."

"Good. And since you won't be fishing, you can come with us to Mass at eight."

Mat swallowed a groan. She didn't mind Mass. Sometimes, she even enjoyed it. Even if she didn't believe in everything the Catholic Church pedaled, she found the ritual of it, the familiarity, soothing. She simply preferred to use her mornings off for sleeping in, especially if she had company. If the way things were going with Graham were any indication, she'd definitely have company. Still, she wasn't one to disappoint her mother. "Okay, Ma."

"Excellent. We'll be sure to save you a seat. Now, what are you up to tonight?"

Mat made a face. "Having dinner with Dom." At least it wasn't a lie.

"Dores says he and Renata are getting serious."

"He's smitten, that's for sure."

"That's sweet. You give him my best. I'll see you Sunday."

Mat pinched the bridge of her nose. "I will, Ma. Love you."

"Love you, too, Mattie. Be good."

Mat ended the call and looked at her phone for a moment. It still struck her as strange that her parents, her whole family really, were so completely okay with Dom's transition. Sure, there'd been shock, initially, but once he'd actually gone through with it, no one seemed to give it a second thought. And since he was now he and not she, of course everyone would be on board with him getting married and settling down. With a nice Portuguese girl, no less.

She shook her head. She didn't begrudge Dom any of it. She was just a little envious, maybe. Mat had made peace with her life, but it was perfectly normal to have those moments of wishing for something more. Like winning the lottery and becoming a millionaire—not a realistic game plan, but okay to think about now and then.

Now, however, was not one of those moments. She had a date to get to, and being late was not her style.

❖

Graham was excited to meet Dom and his girlfriend. Based on the little bit she'd heard, Graham guessed—hoped—she and Renata would have a lot in common. Even more, she liked the idea of a double date. Her girlfriend in grad school had been a doctoral student in biology. The crazy hours she spent in her research mentor's lab made it difficult to align their schedules. Graham didn't hold it against her, but she'd wished they could have been friends with other couples, gone out together.

Of course, if she was being completely honest, Graham also liked the implication that she and Mat were a couple. The more time she and Mat spent together, the easier it was to think of them that way. And Will had been right. She might like the idea of playing the field, but she remained a romantic at heart, wired to want to be with one person at a time. She'd not admitted as much to Mat, afraid of jinxing things. The invitation to go out with Dom and Renata felt like an unspoken confirmation that they were moving in that direction.

She headed out to the living room, where Jess and her friend Cara were debating pizza or Chinese for dinner. "I was going to ask you to break our tie," Cara said, "but it looks like you've got plans."

"I do." Graham couldn't suppress a smile. "But my vote is always pizza."

"Yes." Jess pumped a fist. "Are you going out with your lobsterman again?"

"I am. Along with her cousin and his girlfriend."

"Ooh, double date. That means it's serious," Cara said.

Graham laughed, amused, but also happy to have her own take on the situation confirmed.

"Do you want it to be serious?" Jess asked.

They hadn't talked too much about where Graham wanted things to go, but Jess knew her pretty well. She nodded slowly. "You know, I think I do."

Cara, who was visiting from New Hampshire, grinned. "We won't wait up for you, then."

Graham slipped on a jacket. "Thanks. Enjoy your pizza."

Cara rolled her eyes. "Next time, we're getting Chinese."

Jess picked up her phone. "Deal."

Graham walked down the hill toward Bradford, turning left and heading toward the East End. She tucked her hands in her pockets and looked up at the sky. The sun was setting, but they had a good couple hours of daylight left. She let out a contented sigh. It was hard not to appreciate the beauty of a summer evening.

"Graham."

At the sound of her name, Graham turned. Mat jogged down the street in her direction. Graham smiled. "Hey, you."

Mat caught up to her and gave her a kiss. "Hi."

Despite the brevity of the contact, heat rose in Graham's cheeks. It was the sort of bubbly, elated feeling she thought she'd outgrown. It went remarkably well with the sexual energy that seemed to simmer just below the surface whenever she was around Mat. "Is Dom not with you?"

Mat shrugged. "He headed to Renata's apartment so they could walk to the restaurant together."

Graham smiled. "That's sweet."

"He's definitely in full courting mode." Mat rolled her eyes.

They started to walk. Graham shrugged. "I think it's romantic."

Mat looked over at her. "Should I be taking notes? Is that something you want?"

Want might be a strong word, but she did think it was nice. Or would be nice, in the grand scheme of things. "Nah. This is cool."

Mat slipped an arm behind her waist and gave a little squeeze. "It's nice to bump into you, though."

"Agreed."

When they got to Ciro & Sal's, Dom and Renata were already there. They held hands and looked at each other with adoring eyes. If Graham felt a tiny twinge of longing, she promptly brushed it aside. Dom made introductions and hugs were shared all around, then they headed down the gravel path to the restaurant entrance.

Inside, the air was warm and smelled of tomatoes and garlic. The dim lighting made the space feel cozy. Their table sat against an exposed brick wall and the light fixture above appeared to be an antique cheese grater. Graham took a seat against the wall and Mat slid in next to her. Their knees touched under the table. It was romantic as hell and she intended to let herself enjoy it.

Dom suggested ordering a bottle of wine. Graham happily agreed and turned her attention to Renata while he and Mat settled on one. "Mat said you're in real estate?"

Renata smiled. "I got my license last year. My dad has a small agency and I work for him. I'm hoping to learn and eventually buy the business when he retires."

Graham nodded. "That's awesome. You grew up here, right?"

"I did. Both my parents are from old fishing families, although they got out of the fishing business a couple of generations back. What about you?"

"My aunt—she owns the Failte Inn—moved here in her twenties."

"Is that how you wound up here?"

Graham thought back to her teenage years. Spending time away from her parents had been such a thrill. To be somewhere so queer during her formative years only added to that. "Sort of. I spent time with her when I was younger and loved it. I got an internship with the Dolphin Fleet during grad school, then was lucky enough to land a full-time position when I graduated."

"It gets into your blood, doesn't it?"

"That's a good way of describing it. I'm not sure what I would have done if I'd had to decide between a job offer and moving back full-time." Graham chuckled. "I'm glad I didn't have to."

Renata nodded with what seemed to be more than polite interest. "You're a marine biologist?"

"Technically, I'm a naturalist. My degree is in environmental conservation. More about overall ecology than a single species. And I only have a master's degree, not a doctorate."

Dom chuckled. "That's more than any of us have."

Graham blushed. "In school, there was such a hierarchy."

"I didn't say that to make you feel bad. You should be proud," Dom said.

She glanced at Mat, who nodded. "Thanks."

"So," Renata said, as though sensing Graham's desire to change the subject, "I hear you've been out on Dom and Mat's boat."

"Just once. Dom was sick and Mat was desperate." Graham smiled at the memory of her day with Mat. Not romantic by any means, but it might be her favorite of the times they spent together. Well, aside from some of the time in the bedroom.

Renata laughed. "That's one more time than me. Dom keeps saying it's dirty and nothing special."

"Well, he's right about the dirty part, but still." Graham turned her attention to Dom. "You should take Renata out on the boat. She wants to see where you work."

Dom got a look of alarm on his face. He looked from Graham to Renata, then to Mat. "Okay."

Mat set an elbow on the table and leaned toward Renata. "Do you actually want to or is Graham trying to convince you that you want to?"

Graham let out a "hey" and Renata said, "I do want to."

Dom nodded. "Okay."

Graham narrowed her eyes at Dom. "You're not playing that girls are dainty and delicate game are you?"

Before Dom could say anything, Mat lifted a hand in the universal symbol for stop. "I can tell you right now, man, the right answer is no."

"Thanks, pal, but I've got this one." Dom turned to his girlfriend. "I'm sorry I haven't invited you out. It is dirty, not to mention smelly and not at all glamorous. But if it's important to you, of course I want to."

Renata turned and cupped his cheek. "Thank you." She dropped her hand and grinned. "Maybe just a short outing though. Unlike Graham here, I'm perfectly fine never knowing how to bait a trap."

Their dinners arrived and everyone sampled everyone else's food. Graham talked about her family and learned more about Mat's. She was a lot closer to the Pero clan than Graham had realized, even with the family business. The time flew by and Graham found herself sad and a little surprised when the plates were cleared. But then they ordered a pair of desserts to share, along with coffees. While waiting for them to arrive, Graham excused herself to go to the restroom. "I'll join you," Renata offered.

They stood at the sinks, side by side. Graham offered Renata a smile. "I'm glad we did this."

"Same. So, are you and Mat," she paused, making Graham wonder where the question might be going. "Sleeping together?"

Before she could stop herself, Graham laughed out loud. For all the unknowns about what she and Mat were to each other, where their relationship might be going, that was one she could answer. "Yes. Yes, we are."

Renata frowned and Graham feared she made a misstep. She forgot that Mat came from a traditional, probably Catholic, family. But instead of clamming up, or saying anything judgmental, Renata gently grabbed her arm. "Do you have any pointers for me?"

"Pointers?" Was she talking about being with a trans guy? Graham had a few trans friends, but she'd never slept with any of them.

"Dom is sweet and gentle and chivalrous." Renata sighed. "But I cannot get him to make a move."

"Oh." That, at least, was familiar territory.

"How can I convey to him that I don't feel compelled to wait until marriage?"

Graham bit her tongue to keep from laughing a second time. "Um. Have you told him?"

Renata winced. "Not in so many words."

"It's okay, I feel you. Direct can be hard. What if you suggest going back to his place after dinner?"

"You think that will work?"

Graham took a deep breath. "I can't say for sure, but it's a step. He's clearly nuts for you."

"You think?" Renata looked hopeful and, despite being the same age as Graham, so young.

"That part is beyond obvious. You might have to give him a little encouragement, you know? Hand on his leg. Really lean in when you kiss him."

"I can do that."

"Are you going to do it tonight?"

"Yes?" Renata cringed again.

"Do it. I'll make a comment about going back to Mat's and you can follow suit." How funny was it that she was the confident, experienced one in this scenario?

Renata threw her arms around Graham. "Thank you."

She was tempted to ask Renata for ideas on how to get Mat to look at her with the complete adoration that Dom seemed to have for her, but she resisted. Some matters were more complicated than others.

They returned to the table and had dessert. After, the four of them walked back toward the center of town. She tucked her arm through Mat's, watched Renata do the same. "Thinking I might need a night cap," she said, loud enough for Dom and Renata to hear. She turned to Mat. "Want to head back to your place?"

Mat gave her a quizzical look, but Graham squeezed her arm a bit and winked. Mat narrowed her eyes, but said, "Sounds good to me."

"I'd love to do the same at your place." Renata gave Dom some serious bedroom eyes and Graham gave her a thumbs-up behind Dom's back.

"Uh." Dom stuttered in a completely endearing way. "Sure. That would be great."

They walked the rest of the way to Mat and Dom's building. Before Dom could say anything about not splitting the party up just yet, Graham said, "This was so much fun. We should do it again soon."

Renata nodded. "Agreed. You two have a good night." She took Dom's hand and led him in the direction of his door.

Once they were inside, Mat turned to Graham. "Care to tell me what that was all about?"

Graham smiled. "Just helping my new friend Renata get what she wants."

Mat raised a brow. "And what exactly does she want?"

"Your cousin, naked and on top of her. I guess he's a little old-fashioned."

Mat laughed out loud. Really laughed, until she had to wipe tears from her eyes. "That's one word for it. Dare I ask what advice you gave her?"

Graham lifted a shoulder, made some bedroom eyes of her own. "I told her not to be afraid to make the first move, make it clear what she wants."

"I see." Mat nodded. "And what would that look like, exactly?"

Graham closed the distance between them. "I told her to touch him." She put a hand on Mat's rear end. "Kiss him with her whole body." She leaned in, pressing her breasts against Mat's as she covered Mat's lips with hers.

"Very effective," Mat murmured against her mouth.

Graham took Mat's hands in hers and backed them toward the bedroom. "Baby, you ain't seen nothing yet."

Chapter Fifteen

Graham spent most of her week looking forward to lunch at Failte. In addition to seeing Aunt Nora and Will, she'd get to see Emerson and Darcy. And after lunch, they'd talk wedding. She didn't know a lot about weddings, but she was excited to be included in the planning.

When she arrived, Darcy and Emerson were already there. They'd brought along Darcy's son, Liam, who Graham had met a couple of times when they came out for whale watches. Graham remembered him being eager, but also attentive. She'd wondered at the time if it was a personality trait, or a specific interest in whales.

Will refreshed introductions and Graham congratulated Emerson and Darcy on their engagement. "I'm a huge fan of your work," she said to Emerson. Then, to Darcy, "Yours, too, actually."

That earned her a laugh. Darcy gestured to her son. "Turns out, Liam is quite a fan of yours."

"Is that so?" Graham smiled at him.

He nodded with enthusiasm. "I was wondering if you might be willing to talk with me about your career?"

Graham smiled at the formality of the question. "My career?"

"He's doing a science camp this summer and they have a project to research a potential career," Emerson said by way of explanation.

"I think a real-life interview is way cooler than just looking stuff up on the computer and I am definitely interested in your job," Liam said.

"I'd love to, buddy. We can talk today if you want, but if your mom is cool with it, I could also give you a behind-the-scenes tour."

Liam's eyes got huge. "You could?"

"Absolutely. I mean, I know you've been out a couple of times, but if you came early one day, I could show you how we record and track all the sightings, what that teaches us about the whales' migration and their feeding habits."

"That would be so cool." He paused after each word, putting extra emphasis on "so."

"I think that might make you his hero," Darcy said.

"It would be fun." Graham looked at Liam. "I remember the first time I met a marine biologist. I was obsessed."

"I'm torn between wanting to be a marine biologist and a regular biologist." Liam looked up at the ceiling. "Or an astronomer or a doctor."

Graham nodded. "All very cool jobs."

Darcy shrugged, but gave Liam a look that was pure love before looking back to Graham. "We seem to be homing in on a theme, at least."

"I think I still wanted to be a ballerina at his age."

"Oh? Did you dance?" Darcy asked.

Graham laughed. "No. I have terrible rhythm. It wasn't until I was twelve that my mother broke the news to me. Fortunately, I'd discovered nature documentaries by then and had a new focus."

Liam chimed back in. "I love nature documentaries! You should come over and watch with us. Mom is only kind of interested, but Emerson and I watch them together all the time."

Will raised a hand. "I'm not super smart like all of you, but this sounds fun. Can I come over, too?"

Graham watched Emerson give her sister a look that seemed affectionate and scolding at the same time. "You're plenty smart and in lots of different ways, but yes. Of course you can come over."

Nora emerged from the kitchen with a huge plate of sandwiches. "I made soup, too. Minestrone. Would anyone care for some?"

Everyone's hands went up. Graham stood. "I'll help."

An hour later, Graham was stuffed and ready for a nap. She wouldn't, of course, but she did allow her mind to drift while the others—Nora and Darcy, mostly—started ironing out logistics for the wedding.

Nora frowned. "I'm sorry that I don't have very many dates to offer you. Most of my summer bookings were made months ago."

Darcy shook her head and smiled. "September is perfect. It's actually the best time for me to take a few days off from work."

Emerson nodded. "I'm sure the Sunday after Labor Day is still a popular time. Are you sure it won't cause any trouble?"

Nora tapped her notebook with her pen. "I'm full Saturday night, but have only two couples staying Sunday as well. That leaves one for you and two for any guests you have coming in from out of town. Tisha's still here to lend a hand. It's going to work beautifully."

"I'm completely at your service, too," Graham said. "I consider you friends by association and I love throwing a party."

Darcy took a deep breath. "I can do some of the food myself ahead of time so you're not saddled with everything."

Nora's face got very stern and Graham had to suppress a laugh. Apparently, Darcy still didn't know Nora very well. "You will do no such thing. This is your special day and you're already being about as low-fuss as is humanly possible."

"Agreed." Will, whose arm had been draped behind Nora, gave her shoulder a squeeze. "Let us do this for you."

Emerson smiled. "We really can't thank you enough. Alex is insisting on doing the cake, though. Is that allowed?"

Nora laughed. "Of course. I'd say it's her prerogative, even. I'll coordinate with her on getting it here and anything she might need."

They talked about numbers of guests and the menu, where to rent chairs and who would perform the ceremony. Graham half-listened, wondering about what her own wedding might look like one day. As a little girl, she'd dreamed of something big and fancy. Now that she'd grown up, her priorities had shifted. Now, it was about finding the person she wanted to spend her life with and being surrounded by family and friends.

She didn't intend it, but Graham's thoughts turned to Mat. She chuckled at the idea of Mat knowing where her mind had gone. She might not have a ton of experience with relationships, but she knew better than to go there anytime soon.

Graham walked back to her apartment in an excellent mood. It was so much fun to team up with Nora and Will, especially for two people she liked so much. She hoped the whole wedding planning thing might make her closer to both Emerson and Darcy. She loved Jess, as well as her friends from work, but she liked the idea of having grown-up friends. She thought they saw her as the same, not just Nora's niece or someone who might offer to babysit Liam from time to time. Not that she'd mind the latter. The kid was a riot, and not only because he seemed to idolize her.

For at least the third time that day, Graham wondered what Mat was up to. Work, probably. She said she took at least one day off per week, but Graham wasn't so sure. Unless, of course, the weather dictated it.

As if summoned by Graham's thoughts, Mat chose that exact moment to text her. *What are you up to?*

Graham smirked as she typed her response. She wasn't going to talk marriage with Mat, but there was no reason she couldn't tease her a little. *Planning a wedding.*

Not yours, I hope? Mat punctuated the question with a bride emoji, followed by the one that evoked Edvard Munch's *The Scream.*

Graham frowned. She'd been joking, but she was left questioning the apparent vehemence in Mat's reply. She hoped it meant Mat didn't want her marrying anyone else and not Mat being horrified by weddings in general. *Sister of a friend. They're doing it at my aunt's inn, so I'm helping.*

That's very nice of you. Another text came immediately after. *Speaking of nice, how would you like to join me at a big family shindig? Completely casual, but definitely big.*

Graham's brain dissected the invitation, trying to suss out any underlying meaning. Was the party casual, or the invitation? And why—after all her insistence on not overthinking things—did she continually find herself doing exactly that? She huffed, then renewed her commitment to be cool. *Sure. Day and time? Local, I assume?*

Excellent. And, yes. Sunday at one. Come to my place at 12:30 and we'll go over together?

Graham waited for a moment to see if Mat added a comment about bringing a bag. She didn't, but that was okay. She'd offered. There was no need to repeat herself. *How casual is casual?*

Um, shorts or jeans?

Graham shook her head. Not helpful. *Casual dress okay?*

Of course.

Something about the exchange felt off—not bad, but different from her usual back and forth with Mat. She shrugged it off. She'd just been invited to a family gathering. As far as she was concerned, that was a good sign. She let herself enjoy looking forward to it, along with the late summer sunshine, the rest of the way home.

Chapter Sixteen

Graham walked up Mat's driveway and told herself for the hundredth time not to be nervous. This wasn't a big deal. Mat had invited her by text, after all. If it was a big deal, they would have talked about it. She closed her eyes for a second and took a deep breath. Don't be nervous, she told herself.

Before she got to the door, she saw Dom hovering nearby. Hopefully, that meant he'd be coming, too.

"Hi." He smiled, but something in his face mirrored the nerves she felt.

She returned the smile, but wasn't feeling it. "Hi. Is everything okay?"

The smile turned into a grimace. "I—"

His reply was cut off when Mat's door opened. She emerged and gave Graham the strangest look, like she was surprised to see her. "Hey."

"Hi." Graham let the word drag out, more question than greeting.

"Are we supposed to have plans today? Did I forget?" Mat asked.

What was happening? Graham's nerves morphed into confusion. "You—"

This time, Dom cut her off. "I have a confession."

Mat and Graham turned in unison to look at him. Mat's gaze remained fixed, while Graham looked back and forth, trying to glean meaning from their facial expressions. "You didn't," Mat said.

While Mat and Dom seemed to share some sort of understanding, Graham felt even more in the dark. "Didn't what?"

Dom offered her a smile. "I'm the one who invited you to come today."

Although she grasped the meaning of his words, understanding didn't follow. "Like it was your idea?" Graham looked to Mat for confirmation, but she was busy shooting eye daggers at her cousin.

Dom's smile turned sheepish and he shrugged. "My idea, but also me doing the inviting."

"But it was Mat who texted me."

"Really, dude? You hijacked my phone?" Mat said to Dom.

Graham resisted the urge to press her fingers to her eyes. She was all nervous about meeting Mat's family, about what it might mean, and Mat hadn't even invited her. She felt a sudden need to escape. "I'll go home."

"Wait." Graham just made out Mat's statement.

At the same time, Dom blurted, "They're expecting you."

"What?" Mat's tone pitched from incredulous to something resembling panic.

"I invited Renata and mentioned to my mom that you'd be bringing your girlfriend, too. For the record, she seemed excited. And I'm guessing she's told your mom by now."

Mat pinched the bridge of her nose and tried to process the last ninety seconds. What was supposed to be a laid-back family party at her aunt and uncle's house had turned into something much more complicated. Part of her brain screamed that she needed to undo what Dom had orchestrated. Another part urged her to wring his neck. But a quick look at Graham quieted both those parts.

She looked sad and, worse, embarrassed. Mat might not be the chivalrous type, but she also prided herself on being the kind of woman who did not put that look in another woman's eyes. Even if Graham pretended to be okay with it, Mat knew better. And since Dom had already primed the pump, half the damage was already done.

"You should come."

Graham narrowed her eyes. Mat couldn't tell if it was anger or suspicion. "Really?"

With less than a second of hesitation, Mat made up her mind. She'd deal. It would be fine. And she could always wring Dom's neck later. "Absolutely. It'll be fun. Assuming, of course, you forgive my cousin for being a total ass."

Graham looked over at Dom, who'd resumed his puppy dog look. Mat expected her to smile and let it go. That's what people usually did when Dom pulled something. She figured it had to do with his charming nature and aw-shucks tendencies. But Graham folded her arms. "Why did you do it?"

"I wanted to bring Renata and figured it would be less pressure if there was someone else she knew. And I knew if I asked Mat to invite you, she wouldn't because she's weird about stuff like that."

"With good reason," Mat said.

"Okay, that's fair. But it was a long time ago."

The last thing Mat wanted to do was rehash her past in front of Graham. "Fine. You're selfish, but for a good reason."

Graham nodded slowly. "Agreed. Your methods are suspect, but I support your cause."

"Does that mean you'll come?" Dom looked at her hopefully.

As much as Mat didn't want to bring Graham to a family function, she found herself hoping Graham would now say yes. Which was kind of ridiculous, but here they were. She decided to add her own encouragement. "Please. I'd really like you to."

Graham looked back and forth at them. Mat feared she might ask more questions, but she didn't. Instead, she shrugged. "All right. I assume Renata is expecting me, too."

Dom beamed. "She is. And she'll be here any second."

Mat shook her head. "Bit of a dangerous game you're playing, don't you think?"

Dom shrugged, his perpetual optimism showing on his face. "It worked, didn't it?"

Graham laughed. Mat hoped that meant she really was okay, and not simply faking it to avoid an even more awkward situation. "Should I be bracing myself for any other surprises?"

"What kind of surprises? I want a surprise."

Mat turned in the direction of the voice. She'd not even heard Renata approach. She looked pretty and so happy to see them all. Mat sighed. It was a good thing she'd already decided Renata and Dom were perfect for each other. It made this whole thing much less infuriating.

Dom slid an arm around her waist and kissed her cheek. "If I told you, it wouldn't be a surprise now, would it?"

Mat chuckled. She gave him points for a quick recovery. "Shall we?"

To Graham's credit, she seemed to recover quickly, too. She complimented Renata's dress and asked about who she'd be meeting. Mat made a point of taking her hand as they walked, since Dom and Renata walked ahead of them, fingers entwined. It took just a few minutes to get to her aunt and uncle's house. A couple of her cousins' cars were already in the drive, along with her parents'.

"Don't feel like you have to interact with anyone," Mat said to Graham. "They can be overwhelming on a good day."

Graham looked at her like she'd said the sky was green. "That's silly. Of course I'll interact. In case you forgot, I interact with people for a living."

"Right." Mat squared her shoulders. She might have overcome the tension of Graham's unexpected arrival, but it was quickly replaced with an entirely new case of the nerves. Her girlfriend—and when had she even started using that word to think of Graham?—was meeting her parents, something she'd avoided for the last fifteen years. She couldn't decide whether to be nervous on Graham's behalf, or her own.

Dom led the way and they entered the house. Mat expected all conversations to cease and all eyes to turn their way. But they didn't. Close to a dozen people stood in groups or sat on the sofa. Through the doorway leading to the kitchen, she could make out her mother and aunt bustling around. It felt like a regular family dinner. She took a deep breath. Everything was going to be fine.

Dom took the lead in doing introductions, which made things easier. When they got to Mat's father, she held her breath. Dom looked at her expectantly. Damn. "Pop, this is Graham. She works on the Dolphin Fleet."

He looked Graham up and down slowly. Mat couldn't read his thoughts. Graham stuck out her hand and smiled. "It's a pleasure to meet you, Mr. Pero."

"Afonso, please." He took the hand, but didn't return the smile. Instead, he lifted his chin. "Dolphin Fleet. You mean the whale watch outfit?"

"Yes, sir. I'm one of the naturalists."

He sniffed. Mat cringed. Why did she have to mention the Dolphin Fleet? On top of her own regret, she wished she'd taken a moment to coach Graham on her parents, including the importance of avoiding any talk of religion, politics, gayness, or anything even tangentially related to fishing.

"Huh. What exactly do you do? Chase whales, bet on how many you can spot in an hour? See how close you can get?"

In spite of her own discomfort, Mat bristled on Graham's behalf. There was little she found more insulting than having someone not take her, or her work, seriously. She opened her mouth to tell her father to knock it off, but Graham's laugh interrupted. "You make it sound like a big scavenger hunt."

"Isn't it?" His tone had a challenge in it, but it wasn't dismissive.

"I guess we try to make it seem that way for our guests, but it feels more like bookkeeping most days. Mixed with elementary school teacher."

"Bookkeeper? How so?"

Graham smiled and seemed perfectly content to explain her work. "We pay the bills with tours, but the spirit of the Dolphin Fleet is conservation. We track migrations, breeding and feeding habits. We do our best to identify every whale we see and log the day, time, and location. Our data gets pooled with that of dozens of other fleets and helps biologists understand the entire north Atlantic ecosystem."

"Huh."

Mat laughed at the atypically brief reply. "I think you've left him speechless, Graham. That's no small feat."

Graham glanced at her, then back at her dad. Mat imagined her trying to decide if this was teasing or if she'd inadvertently stepped in something. Before Mat could let her off the hook, her father spoke again. "I'm not speechless. I'm thinking about how much whales get babied these days. I wish some fancy scientist was looking out for me."

Mat groaned inwardly. She caught movement out of the corner of her eye and glanced over to find Dom hovering in the doorway, snickering. The second she got him alone, she was going to throttle him. Graham didn't seem to notice. She nodded affably. "Actually, you do. I'm sure it feels like you've got a bunch of cumbersome rules and regulations, but part of what we do is try to keep fishing and lobstering sustainable."

"Ha." He practically spat the word.

"No, really." Graham didn't miss a beat. "You know how the fishing ban shrank by a week a few years back? That was our recommendation. Well, ours and some other scientists."

Mat didn't know that. She was pretty sure her father didn't either, based on his slow nod.

"Most of the people in my line of work want the people in your line of work to thrive. When we get it right, everyone benefits."

She'd teased her father, but Mat found herself fairly close to speechless herself. She'd come around to thinking her work and Graham's weren't at odds, but she'd never have considered them on the same side. Paired with how impressed her father seemed, it felt like wading into uncharted territory.

"Dinner." Her mother's voice carried from the kitchen into the living room.

Mat had never been more relieved to be called to the table. And given some of the awkward family moments in her life, that was saying something. Everyone moved at once, forming a line that extended halfway across the living room. Mat touched Graham's arm. "Let's eat."

"What about your Mom? I haven't even met her yet."

Mat didn't want to admit she was more worried about that interaction than the one with her father. "Oh, you will."

They joined the queue and shuffled closer and closer to the kitchen. When they reached the makeshift buffet, Mat handed Graham a plate. She described things as they went—migas with poached eggs and pataniscas and paella. Graham took a tiny amount of everything. Whether it had to do with being polite or being adventurous, Mat didn't know. But she appreciated it either way.

As was usually the case, the dining room table filled with the older crowd. Mat gestured to a sliding glass door that led to the backyard. "There are a couple of tables out back. Let's go outside."

Graham smiled, looking cool and relaxed. "Sure."

Mat had her hand on the latch when she heard her mother's voice. "Mattie, you haven't introduced me to your friend."

So close. "You looked busy. I was going to after we ate."

She made a clucking sound. "I'm sure you were."

Without missing a beat, Graham shifted her plate and utensils to her left hand. She extended her right and smiled. "I'm Graham."

"Bia." She raised an eyebrow, but took the hand. "I'm glad you were able to join us."

"I appreciate the invitation," Graham said.

Mat gave her points for the smooth delivery, especially given how the invitation had come about. "We're going to go eat out back with the cousins."

Ma nodded. "That's a good idea."

Graham's smile came across both genuine and warm. "It was nice to meet you."

She nodded again. "You, too."

Her mother shooed them toward the door and Mat breathed a sigh of relief. That was one thing Mat could say about her—Bia Pero would never stand in the way of people eating.

They escaped the noisy and crowded kitchen. At least a dozen people sat around the yard, but Mat felt like she could finally take a deep breath. They joined Dom and Renata at a picnic table, along with a couple of cousins who were chill and not overly interested in the fact that Mat had brought a girl to a family party. Fortunately, her brothers weren't able to make the trip. She wasn't sure she could handle them on top of everything else.

❖

Despite her apprehension over meeting Mat's family, Graham thought the day went well. Mat's cousins were friendly and laid back. Her dad was a riot, too. Blustery, but in the way so many dads are. Underneath the bluster, he was a softy. Mat's mother was a different story. Pleasant, but Graham detected a cool reserve. She wondered if that was her general demeanor or specific to the situation and the girl her daughter was dating.

Graham didn't dwell on it, figuring there would be plenty of time to get to know them both in the future. Well, assuming Mat wanted her to get to know them. That part remained unclear. Mat seemed to relax as the day went on, but Graham couldn't shake the feeling she was playing a role more than being herself.

Still, by the time Graham said her good-byes, complete with hugs and thumps on her back and wishes to see her again soon, it was nearly seven in the evening. Mat walked her out, then offered to walk her home. Graham resisted the urge to accept. "It would be silly for you to walk all the way to my place when yours is three houses down."

Graham thought—hoped, maybe—that Mat might protest. She wasn't looking for chivalry necessarily, but she'd have readily accepted an invitation to stay over. She'd have welcomed a sly observation that Mat could walk her home and not bother coming back. But Mat didn't do either of those things. She kissed Graham on the cheek, thanked her for coming, and went back inside to help with cleanup.

Graham walked with purpose until she was a block away from the house, then slowed her pace. There was a good hour of daylight left and she was in no hurry to get home, although she struggled to identify exactly why. At the very least, she should be relieved. Despite the questionable start to the day, she'd managed to have a nice time with Mat's family. And most of them seemed to like her. Like, really like her. Based on what Mat had said about them, Graham should actually be elated.

Yet, she wasn't. Mostly, because Mat didn't seem to be. The initial tension had melted away, sure. But just as Graham sensed her begin to relax, a detached coolness took over. It felt like she intentionally refused to have a good time.

Maybe she was still angry with Dom. Graham still couldn't believe he'd orchestrated the invitation behind Mat's back. By rights, she should be angry with him, too. He'd put her in a situation that was awkward at best. It could have turned out much worse than awkward for all he knew. But even as she thought about it, Graham couldn't muster any hard feelings. For some reason, she had an unwavering sense that his heart was in the right place.

She wasn't so sure about Mat's heart. That was the problem. Mat's reaction to Dom's little stunt gave Graham a knot of unease in the pit of her stomach. Like she resented Graham's presence as much as the surprise of it. Like she didn't want to come across as a jerk more than she wanted Graham along.

Graham shook her head. It was her own fault. They'd talked some about Mat's family, and she got a sense of Mat's desire to keep them separate from the rest of her life. Graham should have known better than to cross that line without a specific invitation from Mat. Even if the outcome had been better than she'd expected. Well, better by her standards. But Graham couldn't know if their hospitality was genuine acceptance.

Instead of crossing over to her street, Graham wandered into town. She sat on one of the benches in front of the town hall and watched the people go by. Most of the families had cleared out, leaving couples and groups of friends heading to and from dinner. Some straight couples remained, but they were fewer and far between.

Although she'd never felt the sting of parental disapproval—at least with regard to her sexuality—she still found solace in being surrounded by so much gayness. She wondered what it must be like for Mat, having that acceptance and disapproval in such close and constant proximity.

Was that what was going on now? Had the collision of her worlds upset Mat's equilibrium? Maybe. It had to be unsettling to have that play out, especially when it was so unexpected. But Graham had a sinking feeling it was more than that. She had a feeling Mat didn't introduce women to her family because they didn't stay in her life long enough to warrant it. And Graham was no different.

Graham let her head fall back. She looked at the darkening sky through the leaves of the tree branches overhead. She caught glimpses of a half moon. No different.

Chapter Seventeen

Mat didn't call or text Graham to make sure she got home okay. Not that she needed to, but ignoring her made Mat feel like a tool. Which, in turn, put her in a rotten mood the next morning. It didn't help that Dom was beyond chipper. She tried giving him the silent treatment, hoping he'd take a hint. No such luck.

After about ten attempts to start a conversation, he pointed the bander at her. "Is this about yesterday?"

"You think?"

"It went fine. I'm not sure why you're still pissed at me," Dom said.

Mat gave him a withering look.

"Okay, I know why you're still pissed at me. But things went great. For me, but for you and Graham, too."

Mat scowled. "It's because my parents wouldn't want to cause a scene at your parents' party. And because I didn't introduce her as my girlfriend."

"You didn't?" Dom seemed genuinely surprised by that.

"Dude, are you really going to tell me you don't know how it works? They don't ask, I don't tell. It's a thing."

"I understand the concept." Dom rolled his eyes like Mat was being the unreasonable one. "I just don't get it. I mean, they know you're a lesbian. You bring a girl to a family thing and they don't put two and two together?"

"They probably do know. That's not the point."

"Could you remind me of the point again?"

Mat shook her head. "The point is that I don't flaunt my sexuality and they don't give me a hard time about it."

Dom got quiet then. Finally, he looked her right in the eye. "I didn't mean to make things hard for you. I guess, well, I guess I thought they'd relaxed some, caught up with the times."

"Yeah, not so much."

"I'm sorry, then. You can be pissed if you want."

Mat sighed. "I'm not pissed. Just, don't do that again, okay?"

"I won't." Dom focused on his work for a few minutes, then looked at her again. "Please don't hold this against Graham. I'd feel really bad if you broke it off with her because I was an ass."

That was just it. She didn't want to break things off with Graham. They were having fun. And Graham wasn't clingy or asking to talk about what they were or where the relationship was going. The main reason she was pissed was that Dom's scheme threatened to throw a wrench in the whole thing. "I'm not."

"Not holding it against her or not breaking up with her?"

"Neither." She looked out at the water in front of them and imagined Graham standing in the living room, going toe-to-toe with her father. The memory gave her a ripple of anxiety, but there was something else mixed in. She couldn't put her finger on it, but it felt a little like pride. Which made no sense, but she couldn't shake it or come up with another word.

"Good. I'm not trying to tell you Graham is the one, but she makes you happy. You shouldn't throw that away because you're afraid to rock the boat at home."

Mat let those words sink in. She didn't give a lot of thought to being happy. Which wasn't to say she considered herself unhappy. She'd just come to see herself as making the best of the hand she was dealt—no complaints, no grand plans. As much as she might not want to rock the boat with her parents, she didn't really feel the need to rock hers either. It had always worked and left her, at the very least, content. Why did that leave her feeling hollow now?

"What? Was that the wrong thing to say, too?" Rather than antagonizing, Dom's face seemed genuinely concerned.

"No, man. You're fine."

"You look like I just ran over your puppy."

"Shut up. No, I don't."

Dom shrugged. "Look, I get why you might not want to spill your guts to me right now. I'm not going to push it."

"No?" It sure felt like he was pushing something. Even if she wasn't entirely sure what it was.

"No. You're going to do what you want anyway. But, again, for the record, you're happier than I've seen you in a long time, and I'm pretty sure Graham has something to do with it."

They continued working and Dom changed the subject. Well, sort of changed the subject. He went back to talking about Renata and her impressions of the family and Renata's invitation to family dinner with them the following Sunday. Mat half listened and thought about what he'd said earlier. The part about her being happy.

If she really thought about it, Dom did have a point. Graham managed to be fun and smart and easy all at the same time. And the more time Mat spent with her, the more she wanted to. That didn't mean she wanted to marry Graham, or even move in together. It just meant they got along better than most of the women she went out with.

Settling into that should have made Mat feel better. On some levels, it did. On others, it made her feel like an even bigger tool for blowing Graham off the night before. She was going to have to apologize, and probably do something nice.

The catch was only fair and they decided to call it a day midafternoon. She let Dom steer them back to shore while she did some minor repair on a trap that needed new netting on the entry. They unloaded the catch they'd managed and cleaned up for the next day, then headed home in Mat's truck.

Dom went to his apartment to shower and go meet Renata for the afternoon. Mat sat in her truck for a moment and tried to formulate a plan for making things up to Graham. She should probably start with figuring out if Graham was as annoyed with her as she was with herself.

What are you up to tonight?

Since staring at her phone and waiting for a reply made her feel ridiculous, Mat went inside to take her own shower. When she emerged, wrapped in a towel, a few minutes later, Graham had yet to respond. Mat chided herself for scowling, for being an uncomfortable mix of worried and annoyed. Then she realized Graham was probably at work, and would be for another couple of hours.

Instead of fidgeting or staring at the television to pass the time, Mat drove herself to the store. She'd make dinner, whether Graham decided to join her or not. By the time she got back to her place, complete with enough food to make at least three different dinners, she'd convinced herself Graham was avoiding her. But just as she finished stuffing things into the fridge, her phone vibrated in her pocket.

Vacuuming. Unless you have something better in mind.

The light tone did more to lift Mat's mood than Graham's availability. *I'll make you dinner. And let you pick the Netflix.*

There was no delay in the response this time. *I'll be there by six.*

❖

Graham knocked on Mat's door and adjusted the duffel bag on her shoulder. When Mat answered in faded jeans and a white T-shirt, she couldn't help but sigh. "Hi," Mat said with an easy smile.

"Hi." Graham stepped inside and set her bag down. The air smelled like something delicious, but she couldn't quite put her finger on it. "I have no idea what's for dinner, but I'm pretty sure it's going to be amazing."

"Just pasta. Nothing fancy." Mat stepped forward and kissed her. "Thanks for coming."

The kiss wasn't unlike others they'd shared—more greeting than anything else—but Graham picked up on an undercurrent of tension. "Thanks for making dinner."

Mat abruptly turned. She went to the kitchen counter and picked up a glass. "Wine?"

"Sure." Graham accepted the glass. Between this and the weird end to the day before, something was up. It didn't seem fair that Mat would be upset with her, but that was the feeling she got. "Is everything okay?"

"Yes." Mat nodded, as though she was trying to convince herself. She looked away for a second, then locked eyes with Graham. "I owe you an apology."

"You do?" Not what she was expecting.

"For yesterday."

"Oh. It wasn't your fault Dom went behind your back. And really, I'm not mad at him either."

"I'm glad you're not mad at him. I am, or was. He shouldn't have put you in that position."

Graham shrugged. She got the sinking feeling Mat had serious regrets that Graham had come along, regardless of the how or the why. "It's fine."

"But that's not actually what I'm apologizing for. I was weird when you showed up, and kind of a jerk when you left."

"You weren't a jerk." It was Graham's instinct to diffuse Mat's discomfort. Even if she'd left the party deflated, that was the result of her own wants, not anything Mat did wrong.

"You're being kind, which I appreciate. But let me own it. I was weirded out because I don't mix family and dating. Dom aside, obviously. But it wasn't you who created that situation. You were gracious and so accommodating about the whole thing."

Graham smiled. "I really did have a good time."

"I'm not going to say you didn't, but I am going to say thank you for being cool."

Graham's shoulders relaxed. "I'll take it."

"Good." Mat picked up the other glass of wine from the counter. "Here's to being cool."

Graham clinked her glass to Mat's, took a sip. It was a Chardonnay, buttery and smooth. "Since we're back to being cool, how do you feel about a wedding?" Despite the teasing tone Graham had been going for, Mat tensed. "Not ours. Relax."

Mat laughed then. "Sorry."

Graham shook her head. Idiot. "I was trying to be funny."

"You were." Now Mat looked guilty. "I swear."

Graham told herself not to be disappointed by the awkwardness that seemed to be part of their dynamic all of a sudden. She was being overly sensitive. If she could just relax, things would go back to normal. "Let me start over. Would you be my date for a wedding that I'm half attending, half working?"

"Half working?"

"It's at my aunt's inn and the couple are kind of friends, so I'm helping out. But I'm also a guest, so I'd love to have a date." Graham was pretty sure she'd managed to make the whole thing sound about as un-fun as possible.

"Sure."

"Yeah?" Graham narrowed her eyes. "You're not just saying yes because I went to your family thing?"

"Is this a family thing?"

Graham shook her head quickly. "Not at all. I mean, my aunt will be there, along with Will. But it's Will's sister getting married, so if anything, it's her family thing."

"Cool. When is it?"

"Weekend after next." Graham cringed slightly as she said it. "I meant to invite you sooner, but—"

"We ended up at my family thing and it got weird." Mat offered her a knowing smile.

Graham's hesitation about inviting Mat to the wedding actually spanned a couple of weeks, but she'd take the out she was given. She returned the smile. "I wouldn't say weird."

"No?" Mat angled her head. "Unexpected."

"Oh, well, sure. That sounds better."

Mat shrugged. "Yeah. It's the least I can do."

Graham didn't want doing things together—things that didn't involve tumbling into bed together—to be on a barter system. At this point, though, she didn't want to press the matter. "Great."

"How fancy?"

"Not very. Like date fancy. The ceremony will be outside if the weather is okay, so I've got a dress I can layer a sweater and a jacket over if needed."

The description seemed to make Mat relax. "I can work with that."

Mat turned her attention back to the stove and Graham watched her. Mat had only cooked for her that one time before, but Graham decided it was something she could get used to. Yes, the dinner part was nice. The watching, though, was sexy as hell.

And she had a date for Emerson and Darcy's wedding. Graham had worried that Mat might say no, or at the very least claim she had to work. But her apprehension had proved unnecessary. Just like her worry about how things had ended the day before. She might be in uncharted waters with Mat, but that didn't have to imply dangerous territory.

Chapter Eighteen

The two weeks leading up to the wedding included half a dozen nights with Mat and it felt like they'd reclaimed the light, easy energy of their first few dates. Good meals, amazing sex, no serious conversations. It wasn't like they'd had a fight in the first place, but it felt to Graham like they'd made up.

The Sunday of the wedding arrived, chilly but bright—a perfect early fall day. Graham invited herself into the shower with Mat. Kissing led to roaming hands over soapy skin. By the time they were done, Mat commented that she needed a second shower. Graham pinched her rear end and promised to show her what dirty was later on.

"Are you sure you don't want me coming with you now? I'm very able-bodied, you know."

"Oh, I do know, but I'm fine. Go have lunch with your parents and brother and come to the inn at two o'clock."

"But how will I ever go that long without putting my hands on you?"

Graham raised a brow and said in a teasing tone, "I imagine you'll survive."

"Barely. It'll be a close call."

"Stop." She didn't really care if Mat stopped. She liked the idea of Mat being unable to get enough of her. Lord knew that's how she felt about Mat.

"Fine. But I'll be thinking of what you just did to me in the shower all day."

"Good." Graham threw on her pre-wedding kitchen clothes and grabbed the rest of her things. "I'll see you this afternoon."

"I'll be there."

Graham headed to the inn and found breakfast service just ending. She took advantage of her timing and helped herself to some French toast and bacon. But instead of taking a seat at the massive dining room table, she pushed through the swinging door into the kitchen. She found Tisha chopping vegetables and Nora loading the dishwasher. "Good morning, bosses. Wedding assistant reporting for duty."

Tisha laughed. "Maybe finish your breakfast before you claim to be reporting for duty."

Graham made a saluting gesture with a piece of bacon in hand. "Yes, ma'am. The bacon is to die for, by the way."

Nora shook her head and smiled. "You know you can make it, right? Put it on a rack on a sheet pan in the oven."

"Why would I do that when I can show up here and get it anytime I want?"

Will came in the back door, cheeks rosy. "What can you get anytime you want?"

Graham lifted her second piece. "Bacon."

"Well, that's true." Will turned to Nora. "Chairs are all set up. What else do you need me to do?"

"We need to move the furniture in the sitting room, then set up the extra tables there and in the foyer."

Graham shoved the last bite of food into her mouth. "I'll help."

She handed Nora her plate and followed Will to the front of the house. The rented tables didn't look like much, but once they had cloths and were set, no one would notice. Altogether, they'd have seating for thirty, which was the number Emerson and Darcy had settled on. Once the tables were done, she went to the kitchen and helped Tisha with food. Although her skills in the kitchen remained amateur at best, she could stir pots and slice baguettes with the best of them.

Before she knew it, Nora was shooing her away to get dressed. Somehow, without Graham even noticing, Nora had ducked out and donned her dressy clothes. On her way to the room Nora and Will now shared, she crossed paths with Will, who looked exceptionally dapper in her best person suit. "You look amazing."

In true Will fashion, she blushed. "Thanks."

"You've got the rings?"

A look of panic flashed on Will's face as she patted herself down. Her shoulders slumped and her face relaxed. "I have the rings."

"Sorry, didn't mean to freak you out. You're painfully responsible. You've got this."

Will nodded. "I've got this."

Emerson and Liam arrived, looking just as adorable as Will. Graham took up her station at the side gate to direct guests and hand out the programs Darcy had designed. It didn't take long for guests to start arriving. Graham smiled and greeted. After holding the gate for a group of six, she looked up and found herself eye-to-eye with Mat.

"Hello, handsome." And handsome she was. Mat wore an outfit similar to the one she had on when they went out with Dom and Renata, but Graham was still caught off guard by just how good she looked.

"Hello yourself, gorgeous. You look stunning."

The wedding wasn't formal by any means, but Graham had gone with one of her favorite dresses for the occasion. It was more elegant than what she'd worn out with Mat thus far. "Thank you."

"Can I hang here with you or should I go in?"

"I'd love it if you kept me company." Mat moved off to her side and they stood together, greeting the remaining guests. At five of, they made their way down the garden path and took a pair of seats near the back.

The ceremony was brief, but touching. Liam had written his own vows for Emerson, and she had prepared words for him. They promised to be a family—first, last, always. In spite of herself, Graham shed a few tears. Something about that much love, that much hope, concentrated in a single moment in time took her breath away.

After the kiss and a proclamation of spouses for life, a cheer went up from the small crowd. On cue, Tisha emerged from the house with a tray full of champagne flutes. Graham grabbed Mat's hand and whispered, "Want to give me a hand?"

"Sure."

Graham led them into the kitchen where more champagne waited. They brought it out, circulating until everyone had a glass. While Will and Darcy's friend, Lia, gave toasts, she and Mat carried a couple dozen chairs into the house, positioning them around the temporary tables. She then helped direct guests inside, past a selection of cheese, crackers, and canapés artfully arranged on the kitchen island.

"I'm playing bartender now," Graham told Mat.

"I can definitely help you there."

They stood side by side in the sitting room, pouring wine and opening bottles of beer. It felt like no time at all before Nora announced the buffet was open. Guests made their way through and found their seats. When everyone was seated, Graham and Mat got food and snagged their own seats, arranged in a way that kept them closest to the bar.

They were seated next to Alex and Lia, who'd left their daughter, Maeve, at home, and a couple Graham didn't know. It didn't surprise her, necessarily, but Mat seemed to have no trouble chatting them up—asking questions and making jokes. She actually seemed more comfortable doing it than Graham. She filed the detail away, under "one more reason to fall for Mat." It was turning out to be a pretty big file.

When the meal ended, Emerson and Darcy cut their cake, a simple but exquisite creation of ivory colored frosting and leaves made out of sugar. "Did you make that?" Mat asked Alex.

Alex smiled. "I did."

Mat nodded. "So, it will taste as good as it looks."

Graham had never had anything that fancy from The Flour Pot, but she'd devoured more than her share of cookies and muffins and pastries. "Agreed."

There was no dancing, but people lingered over their cake and cups of coffee or glasses of wine. Despite being told she didn't have to, Mat helped Graham clear plates. She looked so freaking at ease doing it, Graham wondered if she'd waited tables at some point in her life. The next thing she knew, Mat and Will were at the kitchen sink, sleeves rolled up and laughing like they'd been friends for years. To Graham's mind, the whole thing was completely, utterly perfect.

When everything was cleaned and put away, Tisha bid them good night, leaving Mat, Will, and Graham alone in the kitchen. Will slapped a hand on Mat's shoulder. "We can't thank you enough for your help tonight. I know my sister and Darcy would agree you went above and beyond anything we could have asked for."

Mat shrugged. Now that it was done, she realized how caught up in it she'd been. "No worries. It reminded me of how we do things in my family. Not weddings, mind you, those are a full production. But to celebrate other things, it's like this. Everyone pitches in."

"You've got a big family, don't you?" Will's voice held something that resembled awe.

Mat shook her head. "You don't know the half of it."

"Well, we were glad to have you be a part of ours." Nora nodded matter-of-factly, as though she sensed too much praise would make Mat uncomfortable, which, of course, it did. Which was to say nothing about her comment on Mat being part of the family.

"You ready to get out of here?" Graham asked.

"I am if you are."

Will went to collect their jackets and Nora smiled at Mat in a way she couldn't quite decipher. "Mat, will you let us make you dinner as a thank you? One night next week, perhaps?"

For some reason, that wasn't at all what Mat was expecting. "You really don't have to—"

"We'd love to," Nora said before Mat could finish. "Wouldn't we, Will?"

Will, who'd just returned, nodded. "Absolutely. I have no idea what I'm agreeing with, but I agree wholeheartedly."

Mat chuckled. Nora seemed to have Will wrapped around her finger, not that Will looked like she minded in the least. "That would be nice. Thank you." She might not be gung ho about a cozy family dinner—or was it a couple's dinner?—but she'd been raised better than to turn down such invitations.

"Wonderful. Graham, I'll call you tomorrow to find a date that works for everyone."

They said their good-byes and Mat and Graham headed out. The night sky was overcast and the temperature had dropped considerably. Fall was most definitely upon them.

Graham shivered despite her jacket, prompting Mat to offer hers. Graham waved her off. "No, no. I'm fine. I'm hoping you might warm me up in a bit."

Mat smiled at the suggestive tone. For some reason, it struck her as strange that Graham never seemed to get enough of her. Not bad, just strange. "Does this mean you're coming home with me?"

Graham let out a nervous laugh. "I suppose I should wait to be invited."

Mat grabbed her hand and squeezed. "Quite the opposite. I didn't want to presume you wanted to stay over. I'm sure you're exhausted."

Graham smiled. "Never too exhausted to go home with you."

"I also shouldn't assume we're always going to stay at my place." As she said that, Mat realized she'd never even seen Graham's apartment. "We can totally trade off if you want."

Graham shrugged. "Your place is nicer, and you don't have a roommate."

"I'm sure your place is perfectly nice. You have a point about the roommate, though."

"I mean, we should sometime. At the moment, though, I'd like nothing more than to go back to your place, take off all our clothes, and tumble into bed."

Mat felt the familiar stirring, the one she'd expected to wane by now. "In that case, we should walk faster."

When they got to Mat's place, Graham's mouth immediately found hers. Despite the fatigue, Mat's body responded to the way

Graham tugged at her clothes and seemed hungry to touch her everywhere. She guided them to the bedroom, discarding articles of clothing as they went. Graham's shoes. Mat's shirt. Graham's dress. Mat's pants.

Although the need to get to bed had been frantic, the pace once they got there slowed. Mat chalked it up to the wedding. Even she wasn't immune to the sweetness, the romance, of two people so completely in love. She might not be in the market for one of her own, but she wanted to be tender with Graham, to show her that she mattered.

Graham responded in kind. There was no teasing, no attempt to drive one another higher, harder. They made love, to the extent Mat was willing to use that phrase. Graham came, whispering Mat's name instead of screaming it.

Graham fell asleep almost immediately. Mat expected to lie awake, her brain ignoring the tiredness of her body. Her pulse slowed though, coming down from the orgasm and slipping right into that lulled state just this side of sleep. It was new, this calm contentment. She felt something similar out on the water, on a clear day with the sun glinting off the ocean and a cool salt breeze in her face. To have it with a woman, though, was different. As Mat drifted off, she considered why such a feeling, one that should make her anxious, didn't.

Chapter Nineteen

"It's not a huge deal. I promise." It was just over a week after the wedding and Graham lay sprawled half on top of her, chin resting on her hand.

Mat eyed Graham. That was easy for her to say. As far as Mat was concerned, having dinner with Graham's aunt and best friend—who were a couple no less—felt like meeting the parents and a double date rolled into one. Everything about it triggered her fight-or-flight response. And since she wasn't a fighter, she had a strong compulsion to run. "I just don't feel prepared."

"There's nothing to prepare. It's the first night since spring she doesn't have anyone at the inn. If anything, it's a celebration of being laid back."

Mat thought about the wedding, the one and only time she'd been to Failte. With its perfect gardens and pristine white paint, it felt anything but laid back. Even if she'd gotten a glimpse, and the chance to help out, behind the scenes. But she'd agreed and backing out now wasn't an option. "What can I bring?"

"Yourself." Graham gave her a reassuring look. "Really. I'll swing by your place at six and we can walk over together."

Mat took a deep breath. She didn't want to disappoint Graham. Nor did she want to seem like a coward. On top of that, Graham had handled the party with her family like a champ, especially given the circumstances. She could do this. "Okay. Fine."

"You're the best." Graham rolled the rest of the way onto Mat's chest and kissed her.

"Yeah."

Graham looked at her through lowered lashes. "How about I show you how great I think you are?"

Mat glanced at the clock. Five thirty. She'd be late, but whatever. Dom could wait. As far as she was concerned, he still owed her. "And how are you going to do that?"

In lieu of an explanation, Graham wiggled down the bed, planting kisses all over Mat's torso. She situated herself between Mat's thighs and, without anything else in the way of foreplay, pressed her tongue into Mat.

"Fuck." The arousal was instant, her body going from sleepy to electrified in the span of about two seconds. Mat could feel Graham smile. Then she went to work, starting with long, unhurried strokes. Mat could feel her clit getting bigger and harder. Graham flicked it gently with her tongue, coaxing it. Mat put her hands in Graham's hair, still unused to how immediate her response to Graham was. "God, that feels good."

Graham shifted slightly and Mat let go of her hair. She felt Graham's fingers tracing on either side of her opening, spreading around the wetness. She tightened in anticipation.

Graham eased one and then a second finger into her. Mat clamped down, intensifying the sensations in her clit. In addition to ramping up the pleasure, it gave Mat the feeling of being grounded, anchored in the moment.

Graham slid in and out, keeping her pace easy and smooth. It wasn't a fucking so much as a complement to the movement of Graham's mouth. Mat rolled her hips gently, letting Graham set both the intensity and the pace. It felt so different than being with other women—better, but something else. Easier, maybe.

As if sensing her brain at work, Graham sped up. Her fingers pushed into Mat with more force, the strokes of her tongue gave way to sucking. The added urgency cleared away any remaining desire or ability to think. Mat opened her eyes and raised her head, reveling in how gorgeous Graham looked going down on her.

The visual pushed her over the edge. Mat let her head fall back and she rode the orgasm. Instead of a flash, she imagined it like a sound wave, rippling out from her center until every ounce of her vibrated with pleasure.

When it finally ebbed, she felt spent and raw, like exposed wires. She touched a hand to Graham's head, not sure she could take any more stimulation. Graham eased away, propped herself on her elbows. "You are so fucking sexy."

Mat chuckled at the assertion. "No, that's my line."

"Yeah, what are you going to do about it?"

The playful challenge did wonders for her recovery. "Come here."

Graham crawled up the bed and started to settle next to her. Before she could, Mat moved down. "Oh, no. Keep going."

Understanding dawned in Graham's blue eyes, making them darken several shades. "Are you—"

Before she could finish the question, Mat gently nipped at her thigh. "Please come and put that gorgeous pussy of yours on my face."

Graham seemed to hesitate for a second, but she obliged. She placed a knee on either side of Mat's head and Mat wrapped an arm around each of her thighs. Mat breathed in deeply, certain she could get drunk on the scent of Graham's arousal. She applied gentle pressure with her hands, encouraging Graham to ease herself down. But again, Graham hesitated.

"What's wrong?"

"Nothing. I..."

As she trailed off, Mat had a pang of worry that she'd misread Graham's interest. She loosened her grip and angled her head, looking up at Graham's face. "Hey, no pressure. I don't want you to do anything you're not totally into."

Graham bit her lip in a way that made Mat more turned on rather than less. "It's not that. I just, I haven't done this before."

Oh.

"I feel a little self-conscious is all."

That, she could work with. "It's okay. It can be a little weird at first, but it feels amazing. Or, it should. We can stop anytime if you don't like it."

Graham covered her face with her hand, then moved it away. She looked down at Mat. She was blushing. "I'm afraid I might suffocate you."

"I promise you won't." Mat exerted a decent amount of pressure onto Graham's thighs. "See, I can communicate and move you if I need to."

Graham nodded. "Right. Okay."

"Okay, you want to?"

Another nod.

Excellent. Mat inched down until she was exactly where she wanted to be. "Just relax and enjoy. This is all about you."

Graham took a deep breath, trying to will away her nerves. She was being sexually adventurous, after all. And trying new things was part of that. "Right."

She let Mat guide her, heard her sigh. It occurred to her that she would love to have Mat like this, which further reduced her uncertainty. And then Mat slid her tongue into Graham's wetness and she stopped thinking about anything but how good that felt.

She closed her eyes. It did feel good. Like, really, really, good. And unlike anything else she'd ever done with a woman in bed. Or out of bed.

After a couple of long, gentle strokes, Mat started making lazy circles with her tongue. Graham, who'd been so hesitant to move, couldn't seem to stop herself. She rocked slowly, moving her hips in time with Mat's mouth.

She heard Mat groan, felt the vibration of it against her clit. Graham let out a moan of her own. Mat tightened her grip slightly. Graham opened her eyes and looked down. With the soft light of early morning coming through the windows, she could appreciate how sexy Mat looked between her legs. Somehow, Graham managed to feel powerful and yet also completely at Mat's mercy. It was a total turn-on.

And then there was Mat's mouth. She'd started sucking Graham's clit, bringing Graham excruciatingly close to release. But then she shifted. Graham whimpered. Barely a second later, Mat's tongue plunged into her.

"Oh, God." Soft, but forceful. Like being consumed and replenished at the same time. It was perfection. "Oh, Mat. Yes. Please, yes."

Mat was relentless. She drove Graham higher and higher. Graham lost track of her plan to keep her movements controlled, to make sure she didn't smother Mat. She lost everything but the sensations coursing through her, the tangle of nerves at her core that threatened to short circuit her whole system.

When the muscles in her legs began to quiver, she reached forward, grabbed hold of the headboard in an attempt to steady herself. It was fruitless. The orgasm ripped through her. Her whole body quaked. She called out Mat's name.

When it ended, Graham was left weak and stiff. Spent. She gingerly eased herself to the side of Mat, then flopped back, putting herself head-to-toe with Mat. Her breathing remained choppy and her heart continued to thud against her ribs. "Okay, then."

Mat gave her knee a gentle squeeze. "I'm taking it you were down with that."

"Understatement of the century." Graham rolled to her side, draped her arm over Mat's legs. "I'm hoping you'll let me try being on the other side."

Mat sat up. "Definitely, just not now. I'm already late."

Graham picked up her head to look at the clock. "That's too bad."

"Next time. I promise."

"Fine." Graham pouted, but she laughed at the end.

Mat climbed out of bed and started to pull on work clothes. "I promise I'll think about it all day."

Graham followed, donning her outfit from the night before. She'd taken to bringing a bag, but didn't always bother with a change of clothes, especially on a workday. Mat left so much earlier,

Graham had more than enough time to go get ready in the comfort of her own place. "Maybe not while we're having dinner at my aunt's."

Mat winced. She'd forgotten that's what started this whole conversation. "Agreed."

Graham crossed the room and kissed her. "I'll see you at six."

"See you then."

❖

"Dinner with the fam. Sounds serious." Dom handed her the last tote of bait and hopped on board.

"You realize the irony of your saying that, right?"

Dom spread his arms and shrugged. "I have no idea what you're talking about."

Mat shook her head. "Part of the reason I got roped into this is the stunt you pulled. 'I've hung out with your family,' she says, 'so you should hang out with mine.'"

"I thought the family dinner went well." Dom gave her a look that said he wasn't going to give her an inch. "I think you make way too much out of stuff like this."

"Can you blame me?" She hated pulling out the past, especially since Dom had endured plenty of his own family strife when he announced wanting to transition.

"No, but all that was a long time ago. I think your parents and mine have evolved since then. Slowly, painfully perhaps, but evolved nonetheless. I think you're holding a grudge."

She didn't know if it was because, once he'd actually transitioned, it became less of a thing or because he simply had a more forgiving, easygoing personality. Either way, Mat envied his unflinching efforts to bring his family around. And from what she could tell, it was working. "It's not a grudge. Let's just say I'm risk averse."

"Dude, you're the one who taught me the best rewards sometimes require the most risk."

"I was talking about fishing."

"Actually, you were talking about getting laid."

Mat chuckled as she remembered the conversation. They'd been in their early twenties. Dom had started to transition, but was read as male only about half the time. He'd taken a break from dating to avoid lengthy explanations or awkward backpedaling from people whose expectations didn't match up with reality. She'd given him a pep talk to inspire him to put himself out there. "Right. I stand by it as a rule for picking up women. Family is a different beast altogether."

Mat steered the boat into open water and headed in the direction of the traps on the day's schedule. Dom connected the hoses that would fill the barrels with salt water. "Okay. Let me take a different approach. It doesn't need to be a big deal."

"That's what Graham said."

"See, right from the source. If she says it's not a big deal, you should believe her. Maybe she just wants to reciprocate."

Mat sighed. Dreading it wouldn't do her any good. And she'd agreed to go. Backing out would be a dick move. "Yeah."

"Are you nervous that it's at that fancy bed and breakfast?"

Oh, Dom. He knew her so well. "Let's just say it's not helping matters."

Dom leaned over and bumped her shoulder. "Remember, it might be fancy, but the fancy is for the guests. At the end of the day, that lady is in the service industry. She works for them."

Mat nodded. She thought about doing dishes with Will, passing out champagne with Graham. She didn't want to admit thinking about it that way made her feel better, but it did. "Right."

"And I bet the food is going to be amazing."

Dom might do a lot of his thinking with his stomach, but he had a point. "I'll eat extra on your behalf."

Mat pulled up to the first trap and they fell into silence. The easy rhythm of working together helped her to tune out the nagging voices in her mind—the one that worried about spending time with Graham's aunt as well as the one that had been creeping up on her more and more of late. The one that liked to pose a whole different range of what-ifs. What if she really hit it off with Nora and Will? What if things with Graham didn't grow stale? What if they just kept getting better?

"Earth to Mat."

The sound of Dom's voice yanked her back to the present. Mat realized she was clutching a lobster, just above the trap and out of Dom's reach. "Sorry." She hastily set it in the banding box and rebaited the trap.

"Don't apologize. Talk to me."

Mat studied her cousin. He was so much more of a brother to her than any of her actual brothers. It had always been that way. Before she'd had an inkling she was gay and when Dom still seemed content as Dominica. She wondered often if they'd somehow sensed that otherness in each other, before they'd even recognized it in themselves. They'd seen each other through heartbreak and so much more. "I'm afraid of not breaking up with Graham."

The second the words were out of her mouth, she realized how ridiculous they sounded. She shook her head, steered the boat back to the right location, and dropped the trap. Dom moved the banded lobsters to the barrel. "I hear you."

"Really?"

"Sure. It's easy when there's not a lot at stake. When it comes to relationships, you're the queen of making sure there's not a lot at stake."

She couldn't disagree, but having it explained back to her in those terms made her cringe. "That makes me seem like such an ass."

"No, because you're up front about what you want, what you're offering. Usually, the women you hook up with understand that and want the same. Graham is different."

"Is she? I didn't think so, at least at first. You were there that first night." Graham had initiated the flirtation. And by the time they got back to Mat's place, she seemed to know exactly what she wanted.

"I was, but I've also been around ever since. I don't think she was playing you that night, but I also don't think that's her usual MO."

Maybe that was the problem. Graham had said as much, but she'd not given any hints on what her usual MO might be. And Mat had yet to figure her out. She wasn't needy or clingy, but at the same time, she seemed perfectly content to spend whatever time she could with Mat. She was the epitome of confidence one minute, then shy and inexperienced the next. Mat didn't have a handle on her own feelings and she felt even less clear about Graham's. "Yeah. I don't know what to do with that."

Dom offered her a wry smile. "I know you hate when I say this, but maybe you should follow your heart."

He was right. Not that she should follow her heart. She hated when he told her to.

Chapter Twenty

The inn was just as beautiful as she remembered, and that was just from the outside. Mat took a deep breath and reminded herself to relax. It might be a crazy fancy place and Graham's aunt might own it, but it was also where she worked. The idea of Nora changing bed linens and scrubbing toilets made her feel better. She decided to keep that fact to herself.

The front door opened and Will smiled at them. Tall and lanky with a mop of short brown curls, her casually masculine stance put Mat instantly at ease. Her attire helped, too. The dark khaki pants and green sweater weren't all that different from Mat's own attire. She pegged Will as around her age, too. Graham hugged her before making introductions. "Mat, you remember Will."

"Great to see you again." Will extended a hand.

Mat smiled. "Likewise."

"I'm glad we're getting the chance to actually spend the evening with you."

Before she could reply, a voice called, "Is that Graham and Mat?"

Mat turned in the direction of the voice. It belonged to Graham's aunt. Now that she wasn't all dressed up and bustling around putting on a wedding, Mat took a moment to study her. She was pretty in a classic sort of way. Her hair was more sandy-colored than Graham's strawberry blond, and her eyes were green instead of Graham's blue, but they had the same high cheekbones and jawline. "Come in. We're so glad you're here."

Mat took the hand Nora offered. "Thank you for the dinner invite."

"It's our pleasure. I'm sorry we haven't gotten around to it before now."

"Aunt Nora does happy hour in addition to breakfast for her guests. It really cramps her social schedule during the summer."

Nora offered an easy shrug. "I'm sure you can appreciate the drive to work when the work is there."

Mat smiled. Despite the luxury of the surroundings, and the fear that she'd have nothing in common with Graham's family, she relaxed. "Indeed I do."

Nora's smile in return was warm. "I've got a couple of things to do in the kitchen still. Will, would you pour wine?"

"Of course." Will leaned in and gave Nora a kiss. It was obvious she was head over heels in love. Rather than uncomfortable, it made Mat like them even more. Nora went back the way she came and Will gestured to the room to their right.

"Wow." She'd been in the room before, but with all the wedding setup, she'd not really paid much attention to the space itself. It was fancier than she remembered. The furniture looked antique, the wood floors gleamed, and the rug probably cost a fortune.

Will laughed. "That was my reaction my first time here."

Mat looked her way and their gazes caught for just a second. She couldn't be sure, but it felt like Will might be trying to offer some reassurance. Mat appreciated the gesture, even if her trepidation about the evening went beyond their surroundings. "Oh, good."

"Really?" Graham looked at Will, then Mat. "I mean, I know it's big for a house."

Will lifted a finger. "You also saw it when it was a run-down heap. That makes it far less daunting."

Mat smiled at Will, liking her more by the minute. "Thank you."

Will went to a table near one of the windows. "I opened a Pinot Noir, but there's beer if you'd prefer. Or water or soda. Nora has a billion things in the house."

"Wine's great. Thanks."

"What are we having?" Graham took the first glass Will poured and handed it to Mat.

"Guinness stew."

"Yum. I've got to get her to teach me how to make it." Graham looked at Mat. "It's so good."

"Anytime." Nora joined them, carrying a plate of cheese and crackers and pickled vegetables. "Just name the day."

Mat narrowed her eyes at Graham. "Is this something really special or do you not cook?"

"I…" Graham trailed off. She raised her hands and made air quotes, then added, "cook."

Despite the mixed company, Mat couldn't help herself. "That's pathetic."

"What? You're some powerhouse in the kitchen?" Graham's tone hovered on the edge between playful and not.

She could feel Will and Nora's eyes on her. At least she had the sense to have a good answer before diving in. "I think I've shown I'm more than competent."

Graham gave her a look of concession. "Yeah."

"You don't grow up a girl in a traditional Portuguese family and not learn to cook. Besides, knowing how to cook ensures you eat well."

Graham raised both hands. "Okay, okay. You've made your point."

"But you left out the most important one," Will said.

"Which is?" Graham gave her a bland expression.

Will lifted a shoulder. "It's a great way to seduce women."

Graham groaned and Mat couldn't suppress a chuckle. Nora offered Graham a sympathetic look. "You've got time yet. And it's not your fault your mother is a lousy cook."

"Yeah, how did that happen?" Graham asked. "You stole all the talent."

"Your mother has plenty of other gifts. And your dad cooks well enough for the both of them."

"I guess."

Nora looked to Mat. "What about you? Should I take your comment about traditional families to mean you got your instruction from your mother?"

Mat nodded. "Absolutely. I think she still harbors some hope I'll use it to snare a good husband one day."

Nora shook her head. "That's too bad."

Not wanting to bring down the conversation, or become the center of it, Mat waved a hand. "It's all right. As long as we don't talk about it, everyone gets along fine."

Graham angled her head. "You don't think they've come around? They were so nice to me."

Her parents had been nice to Graham. And not polite nice, either. Genuinely interested. And her father had asked about Graham the last time they talked. Mat had written it off, but maybe things were beginning to thaw. "Maybe. I think I'll keep things in their nice little boxes, though. It's much easier."

Mat thought that might get her a laugh, but Will and Nora both gave her sympathetic looks. Graham frowned. Mat was about to try to change the subject when Nora said, "I think dinner should be just about ready."

They moved into the dining room. The large table had been set at one end, making it feel more casual than stuffy. Between the change of setting and the process of serving food, the mood lightened again. She asked Nora about when she'd moved to Provincetown, learned about Will coming to town via her sister, Emerson. Family and friendships and work and play seemed to all blend together for all of them. Mat knew it was strange to see that as such a novelty, but she'd never met people whose lives looked like that. At least, not permanent, year-round residents.

When they finished eating, Will cleared the table, brushing aside any offers of help. When Graham suggested a game night, it was all Mat could do not to laugh out loud. Not that she disliked games. It just seemed so domestic. She imagined the ribbing she'd get if Dom knew how she was spending her night.

They set up *Trivial Pursuit* and decided to play in teams. Between Graham's mastery of science and Mat's prowess in History as well as Sports and Leisure, they were one pie piece away from declaring victory. But then Nora and Will went on a run, collecting two and tying the game. Mat correctly answered a question about Elton John and got them into position to win it all. The category: Geography.

Mat closed her eyes for a second. She'd always hated geography. She opened them to find Graham rolling her shoulders and tipping her head from side to side. "Deep breath, Pero. We got this."

Mat laughed at the absurdity of the whole thing, including the competitive streak she didn't know Graham had. "I hate to say it, but I don't think I'm going to be much help." They'd already missed two chances to secure the blue wedge.

Graham pointed at her. "Think positive. You can't show signs of weakness."

"I think that ship sailed when we couldn't come up with the capital of North Dakota." It had been rather embarrassing, even as someone who didn't put a lot of stock in knowing such things.

"That's what I mean. We both knew that. We need to center ourselves, unlock the door to the back recesses of our minds."

"Are you going to pontificate all night or can I ask your question?" Nora feigned exasperation. At least, Mat hoped it was feigned.

She was about to apologize when Graham turned her finger to point at her aunt. "You hush. You're trying to mess with our mojo." She turned to Mat. "You ready?"

"As ready as I'll ever be."

"What," Nora straightened her shoulders, all business, "is the name for a narrow inlet, usually surrounded by cliffs, common in Scandinavian countries such as Norway?"

Graham gripped her arm, then leaned over to whisper in her ear. "It's archipelago."

Mat shook her head. She could still see the two-page illustration in her fourth-grade social studies book, naming the different formations of land and sea. She'd flipped to it at least a thousand times during the lessons she found dreadfully boring. Even then, she knew she wasn't cut out for sitting inside all day. "It's fjord."

Graham made a face. "Are you sure?"

"One hundred percent. Archipelago is a string of tiny islands."

"Oh, my God. You're right. I can't believe I mixed those up." Graham turned to Will and Nora and declared, "Fjord."

"Correct." Nora slid the card back into the box.

Will hung her head, but fished a blued piece from the plastic bag and handed it to Mat. "Congratulations."

Mat hadn't admitted to being super competitive, but it felt good to win. And it was fun to watch Graham stand up and do the most ridiculous victory dance. When she was done, she leaned and kissed Mat firmly on the mouth. "I always want you on my team."

Instead of echoing the sentiment, Mat said simply, "Thanks." She didn't mind teaming up with her, but the way Graham said it left an uncomfortable hitch in Mat's chest. She knew Graham didn't mean it that way, but her mind instantly produced images of game nights and softball leagues and little kids running around a soccer field. She shook her head. Where had that come from?

Will stood and stretched. "I hope you'll give us the satisfaction of a rematch soon."

Graham stood as well. She turned to Mat and cocked a brow. "I think that could probably be arranged."

Shoving aside thoughts of anything beyond a friendly game a few weeks in the future, Mat smiled. "I'd never want to deny you the opportunity to redeem yourself."

"Are you about ready to get out of here?" Graham asked Mat.

It had been fun, but she was more than ready. "Sure." She looked at Nora. "Are you sure there's nothing we can do to help clean up or anything?"

"I cooked, so I'm off duty." Nora hooked a thumb at Will. "But I'm guessing she's got it under control."

Will grinned. "I most certainly do."

"Then we will bid you good night." Graham reached out a hand to Mat.

Mat got up from the sofa and took it. "Thank you again for dinner."

Nora wound an arm around Will's middle. "We're glad you came. We've been wanting to get to know you."

Will nodded and Mat got the feeling again she'd just survived the equivalent of meeting the parents. It still gave her a certain level of discomfort, even though it seemed as if she'd passed whatever test had been in place.

They gathered their things. Nora and Will walked them to the door. Good nights were exchanged all around. Outside, the arrival of fall was increasingly apparent. The wind had a real bite and it took down a few more leaves each time it blew. Graham shivered a little and made a show of pulling her coat tighter around her. "Brr."

Mat smiled at her. "Right? Winter will be here before we know it."

Graham lifted a hand. "Please. I'm not ready to go there. I am, however, ready to go home and get naked and toasty under the covers with you."

The vague sense of anxiety from earlier hadn't fully dissipated. Graham's reference to "home" didn't help. Mat kind of wanted to go home and sit on the sofa and watch sports and not have to think about it. "I'm kind of beat."

Graham nodded. "Same. I promise I won't try to seduce you. Mostly, I want to cuddle up and steal your body heat."

She could decline, but doing so would probably hurt Graham's feelings. Worse, it might provoke her to ask the dreaded, "What's wrong?" It wasn't like she didn't want to spend the night with Graham. If anything, it might save her from having to think or talk about the weird jumble of things that had taken root in her brain. "I guess I could share a little of my heat."

"You do have plenty to spare." Graham stuck her arm through Mat's, then used the proximity to elbow her gently in the side. "Being as you're so hot and all."

"Cute. You're cute."

Graham shrugged playfully. "I know."

Despite telling herself she wouldn't, Mat spent the time walking back to her apartment thinking about the evening she'd just spent on what essentially amounted to a second double date in a month. Only this one was with Graham's best friend and aunt. The fact that the aunt and the best friend were a couple in the first place struck her as odd, but spending time with them had softened that. Sure, the age difference between them remained obvious, but it no longer seemed jarring. Will and Nora fit together, complemented one another, perfectly. And the two of them together made the age difference between herself and Graham feel negligible.

On top of that, Nora didn't seem to have a problem with her at all. Either that or she was exceptionally gracious and faked it really well. Mat wondered what she might say to Graham the next day, if it was just the two of them. Will seemed to like her enough, too. Not that she really cared about making a good impression.

"Penny for your thoughts."

The sound of Graham's voice yanked Mat back to the present. "I was just savoring our victory."

Graham sighed. She resisted the urge to stop walking, but she did turn her head to study Mat's profile. "You're a terrible liar."

"Stop. I'm telling the truth."

Should she pry? She'd gotten the feeling all night that Mat felt out of her element. No, that wasn't accurate. Mat seemed to oscillate between being perfectly at ease and visibly uncomfortable. Graham sensed it had more to do with Mat's own thoughts than the dinner or the company or the rousing game of *Trivial Pursuit*. She didn't want to obsess—or to be a nag—but she couldn't shake the feeling something was up. "People savoring victories don't usually look so serious."

Mat looked to her, raised a brow. "Maybe I'm plotting my next conquest."

They turned onto Mat's street. Graham chuckled. "I can't believe I have such a stubborn girlfriend."

She'd meant it playfully, mostly, but Mat stopped walking and frowned. "I'm not stubborn."

Graham angled her head. "What's the number one trait of stubborn people?"

Mat furrowed her brow. "What?"

She tipped her head to one side. "Declaring adamantly they're not stubborn."

"Is that so?" Mat narrowed her eyes and looked, for all intents and purposes, mad. Or at least irritated.

Graham swallowed. She didn't actually want to pick a fight. She just wanted Mat to open up, confide in her. She couldn't tell if she was nudging things to the former, or the latter. She decided not to push too hard, but not to backpedal either. "That's been my experience."

"I'll show you what stubborn people do."

Mat came at her and Graham thought for a second they were going to wrestle, right there in the middle of the street. But instead of throwing her to the ground, Mat scooped her up. Like, literally scooped her up and threw Graham over her shoulder, then started walking up the driveway. Graham squealed. Mat swatted at her rear end. Not hard, more a playful spank than anything that actually hurt, but it made Graham squirm and squeal again.

"Keep that up and all the neighbors will hear and start peering out their windows."

Graham looked around. She couldn't see anyone watching them, through the windows or otherwise, but the comment had her biting her lip to keep quiet. "What are you doing?"

"I'm carrying you to my bed so I can devour you."

The comment, paired with the feel of Mat's strong arms and shoulders, shut off any thoughts of fights or serious conversations or anything else. Suddenly, Graham wanted nothing more than exactly what Mat had just described. They got to the door and Mat set her down so she could unlock it. Graham licked her lips in anticipation. "If I'm difficult, does that mean you'll have to be extra stern with me?"

Mat opened the door, then turned and looked in her eyes. Graham saw heat in them, hunger. "Is that what you want? Me to be extra stern?"

Now equal parts embarrassed and aroused, Graham looked down. "Maybe."

Mat laughed. Such a seductive sound, it was all Graham could do not to swoon. "Well, now I'll really have to show you what it means to be stubborn."

Once again, Graham found herself hefted over Mat's shoulder. Mat walked into her place, kicked the door shut behind them. Without turning on any lights, she made a beeline for the bedroom. She tossed Graham onto the bed with little ceremony. Before she could put up even a token protest, Mat pulled off Graham's shoes, unbuttoned her jeans. She worked them down Graham's hips and thighs, then tossed them to the floor. Graham's panties went next, followed by her sweater. Mat remained fully clothed.

Graham opened her mouth to comment on that fact, but Mat dropped to the bed. She nudged Graham's legs apart and settled herself between them. She nipped Graham's inner thigh with her teeth then, without a word, plunged her tongue into her.

"Oh, God." Graham nearly came off the bed at the intensity of it, but Mat held her in place. There was no gentle easing into things, no teasing foreplay. Mat's mouth worked her, demanded that she keep up.

The orgasm ripped through Graham before she realized it was coming. The strength of it, paired with the surprise, left her unbalanced and out of breath. But Mat remained relentless. She got onto her knees, putting her fingers where her mouth had just been. She pressed one, then a second into Graham. Even if her brain couldn't keep up, Graham's body responded. She clenched around Mat, wanton and desperate.

"That's my good girl." Mat looked into her eyes, fierce and demanding. "Tell me what you want."

"More." The word escaped Graham's lips, again her body seeming to keep a few steps ahead of the rest of her. Mat obliged. Graham groaned. Mat's other hand grazed her belly, then slid down. Her thumb made slow, deliberate strokes over Graham's clit, keeping time with her fingers. "Oh, yes."

Mat smiled—confident and maybe a little smug. "Don't come yet."

The command rippled through Graham like its own orgasm. Who knew she liked being told what to do? She resisted the urge to bear down, knowing it would send her tumbling over the edge. "Please."

She thought Mat might add a fourth finger. She braced herself, caught on a tightrope of anticipation and longing. Instead, Mat pressed her pinkie against Graham's other opening. She didn't push in, but rather held it there with just the right amount of pressure. Graham's vision blurred with pleasure. She closed her eyes and let her head roll from side to side.

"Now." Mat's voice held authority, power. "Come for me now."

Like a floodgate, Graham opened. Heat poured from her and she rode the tide of it. Her muscles quivered, the shock waves ripped through her. She heard a noise—something primal and raw—then realized it had come from her.

When her pulse finally slowed, when the roar in her ears subsided, Graham opened her eyes. She found Mat watching her, but Graham couldn't read her expression. For some reason, it made her feel vulnerable, exposed. "I thought we were just going to cuddle and go to sleep."

Mat smiled. It was cocky still, but there was something else to it. Tenderness, maybe. It melted Graham, weakening the thin hold she still had on her heart. Mat lifted her chin. "You started it."

Graham swallowed, told herself to keep the moment light. "Mmm, I'm pretty sure that's not what happened."

"But I'm stubborn, remember? You stand no chance of convincing me otherwise."

"Right. So." Graham frowned, not sure what to say next.

"But you can have your way now." Mat stood long enough to shed her clothes. Graham had forgotten she was still dressed. Then she crawled into bed and pulled up the covers.

Graham half sat, propping herself on an elbow. "Wait. Don't I get a turn?"

"What if I promise you a turn tomorrow?"

Graham narrowed her eyes. They hadn't been together all that long, but she'd never known Mat not to be in the mood. "Are you sure?"

Mat nodded. "I really am beat. I promise it has nothing to do with how sexy you are. You're off the charts in that department."

Graham pointed at her. "Don't try to distract me with flattery."

"I'm not, I swear." She lifted three fingers like a scout. "I'm just perfectly content to snuggle and—how did you phrase it?—share warmth."

Graham wasn't convinced, but it didn't feel like the time to press. The evening had been so great on so many levels. She really didn't want to start picking it apart. Graham curled into Mat's outstretched arm and Mat pulled the blankets snugly around them. Graham gave in to how perfect it felt. "God, you feel good."

"Good. Now relax and go to sleep."

She poked Mat gently in the ribs. "So bossy."

"Yep."

In spite of herself, Graham's eyes grew heavy. She let herself nuzzle deeper into Mat's embrace. Maybe they hadn't talked about love yet, but this certainly felt like it. She could be patient. The thought of a thousand nights like this carried her to sleep.

Chapter Twenty-one

Asking Dom to skip their off day again was unfair and Mat knew it. But she couldn't help that being on the water was the only thing keeping her sane these days. She also knew that, if she asked, Dom would grumble, but he'd say yes.

After pacing in her apartment for twenty minutes, she made up her mind. They had an unspoken rule about going out alone. Okay, so maybe somewhat spoken. But there were plenty of fishermen who did. It made the work slower, but not impossible. And it wasn't inherently more dangerous. It just meant no one was around to help if something went awry. She was careful. Things didn't go awry.

She'd give Dom his cut of whatever she hauled. That should be enough to keep him from giving her a hard time. And would assuage any guilt she had about breaking their code. Feeling better about the decision, she changed clothes and headed out.

The sky was overcast, the air cool and damp. The brutal temperatures of November and December remained a few weeks away, but Mat was grateful to have switched over to her winter gear. The layers that would feel like nothing soon enough kept her nice and warm this morning.

With the drop in temperatures, the number of lobsters in each trap grew more consistent. Unlike humans, who tended to hunker down and keep close to home, lobsters seemed liberated by the cold. They wandered out of their caves and found their way to her bait.

She kept her pace slow and methodical. The cost of a careless mistake could be infinitely greater when alone, and really, it wasn't the number of traps she hauled that mattered. At least not today. The routine of the work, the very fact of being on the water, had its usual effect. Her mind cleared of the nagging voices and doubts, the persistent questions about what the hell she was doing.

Happy with her catch, and the state of her mind, she headed back to shore. On the way, her mind kicked back into gear. It conjured images of being with Graham that included everything from the boat to her bed to family dinners and celebrations. Instead of trying to shut them down, she let herself wonder what it might be like.

Could Dom be right? Had her parents mellowed? Might they be more welcoming now than they were all those years ago? They'd come to accept Dom. And now that he was with Renata, everyone in the family seemed on board.

She imagined sitting them down and essentially coming out all over again. She wasn't incapable, or really even afraid. She just couldn't imagine it going well. It didn't seem worth the grief she'd put them—or herself—through in the process. Or at least it hadn't.

Graham changed things. Her sweet smile and ridiculous sense of humor, her intelligence and kind heart. And the chemistry. Dear Lord, the chemistry. If she was being honest with herself, she could admit that sex with Graham existed on an entirely different dimension. It was good, yes, but it stirred something in her that she hadn't even known was there.

With her mind on that tangent, Mat approached the harbor. She kicked into idle to call her uncle and realized she'd missed at least a dozen texts from Dom. They started casual, but morphed through irate to full-on worried. She cringed, feeling bad she'd sneaked off without telling him. As she steered into the unloading zone, she realized he was there, waiting for her.

Since their uncle was there, too, Mat offered a friendly wave and kept her tone light. Dom followed suit. Together, they hoisted the barrel and got it onto his truck. After, Mat moved to their slip and started cleanup. It didn't take long for him to join her.

"Are you fucking insane?" The edge in Dom's voice radiated anger.

She'd expected him to give her a token hard time. And then thank her for giving him a pass, for earning him money while he did nothing. But he was none of those things. "Dude, relax."

"I won't relax. And don't dude me."

Mat lifted both her hands. "Okay, okay. Christ."

"I'm serious, Mat. You could have gotten yourself killed."

Mat appreciated his concern, but she bristled at the statement. "Being a little dramatic, aren't we? I was careful. I went slow. I'm not a fucking moron."

Dom's face softened, if only a little. "I didn't call you a moron."

Mat raised a brow. "No, just insane."

"We don't go out alone." Dom heaved out a breath. "You've heard the stories."

She had. From the time she could walk, she'd heard stories. Some funny, some heroic, some tragic. She'd been raised to appreciate what the sea could offer those who worked it, but also to respect what it could take away. As a kid, it had filled her with a sense of adventure. As a teen, it felt cheesy and over the top. But she'd settled into adulthood and the reality behind some of those tales kept her centered. With less defiance than she'd felt a moment before, she said, "I was careful."

Dom's features softened even more. "I never said you weren't. But it's not just you out there. Things can happen."

"All right, all right. I'm sufficiently shamed."

"Shamed enough not to do it again?"

She really hadn't wanted him to worry. "I won't do it again. Promise."

"Good." Dom rolled his eyes, but smiled. "Now tell me, how much did I make?"

Mat folded her arms. "A couple hundred. I told you, I went slow."

"Eh." Dom shrugged. "Not bad for an afternoon of making love to my fiancée."

"Such a—" Mat cut herself off as the second half of the statement registered. "Wait. What?"

Dom grinned a goofy, over the moon kind of grin. "I asked Renata to marry me and she said yes."

A torrent of emotions whipped through Mat's brain. Joy, but also worry. And she couldn't ignore the pang of envy. "When? How? You don't think it's a little quick?"

Dom's smile didn't waver. "When you know, you know."

She let his words sink in. Did she believe that? They'd never been true for her. The one time she thought so, she'd been not only wrong, but alone in her feelings. That was one of the reasons she didn't think she was built for love. Until recently, the idea hadn't bothered her much. Now? Now she didn't know what to believe. Except that she didn't want to saddle Dom with it. She forced a smile. "I'm really happy for you, man. Congratulations."

He shrugged and seemed to get bashful. "Thanks."

"I can't think of anyone who deserves a happily ever after more than you." As Mat said the words, she realized how much she meant them. She gave him a hard time, but mostly because he felt like a little brother and doing so was both a right and a responsibility. But she loved him and, more, admired him. He'd weathered plenty of storms—the family fallout from his transition, the breakup with his girlfriend at the time—and hadn't grown bitter. If anything, he kept his heart even more open. He'd earned his current happiness tenfold.

Dom frowned. "You say that like you don't deserve to be happy."

They'd finished putting the boat in order. Mat took a final look around before stepping onto the dock. It was her turn to shrug. "It's not that I don't. I'm just not sure I'm cut out for domestic bliss."

Dom followed. He sighed in a way that seemed more worried than annoyed. "How can you possibly say that? You've never even tried."

Chapter Twenty-two

Days passed and turned into weeks. September gave way to October and the number of people in town seemed to dwindle at the same rate as leaves on trees. Graham spent more nights with Mat than not. The routine of work shifted as the seasonal staff left, but Graham didn't mind. Mat continued to work crazy hours in a seeming race against the arrival of winter.

Her cooking lessons with Aunt Nora seemed to be working and she made dinner at Mat's at least a couple of times a week. They alternated that with Mat's cooking and takeout. They went out with Dom and Renata and even had dinner at Renata's place one night. Nights were spent making love and falling asleep together. In almost every way, it was everything Graham wanted. But even as she reveled in the connection, she sensed that something was off.

Perhaps off wasn't the right word. She had no qualms about the time they spent together. It was fun and easy and the sex was hands down the best she'd ever had. It was more like there might be something missing. A depth in their connection. Mat artfully kept things light. And while Graham didn't have a burning desire to make them heavy, she couldn't help but feel like she was being held at arm's length from Mat's heart.

It was one thing to be patient. It was another thing entirely to be in some elaborate dance of evasion. And as time passed, it felt more and more elaborate, and more and more evasive.

Graham decided it was time to do something about it. She chose a night when they'd gone to bed early. Even after the crazy good sex, she felt awake and alert. Trying to keep it casual, Graham draped an arm over Mat's chest and rested her chin on it. "Are you going to tell me what's bugging you or am I going to have to guess?"

Mat frowned. "What makes you think something's wrong?"

"You've been distracted the last couple of weeks. You have something on your mind and you're not very good at hiding it."

"I'm sorry."

Graham took a deep breath, telling herself to be patient, but also to persist. "Don't apologize. Talk to me."

Mat shook her head. "I've been thinking about all the reasons I don't do relationships."

Graham lifted her head, searched Mat's eyes for a hint of where she might be going with this. "Okay."

"And we seem to be creeping into relationship territory, if we aren't already there."

Graham willed herself to ask the question she wasn't sure she wanted the answer to. "And that makes you uncomfortable?"

Mat rolled away from Graham and sat up. Graham followed suit, only she hugged her knees to her chest while Mat remained cross-legged. "It's just that all the reasons I don't are still there. And they feel like a ticking time bomb."

Part of Graham wanted to offer reassurance, to say they didn't need to be in any more of a relationship than Mat wanted. But it would be lying. She did want a relationship. Hell, she was pretty close to wanting a forever. Now might not be the time to say so, but she'd be damned if she was going to pretend her feelings didn't exist. "Can you give me some specifics? It might be easier if we're on the same page."

Mat sighed. Graham could see the tension in her body. "When I was nineteen, I was accused of rape."

Graham swallowed and tried to tamp down the instinctive response her brain, and her body, had to that word. "What happened?"

Mat stared at her hands for a moment, then looked at Graham. "Statutory rape. I should clarify."

The air rushed from Graham's lungs. "Yes, definitely a difference there. Will you tell me about it?"

"Her name was Lindsay and she was seventeen. Her family was in Truro for the summer. We fell in love the way two inexperienced teenagers tend to do. Emotionally intense. She'd kissed boys, but it was the first time either of us had sex. And of course we thought it was forever."

Graham imagined a teenage Mat, full of passion and fire. "But the summer ended."

"Yeah. She'd actually graduated high school a year early and was supposed to start college. She tried to tell her parents she was going to take a gap year and work. They saw through that pretty quick and had no intention of leaving their precious daughter with some working-class townie."

"I can't imagine how difficult that must have been." Graham meant it. But at the same time, she couldn't imagine how the experience would have soured Mat on relationships forever.

"It sucked. In retrospect, they probably wouldn't have attempted legal action. At the time, the threat did more than enough damage."

"That's a tough way to have your heart broken the first time."

Mat shook her head again. "I probably should have expected her to buckle, but I didn't. She said it was to protect me. In retrospect, she might have meant it."

Graham reached over and squeezed her knee. "I'm sure it didn't feel like it at the time."

Mat let out a soft chuckle. "It didn't. The worst part, though, was my family."

"What do you mean?" A little voice in her head told Graham this was the crux of the matter, the part that had spilled over and stayed with her still.

"I wasn't out to them at the time."

"And this blowing up was how they found out?"

"Yeah." Mat took a deep breath. "My family is very traditional and very Catholic."

Graham had wondered vaguely sometimes about the unusual mix of the Provincetown community—the descendants of

Portuguese fishermen and the waves of artists and queer people that came later. She'd never detected visible strife, but it seemed like there might be more coexistence than true community.

"I can see what you're thinking. Yes, they live in one of the gayest places in the world. And they're pretty cool with it as long as it's not in the family. You can imagine how horrifying it was for my parents to learn not only that they had a gay daughter, but that the news might be splashed all over the police blotter."

Graham had tried never to take her parents' support for granted. But she'd also never really thought about what it might be like if they weren't. "So what happened?"

"She left and that was the end of it. My mother made it clear both she and my father were disappointed in me. It took years for things with them to get back to normal."

Far more than the broken heart, that did a lot more to explain Mat's reticence when it came to relationships. "But they did get better? You seem so close to them now."

"My family is the most important thing to me. They're not perfect by any means, but they're family and that runs deep." Mat stretched her arms, then laced her fingers behind her head before letting her hands fall back to her lap. "They're also my livelihood."

"Right." Mat might own her own boat, but she relied on the family business to sell her catch. Alienating herself from them would have a negative impact on every aspect of her life. "So where does that leave you?"

"I keep everything separate. I mean, I love my family, but not enough to be celibate."

The pieces finally clicked into place. It wasn't that Mat didn't want to be in a relationship, it was that being in one meant her worlds would collide. Having a girlfriend, much less a wife, meant bringing her home to meet the family. Graham thought back to the day Dom had surreptitiously invited her to a family gathering. Even though Mat played it cool, tension had radiated from her.

"What? I can see your wheels turning."

Graham shook her head. "I was just thinking about the day I met your family. They were so nice to me."

Mat thought back to that day as well, including the fact it never would have happened if she'd had any say in the matter. "You managed to win my father over. He loved that you talked shop with him, that you knew your stuff." She chuckled. "And that you let him be right about a couple of things."

Graham smiled. "He's funny, and really smart." The smile turned into a frown. "Does that mean your mom didn't like me?"

"It—" Mat hesitated. Her mother, usually so forthcoming with opinions about everything from Mat's clothes to the going market price of lobster, had been unusually quiet. Her gut told her it wasn't praise she was withholding. "I don't know about my mother."

"So that means you haven't talked to her about us. Like at all." Graham's shoulders hunched further and she looked more defeated than disappointed.

"It's not you. I don't talk to either one of them about women. At all. That's the whole point."

Graham looked directly at Mat. There was sadness in her eyes, but also something else. Pity, maybe? "How can you say you're really close to them if you keep such a large part of yourself hidden?"

Mat bristled at the insinuation. "Are you telling me you talk to your parents about sex?"

Graham rolled her eyes. "Not actual sex, but relationships. Yeah."

"And let me guess. They were super duper supportive when you came out?" Mat cringed at the bitterness in her voice.

"They were. I know I'm lucky in that sense. And I get that you weren't." Graham sighed. "I'm trying to make you feel better, not worse."

"I appreciate the gesture." Really, she did. "But I know my family and I know what they can handle. I have a system that works. Trust me."

Graham nodded. "Okay."

Her voice was small and it made Mat feel like garbage. "Look, I like being with you. A lot. I can't remember the last time I dated someone exclusively. I don't want to change that. But that's all I can give." She swallowed. "You have to decide if that's enough."

Graham nodded again, with a little more energy this time. "Okay."

"Okay?"

"Okay, I understand how you feel, where you're coming from." Graham took a deep breath. It felt to Mat like resignation. "I need to think about it and decide if it's enough."

The small knot of discomfort in Mat's gut grew. She didn't want to lose Graham from her life. But at the same time, she knew her limits. She might come with some baggage, but she was honest. She went out of her way to make sure she never strung a woman along. That had always worked in her favor. At this moment, though, she wasn't so sure. She felt a strong drive to escape, but since they were at her place, there was nowhere for her to go. "It's late. We should get some sleep."

"Yeah." Graham scooted down the bed and extended her legs.

Mat turned and did the same. She pulled the blankets up and over them. "I hope you're not mad."

"I'm not." Graham's voice was flat.

"Disappointed, then." She was no stranger to disappointing people.

Graham once again rolled toward her. "I'm really not. A little sad, maybe, but mostly for you. That's a really hard thing to go through, as a teenager no less. And it seems like you're still paying for it."

Mat looked at her. She didn't want Graham to be angry, but she would have known how to deal with it. Disappointment, too. Those things sucked, but in some ways they made it easier for Mat to maintain the distance she so desperately needed. This was harder. Not pity—she wouldn't tolerate that ever—but something gentler. She shook her head. "I'm fine."

Graham's smile in return was reassuring, but Mat sensed sadness behind it. "You are."

Mat grinned, more than ready to end this conversation. "Actually, huddled in with you in my bed makes me a lot more than fine."

The smile became more genuine. "I'll give you that."

Thank God. "Can I turn off the light now?"

Mat expected a snarky comeback, but none came. Instead, Graham took another deep breath and let it out in a whoosh. "Please."

Mat switched off the lamp and lay on her back. "Come here."

Graham came up close, planted a kiss on her lips, then curled into the crook of her shoulder. "Good night."

"Night." Mat kissed the top of her head and gave her a light squeeze.

Eventually, Graham's breathing slowed to the even rhythm of sleep. Mat continued to turn their conversation over in her mind. She allowed herself to imagine what it would be like to be her brothers, bringing home girlfriends that became wives. She'd not given much thought to children, but the idea of having a family, of having her kids running around their grandparents' house on holidays came into focus. She could envision it with striking clarity and, for the first time maybe ever, wanted it. And the woman who scooped up those children, the one who sat next to her at the table and held her hand as her father said grace over the meal, was Graham.

Chapter Twenty-three

After telling Graham about her past, Mat was plagued by strange dreams. They left her with an inexplicable combination of unease and certainty. Graham didn't press her to talk further the next morning, and she was grateful. She was also grateful that Graham had plans with her roommate for some kind of girls' night. She needed some space.

But as much as she wanted the time alone, Mat found herself restless and irritated by eight p.m.

She decided to go out. She hadn't been out since the night she and Graham first hooked up. Not cruising, necessarily, but she desperately needed a change of scenery. Something—anything—to distract her.

An hour later, Mat stood at the bar, trying to decide if she wanted to see a familiar face or hoped she didn't. She offered the bartender a distracted nod. "Can I get a vodka soda?"

"On the house if you tell me where you've been hiding the last couple of months."

Mat blinked a few times as the comment registered. She gave the woman her full attention. "Brooke. Christ. My brain was a million miles away. How the hell are you?"

Brooke gave her a sly smile. "I'm good, better now that you're here. I'd started to worry about you."

Mat grazed her hand over the back of her neck. "It hasn't been that long."

"I think it has." Brooke finished pouring her drink, then added two wedges of lime the way Mat liked it. She waved off the money Mat pulled from her wallet. "I meant it. It's good to see you."

Mat had hooked up with Brooke once a few summers prior. The sex had been good, but they'd come to a mutual understanding they were better suited as friends. They didn't hang out often, but Mat spent more than one slow night nursing a drink and chatting with her about anything and everything under the sun. "It's good to see you, too."

"So," Brooke said in lieu of a question. But before Mat could respond, a couple of women came up to the bar.

Mat used the interruption to formulate her thoughts. She didn't want to lie about the time she'd been spending with Graham, but she also didn't want it to seem like she'd been put out to pasture. Mat cringed at the phrase, and all the implications that came along with it. Brooke returned and looked at her expectantly.

"I've kind of been seeing this girl." God. Could she sound more ridiculous? Even with the way things were, Mat was glad Graham wasn't there to hear her pathetic explanation.

Brooke's sculpted eyebrow arched. "Really? Do tell."

"We met here, actually." Given the time she and Graham had spent together—in bed as well as out—it felt strange to think they'd met in a bar. Like so many of her past hookups, and yet so very different.

Brooke's eyes got huge. "Here? Is she a regular? A seasonal?"

"Resident, but only the last year or so. Pretty sure she's not a regular here." Although, with the exception of having not seen her before, Mat had no real basis to make such a claim.

Another couple came up to the bar. Brooke huffed audibly before moving away to take their orders. Mat chuckled. She couldn't remember the last time she was the subject of any kind of juicy gossip. On second thought, she could. It had been a long time ago, and not a time she hoped to repeat. Brooke returned as quickly as she left. She gestured at Mat. "And?"

"And what?" She'd come out specifically to avoid thinking or talking about Graham. She wasn't going to volunteer more information than she had to.

"And is it over? Is that why you're here, cruising?"

Mat bristled, although she couldn't put her finger on what exactly irritated her the most. She decided to go with the most obvious. "I'm not cruising."

It came out more belligerently that she'd intended. Brooke lifted both hands defensively. "Hey, now. I didn't mean it as an insult."

Mat shook her head. It wasn't Brooke's fault she was in such a pissy mood. "Sorry. I didn't mean to bite your head off."

More people came in. Brooke groaned this time. "Hold that thought. I'll be right back."

Mat used the second reprieve to get a grip. When Brooke returned, Mat was smiling. "Like I said, sorry for being an ass. It's a weird situation. I'm not entirely sure what it is or what I'm doing. Which is why I'm here. Looking for a night of not thinking about it."

"Okay." Brooke nodded in a way that said she had a million and a half questions, but knew better than to ask them.

"Thanks. What's new with you?"

Brooke's smile went all the way to her hazel eyes. "I've been seeing someone, too."

"Yeah?" Mat braced herself for the inevitable gushing. She didn't begrudge Brooke being happy, or having a girlfriend for that matter, but did everyone in her life have to pair up and settle down at the same time?

"Her name is Audrey. She's a chef."

Mat shook her head. Unbelievable. "At Osteria 160?"

Brooke narrowed her eyes. "You know her?"

Mat nodded and let out a sigh. "I recently got her to sign with us as an exclusive supplier."

Brooke's face took on a look of horror. "She's not who you've been seeing, is she?"

"No, no," Mat said quickly.

She remained skeptical. "Have you slept with her, like before?"

Mat had never been so glad not to have slept with someone. "Just friends, I swear."

Brooke laughed, but Mat thought there might be an edge to it. That was one of the problems with living in such a small town, even one as gay as Provincetown. Everyone knew everyone else and, when it came to sex and dating, cross-pollination was inevitable. After a moment, Brooke rolled her shoulders and tipped her head from side to side, as though shaking off unpleasant thoughts. "My turn to be sorry. I know it's technically none of my business."

"Yeah, but I appreciate the weirdness factor."

Brooke laughed again, and this time seemed to relax. "I'm sure it happens to you all the time."

Mat couldn't argue the truth of Brooke's assessment, but it didn't sit well. Despite keeping her sexual activities a secret from her parents, she'd always thumbed her nose at the value judgments people placed on promiscuity. Commentary about her own behavior never bothered her before, so why should it now? But since she'd already been snippy once that evening, Mat kept her thoughts to herself. "Eh, not all that often."

"Not like I would judge, seeing as how you and I had one of the hookups in question." She rolled her eyes, but smiled.

Mat wanted nothing more in that moment than to get out of there, away from talk about relationships and sexual pasts. But since Brooke had comped her drink, it would be rude to just take off. She decided to steer the conversation as far away from herself as possible. "Tell me about you and Audrey."

It was the right tactic. Brooke's face softened and she talked about the blissful state of her life until more customers walked up in search of libation. Mat finished her drink and tried to think of a graceful exit strategy. She glanced at her watch. It was barely ten. She angled away from the bar for a moment and watched the crowd.

She made eye contact with a few people she recognized, a few she didn't. A woman with long dark hair and deep brown eyes held her gaze. Mat nodded a casual hello. The woman returned the greeting with a slow, seductive smile. Under normal circumstances, Mat would take that as all the invitation she needed. She'd cross the room, buy a drink. Friendly conversation might lead to more.

Tonight her feet remained planted. Whether it was her comment to Graham about seeing only her or something else, she just wasn't feeling it. She looked away before accidentally giving the woman the wrong impression and sighed.

"Is it really as bad as all that?" Brooke's voice behind Mat made her chuckle.

"Apparently." Mat turned and found another drink waiting for her. She didn't have the heart to tell Brooke she didn't even want it.

"That one over there seems interested." Brooke angled her head just a fraction. Mat didn't need to look over to know who she was talking about.

"Yeah. She's hot, too. I just, I don't know."

"Sounds to me like you've got one of two problems."

Mat leaned on the bar and gave Brooke her full attention. "What's that?"

"Either you're coming down with something and you're off your game, or," she paused for effect, "you're in love."

Adamant refusal was probably just as damning as agreement, so she did neither. She took a long drink from her glass. It held more vodka than soda. "Not thrilled with either of those options."

"I don't know." Brooke shrugged playfully. "Being in love isn't so bad."

Mat put her glass on the counter. "If you say so. Are you sure I can't pay you for these?"

"I insist."

Mat nodded. "Thanks. I'm going to get out of here."

"I hope you feel better soon, either way."

"Thanks." Mat slipped on her coat, offered a parting wave, and wound her way through the crowd. She could feel the dark haired woman's eyes on her, but she kept her gaze in front of her. The only thing she hated more than being turned down was having to do the turning down herself.

Out on the street, the night had a definite chill. Mat paused and zipped her coat, not quite ready to head home. Brooke's words remained stuck in her mind.

It wasn't like she hadn't considered the idea she might be in love. She'd spent far too much time with Graham—quiet, intimate time as much as sex or going out and having fun—for it not to cross her mind. On some levels, it didn't even bother her. She'd expected to be overwhelmed by it, that all-consuming manic feeling she remembered from her youth. It was different with Graham, though, more reassuring. It was being able to imagine a future with her, and liking what she saw.

Not that it was all wine and roses. Mat had plenty of anxiety, too. She didn't like feeling she wasn't in full control of her destiny. Nor did she relish the idea of trying to integrate Graham into her family. Even if the anniversary party hadn't been a complete disaster.

"Decided I could use a little fresh air myself." They'd never spoken, but Mat knew who was behind her. The voice was low and silky, casual but confident.

Mat turned and, sure enough, found herself face to face with the woman from the bar. She was even more beautiful close up. "I was actually going to call it a night."

The woman's eyes danced. "Is that an invitation?"

On a thousand other nights, Mat wouldn't have hesitated. She loved women who weren't afraid to take charge, who knew what they wanted. Mat could imagine going home with her, or taking the woman back to her place. It would be easy and uncomplicated and everything she'd always believed she wanted. Now, it felt, not bad exactly, but flat. Underwhelming. "I'm not feeling great, I'm afraid. I think I'd make for pretty lousy company."

"That's too bad." The woman looked disappointed, but only mildly so. "I hope you find a cure for what ails you."

"Thanks. I hope you find what you're looking for." God, that sounded cheesy. She was losing her touch, or maybe she really was under the weather.

The woman offered her a bland smile. "I'll be just fine."

She went back to the bar and Mat stood on the street. She looked up at the sky. Thin clouds moved quickly, veiling the moon without blocking its light. She'd gotten herself into a fine mess all right, with no idea how to navigate it. Mat sighed and started walking, not in the direction of home yet, just walking.

Chapter Twenty-four

The shrinking schedule of the Dolphin Fleet meant that, even with the time she'd been spending with Mat, Graham had time on her hands. She figured Will was in the same boat, so Graham cajoled her into meeting at The Flour Pot for coffee and possibly lunch. When she arrived, the whole place smelled of coffee and freshly baked delightful things. Graham breathed it in and wondered why she didn't make an excuse to come more often, especially now that she sort of knew the owner and the cook.

Will was already there, putting in an order for her usual—black coffee. Graham wrinkled her nose and settled on a chai. While waiting for their drinks, they went over to claim a table by the window, waving a hello to Alex's wife, Lia, who was working at the next table over.

"I'm going to go say hi to the baby," Will said.

Graham eyed the bundle in the stroller next to Lia. "Not without me."

They approached the stroller together. Will leaned down and gave Lia a hug. "How's my favorite mama?"

"So much better now that this one is sleeping mostly through the night."

"Well, you look fabulous," Will said.

Graham, who'd been peeking to see if Maeve was awake, nodded. "Agreed."

"Y'all are both very sweet. Especially since I'm sure you came over to see her and not me."

Will's face grew serious. "I'm sorry. You're probably getting that a lot."

Lia laughed. "I am, but I don't mind. It comes with the territory. Do you want to hold her?"

Graham and Will both nodded. Lia scooped the baby from the stroller. She was wearing a fleece onesie covered with dinosaurs and had a swirl of dark brown hair on her tiny head. Graham thought her heart might melt at the sight of it. Will took her first and looked like an absolute natural. Even though she and Nora had no plans to have kids of their own, it was clear she had the touch when it came to babies.

When it was Graham's turn, she took Maeve into her arms. Brown eyes blinked up at her, looking as serious as any adult's. Her tiny fingers curled and uncurled as she moved her arm back and forth. She'd yet to turn one, but she made noises that sounded like an attempt at real words. Graham sighed and gave in to the urge to smell the top of her head. "She's absolutely perfect."

Lia beamed. "Thank you. I mean, I know I'm biased, but she really is."

Will and Graham's drinks were called. Will nodded at Lia's computer. "We won't keep you."

Graham nodded and, with just a hint of reluctance, settled Maeve back in the stroller. "If you need a babysitter, especially between now and April, you call me."

Lia pointed at her playfully. "Considering I only seem to get work done while she's sleeping, I'm going to remember that."

"I hope you do."

Will grabbed their drinks and they settled in to catch up. Graham held her chai in both hands and took a sip. She loved the first really chilly days of fall—all warm beverages and chunky sweaters. Even if it meant her work season was nearly over and she'd have to find some odd jobs to get through winter. "You're looking extra blissful today."

Will shrugged and offered a bashful smile. "I'm good."

Graham had the feeling Will was one of those people who didn't like to brag about how happy she was. She wondered if it had to do with jinxing herself or not wanting to come across as smug. "It's okay. You don't have to hold it in. One, you deserve it. Two, knowing you're happy makes me happy."

Will's smile grew. "I'm so freaking happy."

Graham returned the smile. It really was infectious. "Good."

Will set down her coffee. She folded her arms and leaned forward on the table. "What about you?"

"What about me?"

"Are you blissful?"

"Um." She wasn't unhappy, but she wouldn't use the word bliss, either. "I don't think I can put myself in the same category as you."

Will frowned. "It's not meant to be a comparison. Or a competition."

"Competition, no. But I don't think it's wrong to look at what you and Aunt Nora have and want that for myself." She lifted a shoulder. "At least in the long run."

Will's face was full of empathy. "I hear you. I give you lots of props trying the no strings attached approach, but—"

"But you know me better than that." Graham sighed. "You can say I told you so. I don't mind."

"You know I don't want to say that." Just the idea seemed to make Will uncomfortable.

"I know. You're unflappably nice."

"Stop." Will smiled sheepishly and blushed a little.

"Okay, fine. Will you tell me the truth, though? Like, complete honesty?"

"The truth about what?" A shadow of worry came into Will's eyes.

"Mat and me. Am I pinning my hopes on something that doesn't stand a chance?"

The look of worry intensified. Will took a sip of her coffee, studied her cup. Eventually, she said, "I don't know."

Graham could tell that it pained Will to say that, which made it even worse to hear. "I think I'm in love with her, Will. What am I going to do?"

Will reached across the table and squeezed Graham's hand. "I'm afraid I don't know that either."

"Yeah." She didn't expect Will to have the answer, but it would have been nice to hear something wise and reassuring.

As if sensing her thoughts, Will continued. "There's something to be said for persistence, and for being patient. That's what I had to do with Nora."

Graham remembered the weeks following Aunt Nora's car accident. Nora and Will had been broken up at the time, but Will kept showing up, day after day. Not in a pushy, stalkery way. She proved to Nora that she wasn't going to cut and run and, eventually, Nora trusted her enough to share her heart.

As much as she wanted to see the parallels, there were some critical differences. Mainly, she never doubted that Nora was in love with Will. She was stubborn as hell, but Graham knew in her heart they loved each other. She did not have that same level of certainty when it came to Mat's feelings.

"—standing up for what was in my heart."

Graham blinked at Will. "I'm sorry. I totally zoned for a second. What did you say?"

Will smiled and seemed not the least bit annoyed that Graham had tuned her out. "I said it wasn't just perseverance. I got to the point where I had to own the fact that I wasn't satisfied, that I wanted more."

Graham made a face. "Wait. Are you telling me to be patient or to give her an ultimatum?"

"Neither. First, I would never tell you what to do. Second, I think the answer is most often somewhere in the middle."

"Yeah." So not helpful.

"Hey, now. I meant that in a positive way."

Graham didn't doubt Will's intentions for a second. But she wasn't sure this chat was bringing her any closer to a decision, much less a course of action. "I know. I appreciate it."

Will quirked a brow. "I'm pretty sure you're lying."

Graham laughed at the assertion, mostly because it was true. "I do appreciate the company, and the pep talk. Even if I sort of just want to be told what to do."

"If this is a pep talk, can I say that you deserve someone who adores you, without qualification?"

"And you don't think Mat is that person?" As much as she wanted advice, she dreaded that would be Will's take on the situation.

"I don't know her well enough to know if she is or she isn't. I'm not a fan of her being standoffish the second you seem to be getting serious." Will paused, sighed. "But the way she looked at you that night we all had dinner felt like she was a woman in love, or close to it."

"So, what do I do?"

"You decide if Mat, and what you have, is worth fighting for."

Graham's shoulders slumped. "What if we don't have it yet, but I think we could?"

"Then you have to decide how long you're willing to wait." Will shrugged. "As well as how hard you're willing to push."

Graham nodded. "I've never felt this way about anyone. And I don't think I'm imagining that she feels the same."

"But you're not sure she's brave enough."

The word brave stopped Graham in her tracks. "You know, I've been so worried about whether she wanted it badly enough, I never thought about whether she had to be brave."

"Family dynamics can be hard."

"You're right. I have to remember that." That one comment made Graham feel better about her potential future with Mat than any reassurance Will could have offered. Especially given Mat's history, it made perfect sense that she'd be hesitant to wade into those waters again.

"Now, do you want to get some lunch? I have it on good authority the portobello mac and cheese is amazing." Will angled her head in the direction of the kitchen.

"Are you enjoying having a sister-in-law?"

They walked back to the counter. "I am. It's almost as much fun as having a nephew."

Graham smiled. "I always wanted nieces and nephews."

"Mat comes from a big family, right?"

"Yeah." She hadn't met Mat's brothers or their kids, but she'd fantasized about becoming part of such a large and close-knit clan.

Alex had replaced Jeff at the register and she offered them both a smile. "Hey, you two. What can I get you?"

"Hi, Alex." Graham perused the menu, even though she'd already made up her mind. "I'll have the mac and cheese, please."

Will didn't even pretend to look at the other offerings. "Same for me."

"Coming right up." Alex punched their order into the small screen.

Will took out her wallet, but Graham waved her off. "You're providing free therapy. The least I can do is buy your lunch."

"You've done as much for me a dozen times at least." Will put her wallet away. "I'm agreeing, but with the understanding I get to reciprocate soon."

Graham rolled her eyes, but laughed. "Fine."

With no one else in line, Alex disappeared into the kitchen. But instead of returning with their food, Darcy emerged. Graham watched Will's face light up and they exchanged a hug. Graham was thinking how nice it must be, having a sister-in-law. But before she could give much thought to her own wants in that department, Darcy gave her a squeeze as well. "You have to stop buying your food before I know you're here. How am I ever going to treat you to lunch?"

Graham smiled. "You don't need to treat me to lunch. I helped because I wanted to. I love Will and Aunt Nora, so I love you and Emerson by extension."

Darcy shook her head. "Not good enough. Will you come over for dinner? You and Mat, we could make it a double date." She looked at Will. "Or a triple."

Darcy's invitation was exactly what she'd dreamed of when she decided to make Provincetown home. It felt so close, and still just out of her reach. She sighed. Maybe not for long. "I'd love that."

"You have my number, right? Text me a few dates that would work for you and we'll make it happen."

"Sounds good."

Alex returned, carrying two bowls. She handed them to Will and Graham and they returned to their table. Graham took a bite of her food. So good. She let out a sigh and smiled.

"It's delicious, right?"

"It is." Graham realized, though, it wasn't her lunch that was making her smile.

Will definitely picked up on the change. She studied Graham. "What are you thinking right now?"

"I'm thinking that some things are worth the wait."

Will angled her head. "I don't disagree, but I'm curious what tipped the scales for you."

Graham searched for the words to express the shift she'd just experienced. "I'm not sure they tipped. I'm just feeling a bit better about knowing what I want. Does that make sense?"

Will nodded. The sympathetic look was back. "I know exactly what you mean."

❖

After her sorry attempt at a night out, Mat found herself thinking more and more about her conversation with Graham. At the time, Graham hadn't pushed for more of a relationship than they had, but it still left Mat feeling antsy and inadequate. Her initial reaction was to blame the unease on Graham, on her wanting and needing more than Mat had to give. Yet, the more she thought about it, the weaker that argument became.

That left her to grapple with her own feelings—not a preferred pastime. So when Dom asked if she wanted to spend the day with Renata and him babysitting her nieces, she jumped on it. She figured the distraction of three kids under the age of ten would keep her mind far from Graham and what their future might hold. It was a perfect plan until Renata announced their agenda.

"Graham got us discounted tickets for a whale watch," she said with a mixture of excitement and awe. "I've never been on one. Have you?"

Mat sighed, just barely managing to stop it from turning into a growl. "I haven't."

They bundled into jackets and hats and mittens and piled into Renata's sister's van and drove down to the pier. Dom said, "Renata made sure we picked a time that Graham would be working. We'll get to see her in her element."

"Great." Mat felt anything but great. She actually felt a strong urge to bail on the whole thing and spend her day working.

They parked and the six of them made their way toward the designated dock of the Dolphin Fleet. Mat's trepidation didn't have much chance to take hold. Jacinda, who was seven and wore bright purple glasses, grasped her hand and asked her one question after another about her job catching lobsters and going to work every day with Dom.

They boarded the boat and headed to the top deck. Sure enough, Graham was there, organizing what Mat imagined were the props she used to teach laypeople about marine life. She wore a blue and white windbreaker with the Dolphin Fleet logo stitched onto it. Her hair was braided and she had a knit cap pulled over it. Hardly a sexy look, but it didn't stop Mat from having to swallow the lump that appeared in her throat.

"Hi, Graham." Dom's voice was enthusiastic and both he and Renata waved in her direction.

Graham looked their way and returned the wave. When her eyes landed on Mat, her smile changed. It was knowing, sure. For the briefest of moments, the kids and her cousin and the strangers filling in around them vanished. All Mat could see was Graham and, instead of frightening her, it made her inexplicably calm.

The moment passed and all the noises and people returned. Mat felt a hand clamp down on her shoulder and realized Will had come up behind her. Right. Will worked here, too. "Hey, Mat. I didn't realize you were spending the afternoon with us."

"I didn't, either." Mat laughed at the ridiculousness of that statement. Maybe the universe was trying to tell her something.

"Well, welcome aboard."

"Thanks."

Graham joined them, introducing herself to the little girls. She shook their hands and asked them their ages. It surprised Mat how natural Graham was interacting with kids. Then she remembered Graham did it every day. Of course she'd be good with kids.

Before long, the boat was in motion. The wind had a real bite and Mat was glad she'd decided to grab her own gloves and hat. They puttered out of the harbor and around Long Point toward open water. She watched Graham give her talk, an impressive overview of marine life and habitat, along with breeding, migration, and feeding behaviors of humpback and minke whales. As if on cue, she wrapped up just as sightings began.

The girls decided to stay on the top deck so they could see in all directions. Mat tried to focus on their conversations, but found her gaze drifting to Graham again and again. Armed with binoculars and a notebook, she and the other naturalist announced sightings, identified the whales based on their tail patterns, and logged everything. It wasn't the manual labor of lobstering, but there was more to it than Mat might have conceded before.

Twice, Mat glanced from Graham to Dom, only to find him watching her. It was hard to be annoyed, though. He always smiled at her and, rather than smug or mocking, he simply seemed happy. As did Renata and the girls. It was a gorgeous day, if on the chilly side, and watching whales proved to be a lot of fun.

The girls treated Graham like a rock star. They stood near her and asked questions. Many of the other kids did as well. It was cute to watch. They also insisted on having their picture taken with her and some of the artifacts she used in her lesson. When the captain announced they had to head back to shore, Mat decided to snag a few seconds of her attention.

"I was surprised to see you today." There was no accusation in Graham's voice, only curiosity.

"I offered to join Dom and Renata so they wouldn't be outnumbered. I didn't realize this was the day's activity."

Graham's eyes sparkled. "Your first whale watch, right? What did you think?"

Mat would have come up with something nice to say, but the truth of the matter was that she'd been impressed. She considered herself an expert on Cape Cod Bay, but she'd learned a few things. On top of that, Graham was really good at her job. She was enthusiastic without being obnoxious and managed to convey information that kids could digest without boring the adults to tears. "I don't want to say better than I expected, because then you'll think I had really low expectations. But it was better than I expected."

Graham laughed and the sound—pure and genuine—went right to Mat's gut. "High praise."

"See, I knew it would sound bad. It was really good. Fun and educational."

Graham laughed again. "I'll take it."

The journey back to land seemed to take no time at all. Before Mat realized it, they were docked at MacMillan Pier. People began filtering toward the exit, but Mat held back. "Are you off now?"

Graham smiled. "I am."

"I think I'm roped into an early pizza dinner. Not the most exciting of evenings, but you're welcome to join us."

Graham let her gaze travel from Mat to Dom and Renata, to the three insanely adorable little girls. She'd not been looking for a sign, some cosmic reassurance that things with Mat were going to turn out okay. Still, it felt like she might be getting exactly that. "I'd love to."

She wished Will a good night and walked with Mat to the parking lot. She climbed into the back of the minivan, sandwiched between Sarah and Leonor. From her seat, she was able to watch Jacinda bask in Mat's attention. She empathized with the little girl's crush while indulging in thoughts of having a little girl of her own.

For all that Mat claimed not to want a family, she was a natural with kids. Graham knew better than to equate one with the other, but she couldn't help but wonder what it might be like. And if Mat's assertions truly matched what was in her heart.

They ended up at a tiny pizza joint in Truro. The seven of them crowded around a table that wasn't quite big enough and debated the relative grossness of mushrooms and anchovies. Graham laughed and learned about the girls' dance lessons. She squeezed Mat's knee under the table and exchanged a few flirtatious looks with her.

By the time they ended up back at Mat's place, Graham was exhausted. "I'm not sure how people do it," she said.

Mat shrugged. "I think it's harder when both parents work, but not impossible. Especially if you have a big and supportive family." She smiled. "Like you."

"I'm pretty lucky, I guess."

Graham kicked off her shoes. "I was actually talking about you being the supportive family. I mean, I know the girls aren't technically your family, but you all pulled together and gave their parents the day off."

"When you put it that way." Mat hung up their jackets. "I guess I take that part for granted. I've looked after kids since I was old enough to be left alone with them."

"It's kind of genius, really. Training the next generation of parents." Graham thought of the few minutes she spent with Maeve earlier in the week. She certainly loved the idea of spending time with Lia and Alex's daughter, but she'd be lying if she said she didn't think of it as practice.

"Yeah, I guess that's one way of looking at it."

Graham sighed. She wanted to press Mat a bit, try to get a read on her feelings on babies and marriage and all those things. Or maybe more accurately, a read on whether Mat's no way, no how outlook might soften over time. "I guess the opposite could be true as well."

Mat angled her head. "A reality check, you mean? A reminder of just how much work it is to raise a family?"

"I imagine it has that effect on some people." Graham shrugged, avoided making eye contact.

"Not you, though."

She looked up and found Mat's gaze fixed on her. "Not me."

"For the record, you were really good with the girls. They'd never met you before and, by the end of dinner, wanted to be your best friends. I'm sure you'll be a great mom someday."

Graham searched Mat's face for meaning, but couldn't find any. "Maybe one day."

"So, did you want to watch a movie or something?"

Maybe it counted for something that Mat assumed she was staying, wanted her to stay. "If you do."

Mat closed the short distance between them and wrapped her arms around Graham's waist. "I'd be more inclined to call it a night, crawl into bed early."

Despite the unsettled feeling in her heart, Graham's body responded immediately. It seemed cowardly to give into it, to shut off the doubts and the worry and the longing for something more. But the certainty of their physical connection meant something. Graham refused to believe they'd still be this much in sync if there wasn't something below the surface.

Graham let Mat pull her into a kiss, lead her to the bedroom. She gave herself to the moment, to a passion so unlike what she'd experienced before. The fire of the first few times remained. If anything, it had intensified. That had to mean something. She held onto that as she gave herself to Mat. And after, under the blankets and in the warmth of Mat's arms, Graham let herself bask in the belief that they stood on the precipice of having it all.

Chapter Twenty-five

After the day spent with Dom, Renata, and her nieces, Mat couldn't shake a feeling of restless anticipation. She spent a day trying to ignore it, another trying to work through it. But every time her mind wandered, it found its way to Graham. The image of her giggling with Jacinda over pizza. Watching her work and the quick thrill of sharing a moment of eye contact. The soft certainty of her body as they drifted off to sleep.

The truth of her feelings hit her like a punch to the stomach during a fight—not completely out of nowhere, but still enough to knock the wind out of her. As she sat with it, though, it started to feel good. Even more surprising, it felt natural. She could see a future with Graham and it felt real, not out of reach.

It was that feeling she held onto when she invited herself to lunch at her parents' house. She picked Wednesday, in part because Sunday seemed too far away and in part because she didn't want to deal with other members of the family showing up, announced or otherwise. She also didn't have plans with Graham the night before. Since she didn't trust herself not to be stressed and distracted, that was for the best, too.

After a restless night and a morning of too much coffee and not enough to do, Mat paced back and forth in her living room. Despite the certainty in her heart, her stomach twisted and turned, making her glad she'd skipped breakfast. She told herself to relax. She told herself a thousand things had changed since that horrible day all those years ago. She was an adult. Graham was, too. It wasn't like her parents would disown her at this point. She already knew they disapproved of her relationships with women. This would simply give them something more concrete to disapprove of.

She glanced at her watch. Might as well head over before she wore a path in the rug.

She found her father in his usual chair, reading the paper. Cooking noises came from the kitchen, along with the aroma of linguica and onions. "Hey, Pop."

He moved the paper to the side and looked at her. "Mattie, you're early. Does that mean the catch is good or terrible?"

She smiled. "Pretty good. We have a few good weeks still before we start pulling in most of the traps."

He shook his head. "In my day, we hauled until New Year."

"And lost money more days than not doing it." It was her canned response to his canned assertion.

"But we sure ate well."

She couldn't fault that logic. "We'll leave enough in the water for our own enjoyment and the holiday rush."

He folded up the paper and set it aside. "I know you will. You're a smart businesswoman on top of being a damn fine lobsterman."

Mat narrowed her eyes. He might have been the softer of her parents, but compliments were not his style. "You feeling all right, old man?"

He scowled. "I'm fine. Just thinking lately I don't say often enough that I'm proud of you. Thought you ought to hear it."

Rather than making her feel better, the sentiment left Mat unsettled. She liked it okay, but she didn't know what to do with it. "Thanks, Pop."

They stayed like that for a moment—Mat standing in the middle of the room and her father in his chair, neither of them speaking. Just when the silence started to feel really awkward, her mother walked in. "Who died?"

They both looked at her. Mat blinked a few times. "What? No one."

"You wouldn't know it by the look on both your faces."

Mat laughed, some of the discomfort easing. "Pop was saying nice things and I worried something might be wrong with him."

That earned her a laugh from both her parents. Ma wiped her hands on the towel she held and announced lunch was ready. Since there were only the three of them, they sat at the small table in the kitchen. Of course, she had still prepared enough food for at least a dozen people. Mat took a deep breath. If she had any hope of eating, she needed to say what needed to be said. "I need to talk to you both."

Her mother gestured to the food. "Let's eat. We'll have plenty of time for talking after."

Mat couldn't tell if the deflection came from sensing the conversation might be unpleasant or her general obsession with meals and making sure her family ate at every possible opportunity. Dishes were passed and Mat found herself staring at a plate full of food. She swallowed. "I'm seeing someone."

Her mother froze, serving spoon suspended over a bowl of potatoes. "What?"

Mat had no doubt her mother had heard, but she refused to take it back. "I said I'm seeing someone. A woman. Graham. You met her at Uncle Martin and Aunt Dores's anniversary party."

Pop pointed at her with his fork. "The marine biologist? The one with the red hair?"

"She's technically a naturalist, but yes. She's the one."

"She's so young, so," Ma frowned, "white."

It was Mat's turn to pretend she hadn't heard. "Excuse me?"

"I didn't mean white. I'm not a racist."

Mat looked at her skeptically. "Are you sure?"

Ma waved both hands in front of her. "Yes, I'm sure. I just mean she's not Portuguese, not local even."

Mat shook her head. "Ma, that's bigoted."

"I don't have anything against her, but I don't understand why you'd choose to date someone who isn't part of the community."

Mat stared at her mother, too flabbergasted to appreciate the irony of her current situation. "Would you say that if she was black?"

That seemed to give her pause. "Yes, but not because I have a problem with black people."

Mat resisted the urge to bang her head on the table. "Pop? Care to weigh in?" As she spoke the words, she realized that might make matters worse.

"Well, I can see where your mother is coming from. The more people marry outside the community, move away, the harder it is for us to keep the traditions, the culture, intact."

"Exactly." Ma folded her arms, vindicated.

"Luciano didn't marry a Portuguese girl. You didn't have a problem with that."

"His heart was gone long before he met Alana." She sighed. "But you, my darling child, you stayed."

Mat's head swam. She'd expected a tense conversation, hoped for a hint of acceptance if not full-on support. She had no idea what to do with this. "I don't understand. Did you think I was going to find some Portuguese guy, magically turn straight, marry him, and make a bunch of babies?"

"Of course not." Her mother's spine stiffened, as though Mat had insulted her.

Mat took a deep breath, closed her eyes for a moment. As much as she wanted to dismiss the whole thing, say it didn't matter what her mother wanted or expected, she couldn't. She opened her eyes, looked squarely at her. "Maybe you could tell me what you did have in mind."

"It's not like that. I never wanted to run your life." Her tone was defiant.

Mat laughed. It came out brittle and hard. "Really? You could have fooled me."

Her father chose that moment to reinsert himself into the conversation. "I understand you're upset, Mattie, but that's not an excuse to speak to your mother that way."

"Sorry," Mat said, more out of habit than conviction. Then she looked again at her mother, and found her eyes filled with tears. Except when her grandparents had died, and at her brothers' weddings, she didn't think she'd ever seen her mother cry. "Please, I want to understand."

"I guess I thought you might end up with a girl like Carolina."

This conversation made less and less sense. "Ma, she's straight and has two kids."

She flipped her hand from side to side to indicate the jury might still be out on that one. "Her no-good husband ran off and left her. It wouldn't surprise me at all if she cast a wider net to find someone she could count on, someone who'd help her raise those girls of hers."

Mat blinked at her mother, speechless. "You're serious."

"Well, I didn't have it planned out. I just thought maybe you'd decide to have a family of your own at some point."

Mat didn't know whether to laugh, cry, or scream. "So you've decided it's okay I'm a lesbian as long as I end up with a nice Portuguese girl. One you've picked out for me. Hopefully one with kids." She shook her head. "And here I thought you were plain old vanilla homophobic."

"Mattie." Her father's face was stern.

Ma laced her fingers together and rested them on the table. "When we found out you were gay, I admit I didn't take it well."

Mat snorted, but after a sharp look from her father, didn't say anything.

"It was a difficult way to find out, with those horrible people yelling and threatening to have you arrested."

Mat was unable to contain herself this time. "You didn't even stand up for me."

Ma shook her head. "That girl's father was a fancy Boston lawyer. We knew better than to cross him."

Mat shook her own head. "You never said so. You made me feel like a pariah."

"As you should have. You got yourself into that mess and betrayed us and brought shame on the family."

And there it was. In the end, it always came back to that. "I was scared and heartbroken and you didn't even care."

"You were willful and angry and needed a reminder so you wouldn't make the same mistake again." There was something in her voice. Sadness, maybe, but no regret. It turned Mat's stomach.

"You wanted me to suffer." In some ways, that felt worse than being left to fend for herself.

"A little suffering in life isn't bad. God tests us to make us stronger." She lifted her chin, certainty returning to her voice.

"I don't even know what to say to that." So much of her life, her relationship with her parents, suddenly made no sense.

Pop pointed at her. "You don't say anything to it. You understand that your parents did what they did to protect you, as is their duty. You don't question it just because you don't like it after the fact."

The pain of that time, of her parents' disapproval, came roaring back to life. With it, a brand-new sense of betrayal. "But you lied to me."

Her mother slapped her hand to the table, making the dishes rattle. "We did not lie. Coddling you, telling you everything was fine—that would have been a lie. We did what we thought was best."

Mat pressed her fingers to her forehead. "I have to go."

"Matilde Beatriz, you will not storm out in the middle of a meal because you're mad at your mother." Pop used his most authoritative voice, the one that had effectively coerced or cajoled Mat for the better part of thirty-five years. For the first time in as long as she could remember, it didn't work.

"I sure as hell will. I can't believe I've spent so much of my life listening to you, playing along to your version of what it should look like."

Ma's jaw hardened, but Mat could see tears in her eyes. "You're overreacting."

"Oh, no." Mat stood from the table. "I'm clearly not reacting enough. That changes now."

Without another word, Mat left the kitchen. She walked through the living room, stopping just long enough to put on her jacket. She walked out of her parents' house and she didn't look back.

Chapter Twenty-six

It was a mere two weeks before Thanksgiving, Graham's absolute favorite holiday of the year, but she couldn't quite muster the energy to feel festive. Things with Mat seemed to be stuck in some kind of limbo and she didn't know how to get them moving again. She'd been so confident they were getting closer, had broken down the walls that Mat held around her heart. And then boom. For the last few days, Mat had turned weird and distant. She wouldn't say why, or what was bothering her. But she also didn't push Graham away, like she was angry or upset with her. It left Graham feeling adrift, and seriously questioning her own judgment.

Mat had begged off seeing her that day, claiming plans with her family. Not that Graham expected to spend every day they both had free together, but something about it seemed off. She gave in to her longing for clarity and texted Dom. Whatever plans Mat had didn't include the extended family and he offered to get together and chat. Graham pounced on it, thinking there probably wasn't anyone who could provide better insight into the way Mat's mind worked.

Dom was at the place where they stored and repaired their traps. Instead of having him break up his day for her, Graham offered to meet him there. She could bring him some coffee as a thank you and she'd get to see a part of their work she hadn't before.

She stopped at the Portuguese Bakery and picked up some malasadas along with the coffee. She was pretty sure Dom had a sweet tooth and, at this point, she could use some comfort carbs of her own. She drove over to the trap yard with the directions Dom had given her. It sat just outside of town, down a narrow street and a gravel driveway. She followed the path alongside the small building to the fenced in yard out back.

Graham found Dom bent over a trap, tying knots in rope with a look of fierce concentration on his face. Her heart swelled a little at the sight. He was such a sweet guy. It wouldn't be hard to think of him as a brother. "I come bearing snacks."

Dom looked up and smiled that easygoing smile he had. "You're my hero."

She handed him one of the coffees and the bag of pastries. "You're easy."

He winked at her. "I get that a lot."

Graham smiled in spite of the anxiety she'd been toting around for days. "That's not what I hear."

Dom rolled his eyes. "You've been spending too much time with Mat."

"Have I?"

Dom must have read the tension in her voice because he frowned. "Are you worried you're spending too much time together or too little?"

"It's not the amount of time that's worrying me."

"But something is. I can see it all over your face. And as much as I appreciate the coffee, and the conversation, I don't imagine you're here to hang out."

"Being with Mat, waiting for her to come around. Am I crazy?" No point in beating around the bush, and she had been asking that question more and more. The handful of friends she'd confided in—Will and Jess, to be exact—seemed split on the matter. Not unlike her own feelings.

"No." Dom's reply was immediate and emphatic.

"Don't say that just to be nice. You know Mat better than anyone. I want your honest opinion."

He finished knotting the rope in his hand and looked her in the eye. "It is my honest opinion. First, because you're smart and hopeful. Optimism gets way too much flack these days."

Graham chuckled. "And second?"

"I believe in my heart Mat is in love with you."

Graham's stomach lurched, part in joy and part in knowing that if it didn't come from Mat—eventually—it wouldn't do her any good. "I really want to believe you."

"You should. I do know Mat better than pretty much anyone."

Graham looked down at her hands. "She told me about Lindsay."

Dom reached over and gave her hand a gentle squeeze. "That's a good thing. It's not a story she tells lightly, and never to women she's dating."

"But she told me specifically as a way of explaining why she doesn't do relationships."

"And how did you respond?"

"I told her it sounded like a really hard thing to go through at that age." Graham debated telling him the rest, but figured she had nothing to lose. "She told me what she could offer and said I had to decide if it was enough."

"Is it?"

"No." That much she was sure of. "At least not forever. That's where the wondering if I'm crazy comes in."

"What did you say to Mat?"

"I told her I'd think about it."

Dom sighed. "So, what you're saying is you're inclined to be patient, but you don't know if it'll be worth it in the end."

Graham sighed, but offered him a smile. "Something like that."

Dom set down the rope and gave Graham his full attention. "I'm going to let you in on a little secret."

Graham raised a brow, unsure of whether it was a secret she wanted to know. "What's that?"

"When it comes down to it, Mat is a bit of a mama's boy."

Graham had to bite her lip to keep from laughing. "What?"

"She has this air of being super tough and independent, but at the end of the day, she lets her parents' opinion dominate her life."

"That much I gathered. She pretty much told me she's not willing to rock the boat."

Dom shook his head and looked up at the sky. "Yeah, but to hear her tell it, it's because she doesn't care enough about relationships or being in love."

"You don't think that's the case?"

Dom looked her right in the eyes. "I think she's terrified."

Graham let that sink in. Fear was not a word she'd ever associate with Mat. If anything, Mat seemed completely confident and willing to take on anything and everything she set her mind to. "I'm not sure I see it."

"I think a lot of people, especially those with a bad track record in the love department, are hesitant to wade back in, take that risk."

"I get that." Graham had gathered as much from her conversation with Mat about what happened when she was younger. "But should teenage heartbreak still have that much impact?"

Dom sighed. "No, it shouldn't. But she'd be risking her heart as well as the relationship she has with her parents. Or at least that's how she sees it."

Graham's shoulders slumped. "So, I am crazy if I'm holding out hope we'll ever be something more."

"No. I stand by what I said. I've known Mat my whole life. Other than Renata, there's no one I'm closer to. And even with Renata, I probably still know Mat better at this point." His face softened. "She's never felt what she feels for you."

"She's said that?" Would it help if Mat had confided in Dom? At least then she'd know the feelings were there.

"Not exactly, but I can tell."

Graham winced. "I don't mean this in a bad way, but that does not make me feel better."

He came over to where she was standing and threw an arm around her shoulder. "I know it's hard, but I'm telling you, just be patient. She'll come around."

Graham took a deep breath and squared her shoulders. "You're right. I believe it in my heart. And honestly, I don't mind being patient. She's worth the wait."

Dom flashed a grin. "That's the spirit."

"Mama's boy, huh?" Graham shook her head and chuckled.

Dom shrugged. "I love her to death, but yeah."

Graham rolled her eyes, but more in amusement than frustration. "I'm not sure if that makes my life easier or harder."

"I think it depends on how you play your cards, and if you're in it for the long haul."

The long haul. That was one way of putting it. It sounded less romantic than madly in love, but those things didn't have to be mutually exclusive. And she'd meant what she said. Being with Mat was what she wanted more than anything in the world. As long as she had hope, she didn't mind waiting. "Oh, I'm in it all right. I'm not going anywhere."

❖

Mat walked into the trap yard and heard voices. It took only a second to realize they belonged to Dom and Graham. She slowed her pace, not specifically intending to eavesdrop, but wondering what Graham was doing there. And maybe what she and Dom were talking about. She couldn't really hear, but heard "mama's boy" and then laughter, followed by Graham saying something about life being harder.

The realization they were talking about her hit Mat like a sucker punch. Worse, they were laughing at her, at her pathetic way of letting her parents dictate her life. She froze, unsure if she should confront them or run the other way. Embarrassment won out over anger and she turned to go, but collided with a stack of traps already pulled in for winter. They clattered to the ground. Shit.

"Mat, is that you?" Graham's voice sounded light, playful even.

Mat walked quickly, hoping she might make it out of view before either of them came looking.

"Where are you going?" Graham called. Mat turned. Graham looked at her like she'd grown a second head. "We're over here."

To Mat's ear, the teasing tone had an edge. It felt mocking. "I just remembered I have an appointment."

Graham planted her fists on her hips. "What kind of appointment?"

Dom came up next to her. "Yeah. You're supposed to be here helping me winterize."

Something about the two of them standing side by side struck her, and not in a good way. "I've got to go." She started walking again, the desire to escape still winning over the urge to fight.

"Dude, what's wrong with you?"

The scales tipped and rage bubbled to the surface. "If you're going to talk shit about me, you could have the decency to do it somewhere besides my trap yard."

She saw Dom's shoulders stiffen at her use of "my," but she didn't care. He gave her the same look as Graham. "What are you even talking about?"

"Mama's boy? Feels a little rich, coming from you."

Graham took a step forward as if to separate them. "He didn't mean it like that."

Dom lifted his chin. "Actually, I did. You've got this amazing girl who's completely in love with you and you're ready to throw it all away because you're afraid mama won't like it."

Mat didn't think, didn't say a word. Instead, she lunged at him. She didn't try to land a punch. Rather, she threw her full weight at him and tried to take him to the ground. He stumbled, but didn't fall. Even though they'd always been the same height, between the T and his gym habit, he had a good twenty pounds on her and the strength to match. She felt him grab her and couldn't tell if he was fighting back or trying to push her away.

After some grappling, they did end up on the ground. Her jacket protected her torso, but Mat felt the gravel through her pants. It dug into her skin as they rolled around. She tried to hook a leg over Dom's. Getting on top would be the only way to best him.

"Stop it!" Graham's yell got through to Mat's brain, but it didn't deter her. She had so much emotion bottled up inside, it was like a pressure valve had finally broken free.

Mat continued to struggle, but Dom was on top of her. It didn't take long for him to pin her arms. She tried to squirm, but his thighs held hers in place. Defeated, she stilled. She closed her eyes and heaved out a breath. "Get off me."

"Do you promise not to do that again?"

Defeated and humiliated. Great. "Yeah."

"Or try to coldcock me?"

Her sigh came out as a growl. "Yeah."

She felt his weight shift and then he was standing. He reached out a hand. She took it and let him haul her to her feet. "Feel better?" he asked.

Did he have to be so fucking calm? "Not really."

"Are you out of your mind?" Graham sounded equal parts shocked and angry.

Mat didn't look at her. "I'm starting to think so."

"What the hell was that about?" Graham's voice was calm, but Mat could see she was trembling.

"I don't want to be a project for you to take on, or a problem for you to solve."

Graham shook her head. "That's not how I think about you." She sniffed. "Or us."

Mat looked into her eyes and saw a mixture of hurt and confusion. "You say that, and I even think you believe it. But I know better."

Graham's posture changed. Her spine straightened and she lifted her chin. "You're going to stand there and tell me what I think, how I feel?"

"I know how this works, Graham. You've got it in your head that I'm some sad little puppy you can save."

"I don't—"

Mat didn't let her finish. "I know you don't think you do, but it's all over your face. I can see it every time I look at you. I can't give you what you want. And I know with absolute certainty that I will disappoint you." She sighed. "Hell, I already have."

"That is the most arrogant, pig-headed thing I've ever heard. I'm disappointed all right." Graham shook her head again. "I'm disappointed that you think so little of me."

"It's not like that. I know you, Graham. I know girls like you. You're just going to end up hurt."

"You're a fool. You hurt me the moment you presume you know what's best for me, the second you take it upon yourself to decide for me what I need, what I can and can't handle." Without waiting for a response, Graham turned on her heel and walked away. She didn't look back.

Mat was left standing in the trap yard with Dom. Both of their clothes were dirty from the tussle on the ground. She offered him a sheepish smile. "Well, that sucked."

"Uh, yeah."

She looked at him. "I'm right, though, aren't I? She's trying to save me and I'll just end up pulling her down."

"Do you enjoy playing the martyr or is it just old habit?" Despite wrestling with her on the ground a moment before, Dom's tone was kind.

"What are you talking about? That's not what's happening."

"No? Are you so horrible and undeserving of love?"

Her stomach twisted at his words. "Dude, that makes me sound pathetic. Don't be so dramatic."

Dom shrugged. "I'm just calling it like I see it. Graham's in love with you. You, exactly the way you are. But you've got your head so far up your ass you're going to throw it away."

He left the same way Graham had. Mat stood there, feeling more alone than she ever had. Indignation faded, leaving her with lingering doubt. Doubt that she'd done the right thing, doubt that she could ever be what Graham truly wanted, doubt that she even knew what she wanted for herself.

She shook her head. Self-pity would only make matters worse. Since she was at the yard, and there was plenty to do, she got to work. Starting with the pile of traps she'd knocked over in her attempt to avoid everything that had just gone down.

Chapter Twenty-seven

Graham sat on the sofa in sweatpants and a hoodie zipped all the way up. She wore a shirt underneath, as well as slippers and two pairs of socks. Still, she was cold. The chill sat in her bones and refused to let go. It had been that way for days, ever since she walked away from Mat in the trap yard. She couldn't seem to get warm.

Jess emerged from her bedroom and gave her a sympathetic look. "How're you feeling today?"

Graham mustered a smile. "I'm okay."

"Liar."

Graham chuckled and smiled for real. "I'm not bad, really. Just feeling lazy is all. But since I don't have anywhere to be, I figure I can wallow." She sounded pathetic, even to herself. Fortunately, Jess was a good enough friend that Graham didn't feel the need to fake being chipper.

"You're allowed to wallow, at least for a bit. A week." Jess nodded, as though she'd just made an important decision. "You have a week to mope around in your pajamas. Hopefully, Mat will come to her senses by then. If not, then we'll figure out how to snap you out of it."

Graham thought about the handful of breakups she'd experienced. She'd never used the phrase "snap out of it," but the disappointment of those endings had always faded rather quickly. She couldn't imagine that now. The hollow feeling in her chest, paired with the never-ending chill, felt like a part of her, permanent.

She didn't have the heart to say as much to Jess. "What are you up to today?"

Jess gave her a funny look, then looked down at herself. "Uh, work."

Graham blinked and registered the purple scrubs she wore—solid pants and a top with cats all over it. "Right. Sorry."

"Do you want to come with me? You can hang out with Clio. She likes people way more than Athena."

Clio was the cat that lived at the veterinary office. She had six toes on three of her paws and loved when people took the time to scratch between her ears or under her chin. Graham, who'd considered adopting a cat more than once in the last year, had a real soft spot for her. "Tempting, but I think I'll pass. I'm pretty happy not putting on pants."

Jess narrowed her eyes. "Are you sure you're okay?"

She didn't feel okay, but she didn't want Jess to worry. And she wasn't going to turn into some barely functioning hermit. She wasn't that pathetic. "I will be. Promise."

Jess nodded. She didn't look convinced, but she didn't press it. "I'll be home around six. We'll have dinner and watch a cheesy movie. I think the Hallmark channel is already showing Christmas movies."

Graham pointed a finger at her. "Not until Thanksgiving."

"No, I think they started right after Halloween."

"I mean no watching holiday movies until after Thanksgiving. Or Christmas music. Or decorations." Even in her sorry state, some things were sacred.

Jess lifted both hands. "Yes, ma'am. I forgot you had such strong feelings on the matter." She lifted a shoulder. "There's always *Love, Actually.*"

Graham smiled. It was her favorite old standby, and not technically a holiday movie. "Indeed there is."

Jess left and Graham fixed herself another cup of tea. She returned to the sofa and tried to coax Athena to snuggle with her. It didn't work. She covered her legs with a blanket instead and watched five back-to-back episodes of a home improvement show whose premise seemed to test the boundaries of what could be painted white and then distressed. It was oddly addicting and Graham found herself scanning the room for a piece of furniture begging for such treatment. She frowned. Probably not a good look for the IKEA table.

At noon, Graham hauled herself to the bathroom for a shower. Clean clothes would keep Jess from worrying too much. She toweldried her hair and settled on leggings and an oversize sweater. Still not really pants, but sort of.

She wandered back to the living room and studied the sofa for a moment. Instead of giving in to the soft nothingness it promised, she went to the kitchen. She'd make dinner. It would be good for her. It would also be a nice way to thank Jess for coddling her for the last few days. She opened the fridge and stared into it blankly. The usual yogurt and hummus and crème brûlée coffee creamer stared back at her. Graham sighed. She would have to go to the store.

She looked down at her outfit. It counted as being dressed, or close enough. She pulled on boots and her coat, grabbed her wallet and keys, and walked out of the apartment before she could reconsider.

Ten minutes later, she found herself at the Stop & Shop. The wind whipped through the fabric of her leggings and she lamented not going with real pants. Fortunately, it was a quick dash from the parking lot into the store.

Fluorescent light shone brightly and Christmas music was already being piped in via invisible speakers. Graham grabbed a basket and headed to the produce department before stopping and looking around. She had no idea what to make and even less of an idea what to buy. Poor planning on her part.

"Graham?"

At hearing her name, Graham turned and found Renata giving her a quizzical look. Graham offered her a smile. "Hi."

"Hi. Are you okay? You seem," she paused, as though looking for the right word, "lost."

Graham couldn't help but laugh at the accuracy, and absurdity, of the statement. "I decided to make dinner, but didn't get any farther than that."

"I've been there."

"So, uh, how are you?" Graham assumed Renata knew about her and Mat, but she didn't know how much. Hell, for all she knew, Mat and Dom weren't speaking either.

Renata smiled. "I'm good. I've been thinking about you. Dom told me what happened."

It was a relief to have Renata break the ice, much better than having it floating out there all awkward. Graham shook her head and sighed. "I've been better."

"Do you want to come to dinner? I'm cooking at Dom's. Nothing fancy."

The thought of being so close to Mat's apartment made Graham's chest constrict. "That's a very sweet offer."

"But it would be weird. I understand."

Graham cringed. "Was I that obvious?"

Renata smiled, even more kindly than before, if that was possible. "It was silly of me to invite you. Or, thoughtless, at least. You know, if it counts for anything, we're both still pulling for you."

Graham couldn't see how things would work themselves out, but she wasn't ready to give up hope. Not yet. "It does."

"Are you waiting for Mat to apologize?"

Was she? Yes, but it was more than that. "It's more about her deciding what we have means enough to her."

Renata nodded. "That makes sense. Well, if there's anything either of us can do, just say the word."

Graham realized in that moment how much Dom and Renata had come to mean to her. Before she could do anything about it, her eyes filled and a couple of tears spilled over. "Thanks."

"Oh, honey." Renata set her basket down and threw her arms around Graham.

The gesture made Graham cry harder, but also laugh. When Renata let go, Graham wiped her eyes and sniffed. "God, I'm such a sad sack."

Renata pointed at her. "You are not. You're smart and strong and the best thing that's happened to Mat in like forever."

Graham sniffed again. "I wish she thought so."

"She does. She's just stubborn. It's a trait that runs in the family." Graham nodded. She thought about Dom's way of going about things, as well as what she knew of Mat's parents. "Yeah."

Renata picked her basket up. "Are you going to be okay?"

For the second time that day, Graham straightened her shoulders and took a deep breath. "I will be. I still have no idea what to make for dinner, but yes. I'm okay."

Renata hooked an arm though hers. "That's easy. Come with me."

An hour later, Graham was back home with the makings for a simple, hearty soup. She started chopping vegetables, following Renata's instructions exactly. It was a small step toward feeling normal, but she'd take it. She also took the threads of hope Renata had offered her. She needed to be realistic, but she wanted to believe that Renata—and Dom—had insight into Mat that she didn't.

Jess came home from work and didn't even try to hide her enthusiasm that Graham was up and about and seemed more like herself. Graham didn't know if it was the soup or the vote of confidence from Renata, but as she sat at the little kitchen table with Jess eating the best meal she'd ever made herself, Graham felt warm, inside and out.

❖

Mat didn't hear from Graham after they fought. She didn't hear from her the next day, either. Or the day after that. She cajoled Dom into going out with her to haul in another set of traps. The air was cold and damp and biting. By the end, they were both miserable and cranky.

She didn't sleep. Well, that wasn't entirely true. She slept in small, fitful bursts that brought dreams of being lost in dense fog. Each time she woke, her sheets tangled around her body in a way that told her the sleep had been anything but restful. In the morning, she drank the better half of a pot of coffee, adding a sour stomach to her generally sorry state. She needed to get out of the house, put her mind on anything but the fact that she had absolutely no idea what to do. She needed to be out on the water.

Mat contemplated calling Dom, but that would entail him trying to make her feel better. She didn't want to inflict that on him, or herself. She looked at the weather. Cold, but nothing more than cloudy skies and a brisk breeze. Yes, she'd told Dom she wouldn't go out alone again. But she was desperate. She wouldn't go far, or for long. It was more about being on the water at this point than hauling traps. She needed that, needed the wind and the sea to take her mind off the colossal mess she'd made of her life.

Having a plan took a little of the edge off. She got dressed and, even though she didn't want it, made a peanut butter sandwich. After locking her door, she looked up at Dom's apartment, as though he might be watching and catch her sneaking off. But there was no movement in the windows. He and Renata were probably still curled together in bed, naked and warm.

Her mind instantly went to Graham, to the last morning they'd woken up together. Less than a week had passed, but in some ways, it felt like ages ago. Mat tried to shake off the memory, the visceral longing that, if she let it, could bring her to her knees.

One foot in front of the other, she made it to her truck and climbed in. The streets were quiet, the morning misty and gray. Even the pier had little traffic. Many of the yachts and small leisure boats had already been pulled out of the water for the season. The few that remained were lifeless, awaiting their own hibernation.

Mat didn't worry about bait or the other things she'd usually take care of on a work day. If she couldn't haul traps, she wouldn't have to worry about breaking her promise to Dom. Maybe she'd do a little fishing. It was a hobby she rarely had time for, but one she enjoyed on occasion.

She powered up the engine and maneuvered out of her slip. The temperature had taken yet another dip and the clouds were low. She wouldn't be surprised if they had snow within the week. Despite the biting cold, the air felt good on her face. The sharpness of it demanded her attention, keeping her thoughts away from her parents and the shitty choices she'd made in her life. And Graham.

If this was any other moment in Mat's life, any other woman, she'd have already washed her hands of it and walked away. Even now, even with Graham, that had a certain appeal. But just as her mind would start down that path, her chest would tighten and she'd feel the stirrings of what she could only describe as a panic attack. It was unfamiliar territory, and unnerving.

It wasn't even a matter of apologizing. No, she didn't relish saying she was sorry, but she wasn't one of those ridiculously stubborn people who loathed the very idea. She just didn't know exactly what she would be apologizing for. Overreacting, sure. But Graham was mad about a lot more than that. She wanted and expected more than Mat had been willing to give. Even if she fell to her knees and professed her undying love to Graham, Mat wasn't sure it would be enough.

That's what frightened her most. What if she went through the motions, said and did all the right things, and it still wasn't enough? What if Graham wanted more out of life than Mat could offer?

Realizing she'd once again slipped down a rabbit hole of questions and doubt, Mat shifted the engine to idle. She checked the GPS and noted she'd gone a bit farther than she'd intended. In spite of her sorry state, she chuckled at herself. At the rate she was going, she'd wash ashore in Boston before she pulled her head out of her ass.

She went below deck in search of one of the fishing poles she kept and a lure. Ten minutes later, she was positioned at the back of the boat with a line in the water. The rhythmic letting out and pulling in soothed her and she lost track of time. Nothing was biting, but she didn't really care.

When a large gust of wind almost knocked her over, Mat looked around. The sky had darkened, at least to the west. Probably time to call it a day. Even if it wasn't an actual storm, she didn't want to deal with getting soaked and slapped around by choppy waves.

Mat pulled in her line and stowed the pole. She hadn't found any answers, but she'd managed to settle her mind a bit. Regardless of what came next, at this point, she'd take it.

Chapter Twenty-eight

Graham looked at her phone and frowned. Dom. Probably trying to play matchmaker again. Or, perhaps at this point, a better description would be mediator. She almost let it go to voice mail, but relented. It wasn't his fault Mat was being so stubborn and everything was a mess. "Hello."

"Damn it."

Graham pulled the phone away and checked the screen, as if that might explain the expletive in place of a greeting, then returned it to her ear. "Um, you're the one who called me."

"Sorry." Dom's voice was thick with tension. "I was half-hoping you wouldn't answer because it might mean you were with Mat."

"Well, to the best of my knowledge, hell hasn't frozen over, so no. She's still avoiding me. What's going on?"

"I think she might have taken the boat out alone again and there's a band of thunderstorms coming that weren't in the forecast."

Graham processed the words, but it took a minute for their meaning to sink in. A knot of panic gripped her stomach. "Why would she be out alone?"

"She pulled this on me a few weeks ago. I thought we'd come to an agreement, but the *Paquette* isn't in its slip."

"Wait. Pulled what?" Graham understood what he was saying, but part of her brain lagged. Perhaps if she focused on the specifics, she could hold the possibilities at bay. She didn't like the possibilities that were already lurking at the edges on her mind.

"She's been sullen and antsy. But she didn't," Dom's voice cracked slightly, "want to tear me away from Renata. She went hauling by herself. I flipped out and she said she wouldn't do it again."

Graham nodded, although there was no one to see. "Okay. So what makes you think she would go against her word?"

"The boat's gone and no one can get a hold of her."

Right. Crap. "Would she really put herself in danger?"

"Normally, no."

The implication hung in the air. Things weren't normal. Because of her. "What can I do?"

"Nothing at the moment. Especially panic. I'm going to head to the pier, see if I can get her on the radio. She might be completely fine and on her way in."

Or not. Graham thought about their last conversation. Mat had been angry, although it felt like that anger was directed more at the world than at her. But more than that, Graham sensed defeat. It was the latter that worried her now. People who felt like they had nothing to lose had a tendency to do stupid and reckless things. "I'll meet you there."

"You don't have to—"

"I'll meet you there."

Graham threw on clothes and left her apartment without looking back. Walking gave way to a jog and, by the time she hit the center of town, she'd broken into a full run. When she finally reached the harbor master's office, her legs ached and her lungs screamed for oxygen. She took a minute to catch her breath, afraid she'd burst in and be unable to speak. Talk about sowing panic. That minute gave her enough time to look over to where Mat's boat should be. The slip was empty.

A few others were, too. That made her feel a sliver better, like Mat wasn't out on treacherous seas alone. She also glanced at the sky. There were a few dark clouds to the west, but the sun shone and only a light breeze rustled the flags on the other boats in the harbor. Maybe Dom was overreacting. Please let him be overreacting.

"Hey." Dom appeared next to her.

"Hi." He seemed neither out of breath nor panicked. But his eyes held a shadow of worry. "Have you talked with Stuart yet?"

Graham shook her head. "I just got here."

Dom nodded. "Okay. I'm sorry if I got you all upset. That wasn't my intention."

"You didn't." She realized she was lying. "I mean, I'm glad you did. Told me. I'm glad I'm here."

He nodded again and headed into the office. Graham followed. She looked around. Such an important part of what kept the harbor safe and running smoothly, yet in the two years she'd worked off MacMillan Pier, she'd never been inside. That was probably true for most of her colleagues on the Dolphin Fleet, a fact that made her kind of sad. She shook off the feeling to focus on the task at hand.

She tuned into the conversation Dom was having with Stuart. He seemed calm, and she was pretty sure no one had uttered the words Coast Guard. That had to be a good thing. Stuart turned his attention to the panel of equipment that sat along one wall of his office. He turned a few knobs, then spoke into a microphone, calling to the *Paquette* and asking her location.

They waited.

"Shouldn't she be responding?" Graham whispered in Dom's ear.

"Sometimes it takes a few tries. If she's not at the wheel, she might not hear the first time."

A perfectly plausible explanation. Not that it made her feel any better. Stuart repeated himself. Again they waited.

A voice crackled over the speaker, but it belonged to a man with a thick New England accent. "Crossed paths with her about an hour ago. She was headed north. Over."

Dom swore under his breath while Stuart thanked the captain of the *Donna Jane* for the information. Stuart tried a third time and Graham had to fight the urge to rip the microphone from his hands and yell into it for Mat to fucking answer them already.

She was spared from embarrassing herself by the sound of Mat's voice. "This is the *Paquette.* Over."

Stuart relayed the weather forecast and asked Mat's location. Mat responded with her coordinates and a confirmation that she could very clearly see the storm approaching and was heading in. Dom pointed to the microphone, which Stuart activated. Dom leaned over his shoulder. "Be quick about it. I'll be waiting here to kick your ass. Over."

"Just needed some fresh air, man, a little fishing. You'll have to contain yourself. Over."

Dom laughed, but indicated he wanted to say something else. Stuart obliged. "We'll see about that. Over."

Graham joined Dom in thanking Stuart. They stepped back out onto the pier. Graham glanced at the sky. The clouds on the horizon were closer and more menacing than they had been. Still. Mat was on her way back. Graham told herself to relax.

"Sorry I got you all worried and dragged you down here for nothing."

Graham shook her head. "No, I'm glad you did." She looked at the sky again. "Do you think she's going to make it?"

Dom put a hand on her shoulder. "She'll be fine. I probably overreacted. I was mad because we talked about it and I thought she was hauling without me anyway."

Right. There was no reason at all an experienced fisherman couldn't take her boat out alone. The primary danger in their line of work came from the possibility of getting caught up in the ropes and the lift and the weighted traps. Bad weather was coming, but between modern technology and her relative proximity to shore, Mat would be fine. Assuming she didn't do anything stupid.

"Are you going to wait here until she gets back?" Graham asked Dom. She didn't want to leave, but Mat didn't even know she was there. And if their last conversation was anything to go on, she wouldn't be welcome.

Dom nodded. "I am. I'm worried about her. She doesn't go out for fresh air."

"Yeah." Graham had thought that, but it wasn't her place to say so.

"You should, too." Now that his fears were allayed, Dom seemed to give her his full attention. "I mean, if you want to."

Graham sighed. "I always want to be where Mat is. It's the being wanted that's the problem."

"I know it's hard. Are you," Dom stopped, as though he didn't want to finish the sentence. He met her eyes. "Are you thinking about giving up?"

Only about a thousand times a day. And another few hundred during the endless hours of night. But every time she told herself she needed to walk away, the pain that settled in her chest became unbearable. She couldn't go on like this forever. She refused to be the woman who pined for someone she'd never have. But she wasn't at that point. Not yet. "No."

Dom nodded. "Good."

"You don't think I've crossed the line into pathetic?"

He scowled. "Absolutely not. Mat is a stubborn ass, but if I didn't believe you two were perfect for each other, I'd never encourage you to stick around."

"Thanks." A flash of lightning in the distance caught both their attention. Graham swallowed, a lump of apprehension in her throat. "I hope she beats the storm."

"I was just thinking the same—"

Stuart appeared in the doorway of the office. "Oh, good. You're still here."

Graham didn't miss a beat. "What is it? What's wrong?"

"Mat's out of fuel. She just radioed in for help."

Dom dropped his head. "Son of a bitch."

"She said the storm is close and she's going to go below deck and wait it out."

Graham didn't like any part of that plan. "Can't we send someone out now?" She turned to Dom. "How did she run out of gas in the first place?"

"She was fucking careless, that's how. That's what's been worrying me so much—not that she's going out alone, but the fact that she's doing it with only half her brain working. That's how people get themselves killed," Dom said.

Graham felt the blood drain from her face. She felt lightheaded and swore her body temperature dropped five degrees. Even as she told herself Dom was talking in extremes, the reality of the risks Mat took every day hit Graham like a punch to the stomach. "Do you think—"

"Jesus. I'm sorry, Graham. I shouldn't have said that." Dom looked at her with alarm.

Graham chuckled feebly. She must look even worse than she felt. "It's okay. I know what you meant. Really, though. What are we going to do?"

"I'll call my dad about taking his boat. I'll bring her enough diesel to get home."

"How about I call the Coast Guard?"

Graham had forgotten Stuart was still standing there. His face looked more worried now than when they didn't know where Mat was. "Is it getting worse?" she asked.

"Worse than I'm comfortable with. The last thing I want is two boats caught in a storm."

Graham couldn't decide if the suggestion made her feel better or worse. She didn't want Dom going out alone, but she also hated any scenario that called for the Coast Guard.

"They're better equipped for rough seas. And faster." Stuart's voice was confident and sure.

Graham was convinced and it seemed as though Dom was, too. He said, "Okay. What do you need from us?"

"Not a thing. I'll call it in and then we wait."

Wait. Graham looked out at the water. The entire western half of the sky had darkened. Flashes of lightning were constant and the first rumbles of thunder sounded in the distance.

❖

Mat swore. She tried to start the engine even though she already knew nothing would happen. Engines didn't turn over when the fuel tank was empty. When she'd already tried to start it ten times before. When she'd already radioed for help.

How could she have been such an idiot? Because she'd let herself get distracted, be careless.

It was one thing for Dom to know, to give her a hard time. He had that blend of haranguing and genuine concern that made him annoying, but tolerable. Now she'd broken one of the cardinal rules of fishing and everyone—everyone—would know it.

She glanced up at the menacing clouds. Fucking storm. It hadn't been in the forecast. Although, given the strange temperature swings of the last few days, she shouldn't be surprised. But if it weren't for that, she could have radioed in and the only people she'd have riding her ass would be Stuart and Dom. And Stuart hardly counted. He was a good guy and, for a man who made his living with fishermen, wasn't a gossip.

She shook her head. She was doing it again, allowing her mind to run a thousand different directions when she had things to do. God, it was pathetic. She could hardly stand herself. It didn't help that the rain had started, the kind of cold rain that refused to turn to snow on principle. She'd dressed warmly, but not in rain or fishing gear. It didn't take much for her clothes to soak through.

Before another wave of self-loathing took over, she finished stowing anything that wasn't bolted down. Tools, ropes, her logs—everything went into the small hold at the front of the boat. She hated the idea of including herself in that list, but with no fuel, she'd be useless on deck. No, she'd backed herself right into a corner of helplessness.

The good news was that she had no real fear of capsizing. The *Paquette* had weathered a lot. She was a squat, sturdy thing and Mat felt safer aboard her than just about anywhere else. She'd ride it out, then deal with the humiliation of being rescued.

Feeling everything was as secure as it could be, she went down below. She spent a moment securing things in the hold so she'd have less worry about things sliding and flying and otherwise making a mess. After a moment of hesitation, she slipped on a life vest and pulled the straps tight. When that was done, she looked around. Nothing to do now but wait.

The waves picked up, causing the boat to lurch from side to side. The choppiness that never bothered her on deck made her queasy. It had to be the lack of a horizon, the smell of diesel. Those explanations were far preferable to the idea that the weather was more severe than she anticipated, or that she might in any way be in danger.

Although she had no signal, Mat kept her phone on to keep track of time. Minutes passed slowly, to the point of being painful. She'd never done well with sitting quietly. Feeling powerless and trapped made it a thousand times worse. And no amount of fidgeting could stop her brain from spiraling in a dozen directions—her mother's version of things with Lindsay, Graham's face when they fought, Dom's worry. So much for taking her mind off things.

It wasn't long before the rain intensified enough to lash against the side of the boat. Based on the sound it made pinging off the metal, Mat was pretty sure ice and sleet were mixed in. As the boat listed, she tried to relax and let her body move with it. Not only did that not help, she found herself on the wet and dirty floor of the hold.

Mat let out a string of expletives that didn't make her feel better. If Dom were there, he'd call her on it, but maybe also give her points for creativity. They'd at least get a laugh out of things while they waited.

Mat closed her eyes and let her imagination take over. Graham was there, not Dom. And they weren't caught in a storm without fuel. It was late summer and the sun was shining. Unlike the day they went out together and hauled traps, they were out for the sake of being on the water, together. The breeze would be salty and warm and Mat would be able to taste the sea on Graham's lips when she kissed her.

She was yanked back to reality when a wave hit with such force, she thought for a second the boat might actually tip. The lick of fear in her belly was unfamiliar and unpleasant. She made her way to the door and kept her hand firmly on the latch. She wouldn't survive long in the frigid water, but it would be better than going down with the boat. She wasn't much for praying, but her childhood training kicked in. The Hail Marys and Our Fathers proved soothing if nothing else.

Mat lost track of how long she stood like that, poised for action she hoped she wouldn't need to take. Eventually, the roiling lessened. The rain stopped, or at least let up. She let go of the handle and tried to work the cramp out of her hand. She looked around the tiny space, said a prayer of thanks that it wouldn't be the last thing she saw.

When the worst of the waves seemed to pass, Mat decided to venture out. The sky had lightened and the wind had died down considerably. She looked around for signs of damage. Nothing appeared out of order, although flecks of sleet remained on the windows and ledges of the boat. Mat almost lost her footing; a layer of ice had settled on the deck as well. All in all, things weren't nearly as bad as they could have been.

She picked up the radio transmitter and prepared to swallow her pride. "*Paquette* to Coast Guard. Over."

The reply was immediate. "*Paquette,* this is Coast Guard Vessel 136. We are en route to your last reported location. Over."

Mat checked the GPS which, thankfully, was still functioning. "I seem to have drifted south a ways. I'm at," She rattled off her coordinates and ended with, "Over."

The female voice on the other end of the radio repeated the coordinates. Mat confirmed and got reassurance they'd be to her location shortly. Mat thanked her. She switched channels and called up the harbormaster's office to let Stuart and Dom know she was safe. She expected judgment, or at least some mild ribbing, but the only thing she could detect in Stuart's voice was relief.

It was at that moment everything caught up to her—the ordeal of the storm, the fight with Graham, the fight with Dom, her parents. Angry, exhausted tears spilled down her cheeks, the heat of them immediately chilled by the air. She'd spent her entire adult life avoiding entanglements that would make her feel this way and it had all been for nothing. She let her guard down and now she was miserable, and quite possibly alone.

The sound of an approaching boat snapped Mat back to the moment. She swiped away the tears and sniffed a few times. Not the time to fall apart.

The whine of the engine intensified and the Coast Guard lifeboat came up alongside her. The two members of the crew were professional and kind. If they were judging her stupidity, they didn't let it show. They helped her pour a few gallons of diesel into her empty tank and stood by while Mat went to restart the engine.

Instead of hearing it roar to life, she was rewarded with a sad gurgling sound. "Fuck." She turned her attention to her rescuers. "I think the starting block must have taken on some water."

The older woman nodded in a matter-of-fact way. "Not surprising given the last hour. We're not equipped for towing, but we should be able to get someone out here in a few hours. The worst of the weather has passed."

Mat cringed at the cost and the added hassle, but knew she was still making out easy. "Yeah."

"We'll radio it in and you can ride back to shore with us."

"I'd rather not—"

She didn't let Mat finish. "All due respect, ma'am. You're wet and shivering, probably not far from hypothermia. You should come with us."

As much as she didn't want to leave her boat, refusing would make her seem even more stubborn and foolish than she already did. "Yeah, okay."

"Don't worry about a distress flag. They'll be looking for it."

Mat looked around. There was nothing she needed to take with her at this point. "Thanks."

The younger man hooked a pole to her side railing to bring the sides of their two boats close and hold them steady. Mat stepped from one to the other, then turned to look back at the *Paquette*. It seemed foolish, but it felt like she was leaving her child behind.

"They'll take good care of her." It was the woman who said it, and her eyes were full of understanding.

Mat chuckled at being so transparent. "Right."

The younger guy used the same pole to gently push the boats apart. The next thing Mat knew, they were in motion. Relief was the strongest feeling she had as they headed toward shore. Still, she couldn't help but look back at her boat, growing smaller with each passing second. Just as she couldn't tear her thoughts from what awaited her back on land. And square at the top of that list sat Graham.

Chapter Twenty-nine

The storm had pushed the temperature down a good twenty degrees. So now, in addition to being soaking wet, she was freezing. She'd refused one of those foil blankets because the idea of wrapping herself in one was at least one layer of pathetic she could avoid. But now, with her teeth chattering and her soggy clothes plastered to her skin, she realized the ship of self-dignity had sailed a while back.

She took the blanket.

Mat half-expected the entire town to be standing on the pier, awaiting her return. When she saw that wasn't the case, she felt her muscles relax slightly. People were coming and going and, with the sun shining, it seemed no one was the wiser. Almost no one.

She made out Dom, standing with his legs braced and his arms folded across his chest. Next to him stood Graham.

Mat swallowed. Her chest constricted and, for the first time in this whole ordeal, she found it difficult to breathe. Only for a moment had she truly worried about her safety. Even then, the frustration and the embarrassment were tantamount. She'd imagined Dom would be angry, then judgmental. She realized now, though, that she'd made him worry. She felt small and stupid and, perhaps worst of all, selfish.

And Graham. It had only been a few days since they fought at the trap yard, but it felt like an eternity. The yearning in Mat's body, in her very bones, consumed her. The rescue boat pulled into a slip and one of the crew helped Mat onto the pier. She thanked them again, trying not to loathe how insufficient the words seemed.

Mat climbed the ramp to the main part of the pier. Dom and Graham moved toward her. As relieved as she was to be back on land, a feeling of trepidation sat heavy in her stomach. And then she looked at Graham. Their eyes met and Mat couldn't feel anything but longing.

She tore her gaze away long enough to look at Dom. His face held a strange mixture of tension and relief. She opened her mouth to say something, but no words came out. Before she could try again, Mat found herself pulled into a hug. She couldn't believe how warm and strong Dom felt. But before she could process that, he let her go. Another pair of arms came around her. Smaller, but with a grip that felt fierce and protective. And familiar.

It was the familiarity that did her in. Mat's mind flashed to a dozen moments when she'd been wrapped up in that embrace—in bed, on their first real date, after meeting Graham's aunt. The tears came fast and hot and she was powerless to stop them.

Graham's hold on her tightened even more. Mat felt the warmth of her breath near her ear as she said, "You scared me to death."

Mat laughed, but it came out as one of those awkward sounds that sounded a lot like a sob. She pulled back, looked at Graham's face, then Dom's. "I'm sorry."

Dom gripped her shoulder. "You should be, you stubborn son of a bitch."

The insult, and all the love she could feel behind it, made the tears flow even more. She couldn't remember the last time she was such a mess. Graham reached over and smacked Dom in the arm. "Don't be mean."

He laughed. Mat did, too. She offered him a wry smile. "It's how he displays affection. Very macho."

Graham gave a weak chuckle, but her face remained tense. "Right."

Suddenly self-conscious about Graham being there in the first place, Mat made eye contact. "I'm sorry you got pulled into this, and that you worried."

Mat realized she had no idea why Graham was there. She wasn't in her Dolphin Fleet polo, so she couldn't have happened upon Dom coming or going from work. He must have called her, told her. A certain discomfort joined the embarrassment. Combined with the exhaustion and, to be honest, genuine fear stirred up in the last few hours, she found herself overwhelmed by what it might all mean.

Graham closed her eyes and shook her head. "I love you, you stubborn woman. There's nowhere else I'd be."

The words sank in. Even more than the words was Graham's matter-of-fact tone. Like she really did want to be there. Like she hated being there, but understood it came with the territory and was okay with that. Less like a girlfriend and more like a partner.

Suddenly dizzy, Mat closed her eyes and tried to keep the ground from shifting under her feet.

"You look like shit," Dom said. "How about we get you home?"

"I won't argue." Mat wanted nothing more than to sit down. Well, maybe a hot shower, then sit down.

Dom looked at Graham. "Can you stay with her? I'll go get my truck."

"We'll wait right here."

Dom left and Mat, now alone with Graham, found herself at a loss for words. "Graham, I—"

"Shh." Graham slid an arm around her waist. "We have plenty of time for talking. It'll keep."

The permission not to talk it out felt like such a gift. Mat offered her a smile. "Thanks."

Dom pulled around and they climbed in, sitting three across on the old bench seat. The drive home took no more than ten minutes, but Mat grew fidgety. Now that she wasn't worried about her life or being a laughingstock, her mind could fixate on how wet and uncomfortable she was.

They got out of the truck. Graham didn't ask if she should stay or look at her questioningly. She simply took Mat's hand and led her to the door. Mat pulled keys from her sodden pocket, then realized with embarrassment that her hands were trembling. Again, without saying anything, Graham took them from her and let them in. Mat turned to her cousin. "Thanks for, well, thanks."

He nodded and she could see the toll the day had taken on him. A wave of guilt washed over her, colder and lousier than the actual waves that had pummeled her just hours before. But then he offered her a smile, the kind that told her he wasn't done giving her a hard time, but that everything would be okay. "Get some rest. I'll see you tomorrow."

Mat gave in to the urge to hug him. "Tell Renata I'm sorry I pulled you away."

"She's spending the day with her sisters. I think they're looking at dresses." He shrugged, but there was a sparkle in his eyes that told her he didn't mind the idea one bit. "Call if you need anything."

"Will do." Inside, Mat had a sudden urge to gather Graham into her arms and kiss her senseless. The urge to get out of her wet clothes won out, though. She started peeling them off. "I desperately need—"

"A shower." Graham smiled. "You get in and I'll throw your wet things in the washer."

"Thanks." She wanted to say a thousand other things. You don't have to stay. Please stay. I've missed you. I need you and it terrifies me. Not sure any of them were right, she headed into the bathroom.

She left her clothes in a heap on the floor and turned the water on extra hot. Her skin was so cold, though, she had to ease it down a bit to be able to stand it. She stood under the spray for a long while, then scrubbed her skin and scalp. She turned off the shower and she reached for her towel, but it wasn't there. A second later, the bathroom door opened about a foot and it appeared, held out by Graham's arm. "I threw it in the dryer to warm it up," she said from the other side.

"Um, thanks." It seemed like a weird thing to do, but as Mat dried off and wrapped herself in it, she understood the appeal. Had she really never had a warm towel before?

"Do you want me to bring you some clothes?"

"I'll get them."

The arm disappeared and the door closed. Mat took a moment to study her reflection in the mirror. It was the same face that had stared back at her this morning, but it felt different. Like she'd aged several years in the course of a day.

She shook off the feeling and padded to her bedroom. She found her favorite sweatpants and pulled them on, along with a thermal shirt and a hoodie. Since she clearly had given up any notion of looking good, she added wool socks and her beat-up slippers.

Mat found Graham puttering in the kitchen. At the sound of Mat's footsteps, she turned. "I'm warming soup. It's nothing fancy, but your fridge is in pretty dire straits."

Mat chuckled. She'd been living on frozen junk and takeout. "It's perfect. Thank you."

"I boiled water for tea, but could put on coffee if you'd prefer."

"Tea is good. Caffeine is the last thing I want right now."

Graham smiled. "I thought maybe. Sit. I'll get it for you."

Mat did as she was told and watched Graham put tea bags into a pair of mugs, add water from the kettle. She brought them both to the table before returning her attention to the stove. "You really didn't have to—"

Graham turned. Something resembling impatience flashed in her eyes. "I want to. Please don't argue with me tonight. We can argue tomorrow if you want."

The sternness caught Mat off guard. It was weird, but she liked it. Well, maybe like wasn't the right word. She got it. And for some reason, it made her feel better, cared for. "Okay."

Graham ladled up soup and carried bowls to the table. Spoons and napkins followed. Mat hadn't been coddled like this since she was a child. Even then, she only got this level of attention if she was sick. Graham sat across from her, lifted her mug in a silent toast. Mat mirrored the gesture before bringing the steaming liquid to her lips.

Graham didn't force additional conversation. Mat appreciated that, especially since she probably had a dozen questions about what had transpired. They fell into a comfortable silence. As Mat ate, she felt the remaining chill leave her body. Along with it, the tension in her back and shoulders, in her legs, in muscles she didn't even know she had, dissolved.

About halfway through, Graham got up to add hot water to their mugs. It was a casual thing; she didn't even speak. It felt easy, relaxed, domestic. Mat let that last word sit in her mind. She would have expected it to give her a ripple of panic, but it didn't. Not that she'd want this level of attention every day, but at the moment, it didn't feel smothering. It felt good. Really good.

She was just processing that as Graham stood and began to clear the table. "I hope it's not too forward, but I'd rather not let you out of my sight for at least the next twelve hours. How do you feel about that?"

Mat didn't hesitate. "Fine. Good."

"Good. Are you ready to pile into bed? Watch a movie?"

It was nearly dark out, but even in her current state of exhaustion, Mat couldn't imagine going to sleep just yet. "Movie. You pick." She thought for a moment, then added, "Anything but *The Perfect Storm*."

Graham laughed and Mat realized how much she'd missed that sound. They moved to the couch and Graham grabbed the blanket from the back and tossed it over both of them. She picked up the remote. "I know you like action, but I'm thinking tonight might call for a comedy."

After confirming that they'd both seen *The Princess Bride* at least a dozen times, Graham queued it up. The jokes were as cheesy as she remembered and the familiarity proved soothing. Mat's eyes started to droop shortly after Buttercup was rescued the first time and she didn't even bother trying to fight it. She had a vague sensation of Graham's fingers in her hair, of shuffling into the bedroom. Everything else was a blur—a warm, dry, safe blur.

Chapter Thirty

Graham woke with a start. She'd lain awake for a long time after Mat fell asleep. Part of her simply wallowed in having Mat next to her. After so many nights alone, it felt like being home. And after being scared out of her mind yesterday—fearing every horrible, tragic scenario imaginable—having Mat curled against her felt like a gift. Not knowing how long it might last made her not want to miss even a minute.

But her own fatigue had eventually won out. And now here she was, snuggled under the covers in a state resembling bliss. Despite telling herself to simply enjoy it, her mind began turning. What did it mean? What next?

As if sensing her wakefulness, Mat stirred. Her arm, slung around Graham's middle, squeezed and pulled her closer. In spite of her internal monologue, Graham's body responded. The press of Mat's nipples against her back made her own ache to be touched.

Mat's hand slid up, caressed the underside of Graham's breast. Graham bit her lip, wanting more, but afraid of waking Mat completely. She shifted slightly, moving her backside against Mat's abdomen. Mat mumbled something, pushed against Graham.

When Mat's fingers found her nipple, Graham arched, unable to stop herself. Mat eased away and Graham rolled onto her back. She would not cry. She wouldn't.

But instead of rolling away, Mat used the change of positions to roll until she was half on top of Graham. Eyes still closed, she nuzzled into Graham's neck, kissing her way up to Graham's ear. "I missed you."

Graham's mind raced. Joy and hope and a chaser of anxiety coursed through her. "Yeah," she whispered.

Mat slid a hand across Graham's hip to the apex of her thighs. "Is this okay?"

"Yes. Please."

Mat eased into her and Graham sighed. She'd been wrong before. This felt like home. Mat sucked in a breath. "How are you this wet?"

Graham let out a ragged laugh. "I want you. I'm in a constant state of wanting you."

She feared Mat might say something funny or self-deprecating, but instead she pulled Graham into a kiss that felt like it might melt her bones. Slow, but hungry. Passionate, yet gentle. When Mat pulled away, Graham opened her eyes. Mat's stare held an intensity she'd never seen before. "I feel the same way about you."

They made love slowly. It had only been a week, but it seemed like they were getting to know one another all over again. Graham opened to Mat's touch, welcoming her back in. Mat caressed and coaxed, making promises and keeping them at the same time.

Graham came quietly, with a sigh instead of a scream. Mat kissed her forehead, her cheeks. "Please don't cry."

She'd not even realized she was crying. She lifted her hands to cup Mat's face. "It's okay. I'm okay."

Again, Mat's eyes were on her, searching her face. "I don't want to hurt you."

The apprehension, the sadness in Mat's voice, broke her heart. This woman, the woman she loved, could be confident to the point of cocky when it came to every aspect of her life. Except love. When it came to love, she was terrified. Graham felt a peace settle inside her, along with the smallest swell of her own confidence. "Then stop running away from me."

Mat nodded, her expression solemn. "It's the only thing I know how to do."

"That's not true. You've just let yourself get really good at it." Graham held Mat's gaze, waiting for her eyes to cool, for the distance to return. It didn't.

"No one has ever minded before."

Graham didn't know if that was true, but it didn't matter at this point. The only thing that mattered was the two of them, and where they went from here. "Well, I do."

Mat offered a small smile. "I know. I didn't know what to do with that at first."

"And now?"

"And now I realize that it wasn't love or commitment or even a person I've been running from all this time. It's me. I've been trying to escape the parts of myself that threatened to take over, to consume everything else."

"I love those parts. All of them." Graham's heart beat erratically. She thought she understood where Mat was going, but held herself in check. She needed Mat to say it.

"You're the first person who has. I'm sorry I didn't handle that well. I'm sorry I pushed you away." Mat paused for a moment and Graham wondered if that was it. But then she took a deep breath and continued. "I love you."

Graham closed her eyes for a second, let the words wash over her. When she opened them, she found Mat searching her face, a look of worry in her eyes. For all that Graham had been wearing her heart on her sleeve, had said the same words the day before, Mat seemed terrified her feelings might not be returned. "I love you, too."

Mat nodded. Graham had the feeling it was the first time Mat truly believed it. "I promise I won't run away again."

The lightness Graham had been holding back took over, happiness radiating from her core. She wrapped her arms around Mat. "You damn well better not."

Mat laughed then, such a magical sound. Graham hadn't realized how long she'd gone without hearing it. And then Mat leaned in and kissed her. Soft, but sure. It held none of the questions, none of the uncertainty that had come to feel omnipresent in their relationship. The familiar edge of heat soon followed. Hands and mouths roamed. Without words, they explored and pleased. Like so many times before and yet so completely different.

❖

Dom checked in around noon. The exchange was brief. Knowing Graham was still there seemed to be enough to satisfy him, at least for the moment. Even if Dom was happy to forgive and forget, Mat knew they needed to talk, knew she needed to apologize. And, in the grand scheme of things, thank him. It was his patience, his stubbornness, that kept things from slipping past the point of no return.

She'd have to talk to her parents, too. The prospect of that didn't give Mat the anxiety it once had. Ironically, the conversation she'd had with them, as wretched as it was, gave her hope. She knew she wouldn't be disowned. If anything, standing up for herself, for the woman she loved, would probably help matters.

"What are you smiling about?" Graham, who'd gotten up to make coffee and rustle up some food, returned to the bedroom. She wore Mat's ratty robe and managed to make it look sexy.

"You."

Graham set down the mugs on the bedside table. She didn't believe for a second that's what Mat was actually smiling about, but the very fact she'd say so made Graham feel warm and fluttery. "Stop."

"I mean it. Given how much I tried to ruin things, they're going to turn out okay."

Graham swallowed. "You didn't try to ruin them."

"I did. It wasn't you specifically, but I was pretty hell-bent on not falling in love."

Even now, after everything, part of Graham worried that it might not be real. She worried Mat might be riding the emotional high of the last twenty-four hours and would eventually come down. If that happened, Graham didn't know where it would leave them. "And all that's changed with your near-death experience?"

"I didn't almost die."

The lack of conviction told Graham things had been scarier than Mat initially let on. "I'm just saying you've had an intense couple of days. Hell, it's been a crazy couple of weeks. I don't want you to say what you think you're supposed to say."

Graham sat on the bed. Mat sat up and scooted closer to her. "I get why you might be worried about that. But I'm sure about how I feel. I've never been more sure of anything."

Graham wanted to believe her. She wanted it so badly. "Okay."

"I need to tell you something."

And there it was. Graham bit her lip and held her breath.

"The day I found you and Dom at the trap yard, I'd been talking to my parents."

Not where she thought this was going. Graham forced herself to exhale. "Okay."

"I'd decided to tell them about us."

Holy crap.

"And it went badly, but not in the way I expected. Then I find the two of you, joking behind my back."

Graham smiled, although it felt bittersweet. "I asked Dom to talk because I wasn't sure if we were going anywhere. He was trying to convince me that we were."

Mat shook her head. "I'm sorry I overreacted and was a total ass."

"Wait." Graham narrowed her eyes. "What exactly are you apologizing for?"

Mat looked up at the ceiling and Graham worried for a second she didn't have an answer. But after a beat, she took a deep breath and launched in. "I'm sorry I was dismissive at first and wouldn't even consider a relationship. I'm sorry I freaked out when you met my family. I'm sorry I shut you out when I didn't know what to do with my feelings. I'm sorry I wrestled Dom to the ground in front of you. I'm sorry I got myself stranded in a storm and made you worry. And, maybe most of all, I'm sorry I didn't tell you I was in love with you the second I realized it."

Graham blinked, trying to take it all in. "Wow."

"There's probably more, but those are the highlights."

"That's a lot."

Mat smiled ruefully. "Did you forget just how much of an ass I've been? Maybe I shouldn't have reminded you."

Laughter bubbled up Graham's chest. Rather than hold it in, she let it out. A little titter turned into a rolling giggle. That gave way to the kind of laughter that made her snort. Eventually, she was laughing so hard, no sound came out at all. It was like all the emotions she'd been trying to keep under control finally found their escape. And rather than swallow her up, releasing them made her whole.

When she finally stopped, Mat looked at her with a kind of quiet alarm. It was so genuine, so real, Graham couldn't help but lean in and kiss her. It was a language Mat seemed to understand. When Graham eased away and looked at her, the worry was gone and Mat wore a hopeful smile. "So, we're okay?" she asked.

"Oh, Mat." How had she managed to win the heart of this amazing woman? "I'm yours, completely and entirely. We are so much more than okay."

"Well," Mat kissed her quickly, "as someone who technically could have died yesterday, I think that's the best news I've heard this week."

For a split second, Graham remembered the panic of the day before. Just the idea that Mat might have been lost made her shudder. "Promise me you won't ever do that again."

Mat kissed her again. "I promise."

"Good. Because you really did scare me half to death."

"And while we're on the topic of promises." Mat's face grew stern.

"Yeah?"

"I know better than to think I can always be exactly what you want, what you need."

"But?" Please, let there be a but.

"But I promise to try."

"And to not shut me out," Graham said.

"And to not shut you out." Mat took a deep breath. Graham couldn't be sure, but it sounded like one of those soul-cleansing breaths that only come around once in a great while. "I'm really over the moon for you, Graham."

Graham smiled and had one of those deep breaths of her own. "Over the moon and all the way back."

Chapter Thirty-one

One year later.

Mat curled her lip as Graham straightened the knot of her bow tie. Graham gave her a bland look. "Stop."

Mat sighed. "I guess it could be worse. I could have to be in a dress."

Graham dropped her hands to the lapels of Mat's jacket and pulled her close. "That's the spirit."

"That said, you make an exceptionally beautiful bridesmaid."

Graham took a step back and did a twirl. "This is a ton better than the taffeta monstrosity I had to wear to my cousin's wedding when I was in college."

"If anyone could pull off taffeta, my love, it would be you."

Graham beamed at her. "That's very sweet, but trust me. The dress was atrocious."

"I'm sure you looked stunning nonetheless." Mat kissed her, then stepped to the side to check her reflection. She wasn't big on suits, but had to admit this one looked nice. Renata had good taste. Actually, she wouldn't be opposed to wearing something similar for her own wedding. Mat smiled at the thought. It hadn't been that long ago that she'd dismissed the very concept of getting married. Now, here she was, decked out for her cousin's special day with an engagement ring burning a hole in her pocket.

"What are you grinning about?"

Mat wrapped her arms around Graham's waist. She lifted her off the ground and turned a slow circle. Mat set her down and kissed her again. "You."

"Really? That looked more like a cat who ate the canary kind of smile."

Mat shrugged and tried to relax her features. She had everything planned and blowing the surprise seven hours early wasn't part of it. "Just happy."

Graham beamed. "I know, right? It's hard to imagine a more perfect couple."

Mat could think of one, but didn't say so. "Or a more perfect day."

She'd been nervous when Dom and Renata planned a November wedding so they could honeymoon during the off season. Mat imagined a blizzard or, perhaps worse, a sleeting, slushy, muddy mess. But the day turned out sunny and just above freezing. It didn't get much better on the Cape at this time of year. "Agreed. You're going to help Renata get ready?"

"Given the number of sisters and aunts and cousins who will be fussing over her, I think my job is to drink a mimosa and try to keep her sane."

Mat laughed at the assessment because it was spot on. Graham had learned the quirks of her family, of the whole community, quickly. One of the many, many reasons she loved her. Mat slid a hand down her back and cupped her ass. "So, what you're saying is that no one would notice if you were the tiniest bit late."

Graham wiggled away and swatted at her. "You have a one-track mind."

"Not true." Mat shook her head and thought about how just untrue that was today. She needed to get a grip. "Okay, maybe a little bit true."

"Yeah. I'm sure." Graham took a step back but didn't take her eyes from Mat. "I'll see you at the church in a couple of hours?"

"You will. I haven't decided if Dom is going to be as cool as a cucumber or a train wreck, so I may or may not sneak away to find you."

"Stay with him. You're so much better for him than his brothers. We'll have the whole reception."

Mat looked at her hopefully. "And maybe I can get you to sneak away with me for a bit."

Graham folded her arms. "I am not having sex with you in a coat check room."

"I won't try, I promise."

Graham narrowed her eyes but didn't press. "Good."

"Are you ready to go? I'll drop you off."

"I was so hoping you'd say that."

"Give me a little credit." Mat led the way to the living room. She took Graham's coat from the rack and held it for her to slip on. She put hers on next, grabbed her keys. She put her hand on the knob to open the door but stopped. "I love you, you know."

Graham dropped her head, then looked up at her through those gorgeous lashes. "I love you, too."

The getting ready and ceremony passed in a blur. Mat had never seen Dom look more nervous, or more elated. Renata glowed. Mat managed to catch Graham's eye once or twice. Each time, her heart rate kicked up a notch—in part because Graham was so damn beautiful and partly because of what Mat had planned for later.

They stood and smiled and posed through an interminable number of pictures. At the reception, they were forced to sit at a massive head table, bridesmaids on one side and groomsmen on the other. Mat gave the toast she'd slaved over, getting a couple of laughs and maybe a tear or two. Dinner was served. Mat sipped a beer and tried to tune out the conversation Dom's brothers were having about soccer.

After the meal, Dom and Renata took to the dance floor. It gave her an excuse to get up and snag a seat abandoned by one of the other bridesmaids. Graham beamed at them. "Aren't they the cutest couple ever?"

"I think they might be. Well, after us, of course."

The DJ invited other couples to join them. Mat stood and extended a hand. "May I?"

"Yeah?" Graham looked at her with questioning eyes.

Mat didn't hesitate for a second. "Oh, yeah."

They danced to fast songs and slow, top forty hits and a traditional Portuguese waltz. Mat introduced Graham to relatives and family friends she hadn't seen since the last wedding, or maybe it was funeral. Some of them seemed genuinely happy for her. A few of the older set were cool toward them, but it could just as easily be based on the fact that she was wearing a suit and had short hair. Mat realized having a woman she loved by her side made the whole thing easier rather than harder.

After sharing a piece of cake, Mat decided now was her chance. "Sneak away with me for a second?"

Graham looked at her, eyes a mixture of desire and suspicion. "I thought you promised not to seduce me in the coat closet."

"I did. I won't. Promise."

"Okay." Graham tucked her hand into Mat's. "Lead the way."

Mat clasped her fingers. The warmth, the certainty of Graham's hand in hers, made Mat smile. "We do need our coats, though."

"Where are we going?"

"You'll see. Trust me."

They stepped outside. Mat led them along the side of the building and across the street. "Where are we going?"

"You'll see." Mat unlatched the gate. She gestured for Graham to lead the way.

She'd scoped out the deck before renting the place, then again that afternoon when she handed off the supplies. Will, God bless her, had outdone herself. Fairy lights glowed, reflecting warm light against the wood of the deck and the small piles of snow against the rail. The air was still and she could just make out the sound of water lapping against the sand.

"What is this?" Graham, still holding her hand, turned and looked in her eyes. "Where are we?"

"I thought it might be nice to have a special place to stay after the chaos of the day."

"You rented this place? Like the whole place?"

"Not the whole place. I think the building has four units."

"You know what I mean."

Mat smiled. "It's ours for the next three days. Not technically a getaway, since we aren't going anywhere."

"That's so sweet. It's perfect. You're perfect."

Mat swallowed. Her entire body had become a giant bundle of nerves. The reality of what she was about to do hit her like a ton of bricks. "I'm anything but perfect. But I hope I'm perfect for you. Because I've never been happier than I am when I'm with you."

Graham offered her a slow smile. "The feeling is entirely mutual."

Mat reminded herself to breathe. "Good. That's good."

"Are you okay?"

She let out a nervous chuckle. "I think so. I hope so. I mean, I will be."

"What?"

Mat cleared her throat. "The thing is, Graham, I love you."

"We've already established that. I love you, too."

"Good." Mat nodded. The entire speech she'd prepared vanished from her mind. Which was probably for the best. She'd not been all that happy with it anyway. "But, I...it's more than that. You make me feel things I didn't know I could feel, feelings I'd given up on years ago. You've given me hope in love and future and family and I want to spend my whole life doing everything I can to make you feel the same."

"You do give me those things. I feel exactly the same."

"Good, because I was kind of hoping we could make it official." Mat dropped to her knee, opened the little black box. "Will you be my wife, Graham, and make me the luckiest, on top of the happiest, woman in the world?"

Graham looked at Mat, then at the ring in her hand, then Mat again. The rest of her surroundings faded to a dewy blur and her pulse became a mad flutter in her chest. She'd allowed herself to fantasize about this moment, had even started to believe it might happen one day. She wasn't expecting it tonight, though, and it took her breath away. She nodded, blinked away the tears that threatened to spill down her cheeks. "Yes."

Mat looked for a moment like she might fall over. Graham hoped it was relief and not a stab of regret. She blinked a few times, took a giant breath. "Yes? Did you just say yes?"

Graham nodded again. "Yes. A thousand times yes."

"Oh, thank God." Mat took the ring from the box. It was a modest, princess-cut diamond in the most beautiful antique setting. Graham extended her hand and Mat slid it onto her finger.

Graham laughed then, a joyful sound that escaped her lips and permeated her whole body. She grabbed both of Mat's hands and pulled her to her feet. "Come here."

Mat stood. She slid her arms around Graham, between her coat and her dress, and pulled her close. "You said yes."

Graham shook her head, then smiled. "Why do you sound surprised? I've been head over heels for you much longer than you've been for me."

"I'm not surprised, I just." Mat paused, looked away for the briefest moment. "I think I'm still floored sometimes by the fact that you want to be with me."

Graham took Mat's face in her hands. "You are the smartest, sexiest, most hard-working woman I know. Every single day, I wake up and find a new reason to be in love with you."

Mat nodded. "I feel the same way about you. You're my happily ever after."

Graham leaned in and kissed Mat. The feel of her mouth and the press of her body warmed her from the inside out. "And you are mine."

Mat pulled back slightly, but didn't let go. "We should probably get back."

The wedding. Despite standing out in the cold in her bridesmaid dress, Graham had forgotten all about it. "Right. Did Dom know you planned this?"

Mat nodded. "I wanted to make sure he didn't feel like I was encroaching on his special day. I may have told Will, too. She's the one who helped me pull off the setting."

"If Will knows, Aunt Nora probably knows, too." The idea of the two of them being in on it made her smile.

"Is that okay? I hope it doesn't spoil you telling them."

Graham shook her head. "Quite the opposite. It tells me you already think of them as family. And that makes me beyond happy."

"Oh, good. And while we do have to go back to the wedding, it's entirely up to you if we make a big announcement or not. Dom and Renata are cool either way."

Graham thought about it. She liked the idea of basking in her own happiness for a bit before making herself the center of attention. Really, though, it was Mat's family. She should get to decide. "I'd probably wait and tell the people closest to us first. And I believe they would be fine with it, but I'd rather let Dom and Renata have their day all to themselves."

Mat nodded. "Now that you've said yes, part of me wants to shout it from the rooftops, but I agree."

"That said, I'm not taking the ring off. I don't plan to take it off ever."

Mat lifted her hand, kissed each finger. "Good."

They started back the way they came, but Graham paused. "We really get to come back here at the end of the night?"

"We do." Mat squeezed her hand. "Nothing that tops this, but I might have a couple more surprises inside."

Graham grinned. "I can't wait."

Mat stopped. She turned and pulled Graham into yet another kiss. This one was possessive, but sweet. Graham's pulse, which had finally started to slow, kicked up again. "Do you know what I can't wait for?" Mat asked.

"What's that?"

"Everything. I get to spend every day of the rest of my life with you and I can't wait for any of it."

Graham's heart swelled in her chest. She couldn't think of a better answer.

About the Author

Aurora Rey grew up in a small town in south Louisiana, daydreaming about New England. She keeps a special place in her heart for the South, especially the food and the ways women are raised to be strong, even if they're taught not to show it. After a brief dalliance with biochemistry, she completed both a B.A. and an M.A. in English.

When she's not writing or at her day job in higher education, she loves to cook and putter around the house. She's slightly addicted to Pinterest, has big plans for the garden, and would love to get some goats.

She lives in Ithaca, New York, with her partner, two dogs, and whatever wild animals have taken up residence in the pond.

Books Available from Bold Strokes Books

Against All Odds by Kris Bryant, Maggie Cummings, M. Ullrich. Peyton and Tory escaped death once, but will they survive when Bradley's determined to make his kill rate one hundred percent? (978-1-163555-193-8)

Autumn's Light by Aurora Rey. Casual hookups aren't supposed to include romantic dinners and meeting the family. Can Mat Pero see beyond the heartbreak that led her to keep her worlds so separate, and will Graham Connor be waiting if she does? (978-1-163555-272-0)

Breaking the Rules by Larkin Rose. When Virginia and Carmen are thrown together by an embarrassing mistake they find out their stubborn determination isn't so heroic after all. (978-1-163555-261-4)

Broad Awakening by Mickey Brent. In the sequel to *Underwater Vibes*, Hélène and Sylvie find ruts in their road to eternal bliss. (978-1-163555-270-6)

Broken Vows by MJ Williamz. Sister Mary Margaret must reconcile her divided heart or risk losing a love that just might be heaven sent. (978-1-163555-022-1)

Flesh and Gold by Ann Aptaker. Havana, 1952, where art thief and smuggler Cantor Gold dodges gangland bullets and mobsters' schemes while she searches Havana's steamy Red Light district for her kidnapped love. (978-1-163555-153-2)

Isle of Broken Years by Jane Fletcher. Spanish noblewoman Catalina de Valasco is in peril, even before the pirates holding her for ransom sail into seas destined to become known as the Bermuda Triangle. (978-1-163555-175-4)

Love Like This by Melissa Brayden. Hadley Cooper and Spencer Adair set out to take the fashion world by storm. If only they knew their hearts were about to be taken. (978-1-163555-018-4)

Secrets On the Clock by Nicole Disney. Jenna and Danielle love their jobs helping endangered children, but that might not be enough to stop them from breaking the rules by falling in love. (978-1-163555-292-8)

Unexpected Partners by Michelle Larkin. Dr. Chloe Maddox tries desperately to deny her attraction for Detective Dana Blake as they flee from a serial killer who's hunting them both. (978-1-163555-203-4)

A Fighting Chance by T. L. Hayes. Will Lou be able to come to terms with her past to give love a fighting chance? (978-1-163555-257-7)

Chosen by Brey Willows. When the choice is adapt or die, can love save us all? (978-1-163555-110-5)

Death Checks In by David S. Pederson. Despite Heath's promises to Alan to not get involved, Heath can't resist investigating a shopkeeper's murder in Chicago, which dashes their plans for a romantic weekend getaway. (978-1-163555-329-1)

Gnarled Hollow by Charlotte Greene. After they are invited to study a secluded nineteenth-century estate, a former English professor and a group of historians discover that they will have to fight against the unknown if they have any hope of staying alive. (978-1-163555-235-5)

Jacob's Grace by C.P. Rowlands. Captain Tag Becket wants to keep her head down and her past behind her, but her feelings for AJ's second-in-command, Grace Fields, makes keeping secrets next to impossible. (978-1-163555-187-7)

On the Fly by PJ Trebelhorn. Hockey player Courtney Abbott is content with her solitary life until visiting concert violinist Lana Caruso makes her second-guess everything she always thought she wanted. (978-1-163555-255-3)

Passionate Rivals by Radclyffe. Professional rivalry and long-simmering passions create a combustible combination when Emmett McCabe and Sydney Stevens are forced to work together, especially when past attractions won't stay buried. (978-1-163555-231-7)

Proxima Five by Missouri Vaun. When geologist Leah Warren crash-lands on a preindustrial planet and is claimed by its tyrant, Tiago, will clan warrior Keegan's love for Leah give her the strength to defeat him? (978-1-163555-122-8)

Racing Hearts by Dena Blake. When you cross a hot-tempered race car mechanic with a reckless cop, the result can only be spontaneous combustion. (978-1-163555-251-5)

Shadowboxer by Jessica L. Webb. Jordan McAddie is prepared to keep her street kids safe from a dangerous underground protest group, but she isn't prepared for her first love to walk back into her life. (978-1-163555-267-6)

The Tattered Lands by Barbara Ann Wright. As Vandra and Lilani strive to make peace, they slowly fall in love. With mistrust and murder surrounding them, only their faith in each other can keep their plan to save the world from falling apart. (978-1-163555-108-2)

Captive by Donna K. Ford. To escape a human trafficking ring, Greyson Cooper and Olivia Danner become players in a game of deceit and violence. Will their love stand a chance? (978-1-63555-215-7)

Crossing the Line by CF Frizzell. The Mob discovers a nemesis within its ranks, and in the ultimate retaliation, draws Stick McLaughlin from anonymity by threatening everything she holds dear. (978-1-63555-161-7)

Love's Verdict by Carsen Taite. Attorneys Landon Holt and Carly Pachett want the exact same thing: the only open partnership spot at their prestigious criminal defense firm. But will they compromise their careers for love? (978-1-63555-042-9)

Precipice of Doubt by Mardi Alexander & Laurie Eichler. Can Cole Jameson resist her attraction to her boss, veterinarian Jodi Bowman, or will she risk a workplace romance and her heart? (978-1-63555-128-0)

Savage Horizons by CJ Birch. Captain Jordan Kellow's feelings for Lt. Ali Ash have her past and future colliding, setting in motion a series of events that strands her crew in an unknown galaxy thousands of light years from home. (978-1-63555-250-8)

Secrets of the Last Castle by A. Rose Mathieu. When Elizabeth Campbell represents a young man accused of murdering an elderly woman, her investigation leads to an abandoned plantation that reveals many dark Southern secrets. (978-1-63555-240-9)

Take Your Time by VK Powell. A neurotic parrot brings police officer Grace Booker and temporary veterinarian Dr. Dani Wingate together in the tiny town of Pine Cone, but their unexpected attraction keeps the sparks flying. (978-1-63555-130-3)

The Last Seduction by Ronica Black. When you allow true love to elude you once and you desperately regret it, are you brave enough to grab it when it comes around again? (978-1-63555-211-9)

The Shape of You by Georgia Beers. Rebecca McCall doesn't play it safe, but when sexy Spencer Thompson joins her workout class, their non-stop sparring forces her to face her ultimate challenge—a chance at love. (978-1-63555-217-1)

Exposed by MJ Williamz. The closet is no place to live if you want to find true love. (978-1-62639-989-1)

Force of Fire: Toujours a Vous by Ali Vali. Immortals Kendal and Piper welcome their new child and celebrate the defeat of an old enemy, but another ancient evil is about to awaken deep in the jungles of Costa Rica. (978-1-63555-047-4)

Holding Their Place by Kelly A. Wacker. Together Dr. Helen Connery and ambulance driver Julia March, discover that goodness, love, and passion can be found in the most unlikely and even dangerous places during WWI. (978-1-63555-338-3)

Landing Zone by Erin Dutton. Can a career veteran finally discover a love stronger than even her pride? (978-1-63555-199-0)

Love at Last Call by M. Ullrich. Is balancing business, friendship, and love more than any willing woman can handle? (978-1-63555-197-6)

Pleasure Cruise by Yolanda Wallace. Spencer Collins and Amy Donovan have few things in common, but a Caribbean cruise offers both women an unexpected chance to face one of their greatest fears: falling in love. (978-1-63555-219-5)

Running Off Radar by MB Austin. Maji's plans to win Rose back are interrupted when work intrudes and duty calls her to help a SEAL team stop a Russian mobster from harvesting gold from the bottom of Sitka Sound. (978-1-63555-152-5)

Shadow of the Phoenix by Rebecca Harwell. In the final battle for the fate of Storm's Quarry, even Nadya's and Shay's powers may not be enough. (978-1-63555-181-5)

Take a Chance by D. Jackson Leigh. There's hardly a woman within fifty miles of Pine Cone that veterinarian Trip Beaumont can't charm, except for the irritating new cop, Jamie Grant, who keeps leaving parking tickets on her truck. (978-1-63555-118-1)

The Outcasts by Alexa Black. Spacebus driver Sue Jones is running from her past. When she crash-lands on a faraway world, the Outcast Kara might be her chance for redemption. (978-1-63555-242-3)

Alias by Cari Hunter. A car crash leaves a woman with no memory and no identity. Together with Detective Bronwen Pryce, she fights to uncover a truth that might just kill them both. (978-1-63555-221-8)

Death in Time by Robyn Nyx. Working in the past is hell on your future. (978-1-63555-053-5)

Hers to Protect by Nicole Disney. High school sweethearts Kaia and Adrienne will have to see past their differences and survive the vengeance of a brutal gang if they want to be together. (978-1-63555-229-4)

Of Echoes Born by 'Nathan Burgoine. A collection of queer fantasy short stories set in Canada from Lambda Literary Award finalist 'Nathan Burgoine. (978-1-63555-096-2)

Perfect Little Worlds by Clifford Mae Henderson. Lucy can't hold the secret any longer. Twenty-six years ago, her sister did the unthinkable. (978-1-63555-164-8)

Room Service by Fiona Riley. Interior designer Olivia likes stability, but when work brings footloose Savannah into her world and into a new city every month, Olivia must decide if what makes her comfortable is what makes her happy. (978-1-63555-120-4)

Sparks Like Ours by Melissa Brayden. Professional surfers Gia Malone and Elle Britton can't deny their chemistry on and off the beach. But only one can win... (978-1-63555-016-0)

Take My Hand by Missouri Vaun. River Hemsworth arrives in Georgia intent on escaping quickly, but when she crashes her Mercedes into the Clip 'n Curl, sexy Clay Cahill ends up rescuing more than her car. (978-1-63555-104-4)

The Last Time I Saw Her by Kathleen Knowles. Lane Hudson only has twelve days to win back Alison's heart. That is if she can gather the courage to try. (978-1-63555-067-2)

Wayworn Lovers by Gun Brooke. Will agoraphobic composer Giselle Bonnaire and Tierney Edwards, a wandering soul who can't remain in one place for long, trust in the passionate love destiny hands them? (978-1-62639-995-2)

BOLDSTROKESBOOKS.COM

Looking for your next great read?

Visit BOLDSTROKESBOOKS.COM
to browse our entire catalog of paperbacks, ebooks,
and audiobooks.

Want the first word on what's new?
Visit our website for event info,
author interviews, and blogs.

Subscribe to our free newsletter for sneak peeks,
new releases, plus first notice of promos
and daily bargains.

SIGN UP AT
BOLDSTROKESBOOKS.COM/signup

Bold Strokes Books
Quality and Diversity in LGBTQ Literature

Bold Strokes Books is an award-winning publisher committed to quality and diversity in LGBTQ fiction.

Lightning Source UK Ltd.
Milton Keynes UK
UKHW01f2004140918
328925UK00001B/13/P